Laura Kemp started writing to get out of doing a real job. A journalist for fifteen years, she turned freelance after having a baby because she couldn't get out of the house, washed and dressed, until lunchtime at the earliest.

A columnist and contributor, she writes for national newspapers and magazines, and spends too much time on Twitter (@laurajanekemp).

Married with a son and a neurotic cat, Laura lives in suburbia, where she starts every day vowing she's definitely not going to drink tonight.

To find out more visit her website at
www.laura-kemp.com
or join her on Facebook at
Laura Kemp Books

Also by Laura Kemp

Mums Like Us

mums on strike

LAURA KEMP

arrow books

Published by Arrow Books 2014

2 4 6 8 10 9 7 5 3 1

First published in Great Britain in 2014 by
Arrow Books
Random House, 20 Vauxhall Bridge Road,
London SW1V 2SA

www.randomhouse.co.uk

Addresses for companies within The Random House Group Limited can
be found at: www.randomhouse.co.uk/offices.htm

The Random House Group Limited Reg. No. 954009

A CIP catalogue record for this book
is available from the British Library

ISBN 9780099574590

The Random House Group Limited supports the Forest Stewardship
Council® (FSC®), the leading international forest-certification
organisation. Our books carrying the FSC label are printed on
FSC®-certified paper. FSC is the only forest-certification
scheme supported by the leading environmental organisations,
including Greenpeace. Our paper procurement policy can be found
at www.randomhouse.co.uk/environment

Typeset in Palatino by Palimpsest Book Production Limited,
Falkirk, Stirlingshire

Printed and bound by CPI Group (UK) Ltd, Croydon, CR0 4YY

To my husband, who is amazing in every way
apart from when it comes to housework

Acknowledgements

Twenty-five years ago, my mum took a stand.

Working as well as running the house, she decided enough was enough – she would no longer make my dad's sandwiches for him to take to the office for lunch.

It was a small act of protest and it has never left me.

Neither has the memory of the day when my friend came to school and told me she'd had oven chips for tea five nights in a row because her mum was fed up with cooking.

This book was written because of them – and for those of us who have ever thought 'that's it, I'm sick of this, I'm going on strike'. Then gone back to the ironing because of fear, guilt, love and 'it's easier if I do it'.

Of course, there are men out there doing half, the majority or all of the housework. But statistics show, in the main, women are still doing the lioness' share on top of motherhood, and in many cases, a job outside of the home too.

Just because we've traditionally done it and just because we have women's bits doesn't mean we should be the only adult in the house to clean the loo.

By the time my son grows up, I hope we'll have redressed the balance: imagine if our daughters' husbands change the sheets without being asked or expecting a round of applause.

Huge thanks go to my wonderful agent Lizzy Kremer, gorgeous editor Georgina Hawtrey-Woore and everyone at Arrow for sharing the dream. I'm very grateful to Professor Teresa Rees for talking me through the sociology of housework. And finally to my family for putting up with me when I became the book and banged on about the injustice of it all.

See you on the picket line.

'War is women's work!'

Lysistrata, Aristophanes

mums on strike

EIGHT YEARS AGO

Sunday, 1 June

2.37p.m., Tenerife time

It took a few seconds to realise she was, in fact, Mrs Stratton.

At first, she smiled at the coincidence. How funny, she thought, that's Adam's surname, what are the chances of that? The drone of the aeroplane lulled her back to 'Keep Glowing: How To Make Your Tan Last Longer' in the mag on her lap.

Then, sensing someone standing by her seat, she looked out of the corner of her eyes and saw that the air stewardess was talking to her.

'Oh, that's me!' Lisa said, beaming as she received a bottle of champagne with the compliments of the airline. 'Sorry, still getting used to it!'

Little more than twenty-four hours ago, she'd walked up the aisle a Watson, something she'd been trying to escape for twenty-eight years. Now as a Stratton, she saw herself in slow motion, shaking a sleek, salon-styled head of hair as if she was starring in a cheesy advert.

She turned to take him in. Sandy-haired, strong-jawed, slightly stubbly and utterly gorgeous, Adam's head was leaning against the window. His eyes were closed as he caught up on some sleep after the best day of their lives. Lisa's heart fluttered as she saw his hands twitch on his chunky thighs in khaki combat shorts.

What was he dreaming about? she wondered, as she sipped bubbles. Probably about yesterday. She knew him back to front yet she yearned to know his thoughts, his unconscious, his everything.

This is what she'd waited for – true love. Forever.

The seatbelt light went on as the captain warned of turbulence ahead. Ha! There'd be none of that in their marriage. Not an angry word had passed between them during two years, not even when they moved in together six months ago. It was so perfect, Lisa had to be careful not to go on about it to her friends. They shared everything: laughter, trust, chemistry, respect and even the housework.

Her brown eyes stared into the blue sky, reliving her wedding day as if she was watching clips from a movie camera. Her beloved bridesmaid, Cal, giving her a 'something borrowed' garter from her very own wedding just three months before. Adam's first sight of her, when he mouthed 'you look beautiful' as she arrived at his side. His hand trembling as he glided the ring along her finger. Her shivers as he unveiled her. Their first kiss as man and wife, a long and soft seal of love met with applause. And their heads covered in confetti as they stepped out into the sunshine as one, her beautiful strapless ivory gown catching paper hearts on its puddle train.

As if looking at her own wedding album, she saw candid shots of faces she adored. Then, their three-tiered chocolate marble cake; her gorgeous bouquet of red roses made by Cal, a florist; an image of herself and Adam gazing into each other's eyes during their first dance to 'God Only Knows' by the Beach Boys.

She spontaneously giggled when she saw Mum leading Dad on the floor while her in-laws held each other at arm's length doing a foxtrot. How different their families were! It was amazing she and Adam had met in the middle, both a product and in spite of their upbringing. A mummy's boy through and through, Adam had proved that in his speech when he promised he'd pick up his own smelly socks! That'll do me, Lisa thought, considering her own unconventional childhood.

The plane began bumping around, bringing Lisa back to the cabin. She watched Adam breathing and wondered what their babies would look like. One day they'd have kids, but not yet; they'd decided she wouldn't come off the pill for a year or so because they wanted to enjoy each other first. And she might as well make the most of this size 10 body she'd worked so hard on. She couldn't wait to surprise him with her Just Married bikini bottoms.

Adam came to as their seats shook. He stretched, his fingertips brushing the overhead buttons. Then he leaned over, tucked a lock of her long, straightened chestnut hair behind her ear and kissed his wife on the neck.

'Ooh, champers, Mrs Stratton. Lovely,' he said as he poured himself a glass. He topped up Lisa's so enthusiastically that a pool of liquid fizzled onto the lap of her emerald halterneck flared jumpsuit, which she'd chosen months ago as her 'travel outfit'.

'Adam!' she said, tutting as she dabbed the wet patch with a tissue from her handbag.

'I know, what a waste!' he said, his aquamarine eyes glinting with mischief.

'What were you dreaming about, then?' she asked, looking up adoringly at him. 'You were twitching like a puppy! The wedding? Tenerife? Me looking gorgeous on the beach?'

He laughed and kissed her again, this time on the lips.

'If only! You know that couple we saw fighting in the check-in queue? Well, we'd morphed into them and we were having a set-to after I'd dropped a wet towel on the hotel room floor. Then our mums appeared and started wrestling,' he grimaced.

Lisa's shudder was short-lived. The seatbelt sign went off and she squeezed Adam's hand, still breathless at the novelty of seeing the platinum band that signposted she was 'taken'.

Then as she got up to go to the loo, she turned to her new husband to reassure him: 'Don't panic, darling, we'll never end up like that.'

EIGHT YEARS LATER

The Day Before the Strike

5p.m., Tuesday, 13 May

Lisa Stratton shouted 'Tea's ready!' as she dished up home-made spag bol onto four plates.

Silence. Apart from the telly blaring in the lounge.

'Tea's ready!' she called again, slightly louder, spooning out broccoli and peas. Perhaps the kids will eat their veg if they're hypnotised by the sight of their favourite food, she thought. She could but try.

Star Wars knife and fork, a blob of ketchup and apple juice for George. Grown-up cutlery and OJ in her One Direction tumbler for Rosie. Grated Cheddar for George, Parmesan for the rest of them, and garlic bread. The finishing touch was a big sigh.

For once, just once, why couldn't they come when she called them?

'Tea. Is. READY!' she bellowed in a tone which Adam clearly recognised as she's-about-to-blow because it spurred him on to herd them to the table.

11

Five-year-old George wailed because he hated ketchup now. Rosie, almost seven, moaned because she had *sooo* wanted pizza. Adam, forty going on fourteen, teased his wife by asking if his portion was really enough for a strapping man who'd worked his fingers to the bone in the rain today?

Wearily on autopilot, because this scene had happened every teatime since the children had learned to talk, Lisa answered: 'Hilarious, Adam. George, just eat your tea, please, and Rosie, you know we have pizza on Saturdays.'

Once they'd finished their afters of ice cream – chocolate sauce for George, raspberry for Rosie – the kids ran back into the lounge. Rambling on about his latest landscape gardening job, Adam stayed seated as Lisa cleared the table, stacked the dishwasher, wiped the surfaces, added Coco Pops to the online shopping delivery and emptied the washing machine.

'There's something I want to watch tonight,' she said, noting she needed a haircut as she pulled her unruly wavy tangles into a ponytail in preparation for her next task: 'that period drama thing on BBC2. I've been looking forward to it all day. That and a big glass of white wine and—'

Adam interrupted: 'You'll have to record it. There's football on. Big game. Big, big game.'

She swallowed her disappointment; there was no point arguing.

She was too knackered. She could predict the chain of events. If she insisted on her programme, he'd go down the pub and come home pissed and she'd only just changed the bed and she didn't want him sweating booze all over the clean sheets. She had enough washing to do already. She still had mountains of it in the laundry basket even though she'd spent yesterday, her day off, pulling out twisted wet clothes from the depths of the Hotpoint like a midwife. Every Monday was the same, a post-weekend blitz. Not to mention scaling the Everest ironing pile only to reach base camp, working out who needed what for school this week, topping up the fridge and cooking batches of food she could serve up in the week.

'Can you Sky Plus it for me, then?' she asked, pulling the ironing board out from the cupboard with one hand while pushing back escaping toilet rolls and a broom with the other. 'And can you start running the kids' bath for me?'

'Yes, boss,' Adam replied, treading on a runaway grape on the floor and making a 'yuck' face as he went.

Why hadn't he cleared it up? Lisa wondered as she started ironing the school uniform. Because he knows I'll do it, she reflected, not with anger, not yet, just tired acceptance.

Later, once she'd done bathtime, bedtime, swept

the floor, cleared away the toys, laid out the uniform, reminded herself to sort out what they were having for tea tomorrow night and scrubbed congealed Whiskas off Mickey the cat's bowl, she finally sank into the sofa with a glass of wine.

'Adam, did you remember to record that programme?' she asked. 'It's on now and I can't see the red light on the Sky box thingy.'

'Oh, bollocks, sorry, Lees. REFEREE! You'll have to iPlayer it,' he told her, his blue eyes stuck to the football like a great big man-boy.

'Thanks, Adam. Thanks a lot. Sometimes I wonder if anyone listens to me.'

'Course we do, Lees. It's not a biggie, is it? I've said sorry.'

Was she being touchy? She wasn't sure. Was it worth arguing over? She decided not to chance it, she was too shattered, and announced she was going to bed to read. Adam touched her knee, still staring at the game, scratched his nuts with the other hand, and said: 'OK, love, be up in a bit. Love you.'

After she'd rinsed her wine glass, fed the cat and made a cup of tea to take to bed, she saw the disembowelled grape, its guts smeared across the tiles.

She reached for a piece of kitchen roll and got down on her knees, feeling her back protesting as her hand was poised to scoop up its slimy innards.

Hysterical sobbing. George was shouting for her.

He was having one of his night terrors again, when his beautiful curly brown hair stuck to his forehead and his eyes were wide open, trance-like.

Instantly she jumped up and took the stairs two at a time – which needed a hoover, she noticed – remarking to herself that at least she didn't have to get a tissue for his tears now that she had a piece of kitchen roll in her hand.

Day Zero

5p.m., Wednesday, 14 May

Lisa shouted 'Tea's ready!' as she slid fish fingers off the baking tray onto four plates.

Silence. Apart from the telly blaring in the lounge.

'Tea's ready!' she called again, slightly louder, spooning out green beans and sweetcorn, hoping the kids would eat them without complaining because they'd be hypnotised by the sight of chips. Yeah, right.

Star Wars knife and fork, absolutely no ketchup and apple juice for George. Grown-up cutlery and OJ in her One Direction tumbler for Rosie.

Mayo, salt and vinegar. Another big sigh.

'Tea. Is. READY!'

They trooped in and sat down. Every one of them carefully stepping over the squashed grape.

Lisa felt something in her throat. It was similar to anger but worse.

Rosie, completely oblivious, asked: 'Mummy, you said this morning we were having sausage and mash, that's our second favourite. Why aren't we having sausage and mash?'

George chimed in: 'Silly Mummy!'

Lisa considered explaining that the sausages had been in the online shop and they had arrived only ten minutes ago, later than the slot she'd booked so their tea would've been late and she couldn't face them being grumpy and hungry for the sake of sausages and she'd had a hard day at work and her lunch hour had been spent not sat on her bum but rushing around for the good of the household.

Instead, she hissed: 'Because I am not Nigella bloody Lawson.'

Confused, Adam looked up at his wife, wondering what was going on. She never swore in front of the kids.

'Everything all right, Lees? Time of the month?' he asked over-brightly, probably remembering something someone had told him down the pub about women needing to communicate.

She stopped dead, her fork frozen in mid-air. She had an urge to poke him in the eyeballs.

Knackered, harassed, on the edge, she weighed it up.

Did she smooth it over and deny, deny, deny as she always did? Or did she let rip?

'What have I done, Lees?'

Yes, quite, she thought, what has he done?

In a split second she considered the evidence as he sat before her in the dock. Two nuclear mushroom farts every morning without fail for the last ten years and yet he'd never changed the bedding. One of two adults who used the loo in the house but he'd never cleaned the bathroom. Scoffing food she'd prepared from scratch at blimming breakfast time – having got up at midnight in a panic to get some mince out of the freezer – yet he'd never offered to cook the family tea. Getting himself and only himself ready every morning so he could go for a bacon sandwich at the greasy spoon with his best mate Ginger Steve. Together they ran a landscaping company called Adam & Steve's Garden of Eden, while she rushed around sorting out the kids.

And then squelching that grape, assuming she would mop up the mess.

'I have a pair of boobs. Therefore I do everything round here,' Lisa exploded, throwing her chair back and her fork down, adrenalin pumping, horrified she'd lost it in front of the children, hoping they wouldn't be scarred by this in years to come, but she was seriously at the end of her tether. 'You couldn't even pick up that grape. That's it. I've had enough, you lot can sort yourselves out from now on.'

George asked for ketchup because he liked it again. Rosie started crying because she'd knocked her juice over.

Adam stood up, reaching for his wife, then sat down, waving his hands, patting the air around his kids' heads as if that would erase the memory of Mummy going mental.

It was one of his first ever attempts at multitasking, Lisa narrated in her head as though she was David Attenborough voicing a documentary explaining human behaviour to animals.

About bloody time. She walked out of the kitchen, grabbed her handbag off the cabinet in the hall, opened the door of their three-bed terrace and slammed it behind her. Looking down, feeling furious, she realised she was in her slippers. Pink fluffy bunny rabbit ones, with ears which popped up at every crunchy step she took down the soggy gravel path.

She knew she looked ridiculous, aged thirty-six, marching towards the car in comedy footwear but she was past caring.

5.12p.m.
Lisa sped off into the spring evening, not knowing where she was going, her heart racing. She felt taken for granted and unappreciated – no one ever said thank you for anything she did, no one asked her how she was feeling.

Jesus Christ, she'd been driving their battered silver Ford Focus for a few minutes and only just realised she was listening to one of the kids' *Glee* CDs. 'I Think I Wanna Marry You'. What a joke. She smacked the 'off' button.

And then the tears came. Hot, angry, resentful blobs which she imagined were burning holes like lava into her comfy clothes, the grey hoodie and joggers she always changed into when she got in from her job at the gift shop and café.

She put the windscreen wipers on but as soon as she did she knew the blurry vision wasn't from any rain – a shower earlier had given way to a cloudless sky. Oh God, am I losing my marbles?

Out of habit, her internal sat-nav had taken her to the supermarket so she pulled into a space in the car park. She tilted the rear-view mirror and saw her blotchy face, bruised with hurt, the whites of her swollen brown eyes streaked with red.

What a day. That morning, like every morning since she'd had children, had started with a mental inventory of jobs to do.

6.31a.m., before she'd even come to, she'd started a list. Lunch boxes, school bags, gym kits for after-school club, recycling bags to go out, stick a wash on, unload the dishwasher.

In the shower, while she was waiting for the conditioner to do its thing, she'd wiped at the grimy bathwater marks with her big toe and made a note to self in an Anthea Turner voice to 'simply apply bleach to an old toothbrush to bring the sparkle back to your grouting'. A flash of George's ankle when he got up meant he needed new pyjamas.

At lunchtime, she'd had to ring the vet, send a birthday card to one of Adam's relatives and sort the gas bill.

After pick-up, she'd refereed the kids, supervised homework, wiped someone's wee off the seat of the loo, thwacked at some cobwebs with a wet towel and started a shopping list for things she'd forgotten in the delivery.

Each task was inconsequential and not worth getting upset about but together, stacked on top of one another, teetering precariously, they weighed a ton because they mattered, they were a proof of her love.

The camel's back was broken not by a straw but by that squashed grape.

She'd seen her husband deliberately step over it on his way to the table. He'd seen it but he'd just ignored it. The message was clear: that was her job.

So taken aback by his indifference, so frazzled by the expectation to do and be everything, so cross with his apathy, so upset by his insensitivity, that was when she'd snapped.

In the car she could feel streaks of mascara drying like mud on her cheeks. She could see mums steering wonky trolleys with one hand while holding on to a fractious child with the other, directing another to hold on to her coat, the women's heads turning wildly from left to right, checking for traffic or other threats to their offspring.

Her rage had subsided but her resolve hadn't. Her head swimming with evidence, she recalled the time she'd had flu last year and any rest she'd tried to get was interrupted by him asking where everything was – clingfilm, loo rolls, washing-up liquid and batteries. Even though she was weak and running a temperature, she'd still got out of bed to make tea because otherwise the kids would've had chips every night. After she'd spent three days in bed, Adam had asked if she'd had a nice holiday. Too rough to answer back, she'd simply sobbed at the sight of the bomb site he'd created.

In the car, her phone buzzed, a text from Adam. 'R U OK? Come home, we're worried xxx'.

She started the engine, performed a U-turn and drove home, determined things were going to change.

Lisa had gone mad on a few occasions before, striding off in a huff over something or other. But then the sight of her 6-foot 3-inch husband with little boy sticky-up blond hair and bulging biceps the kids used as monkey bars had made her think how vulnerable and helpless he was, bless him.

This time, her eyes were harder. She felt steely, like the Terminator. Apart from the bunny slippers.

As she approached the front door, she heard Adam's voice telling the kids to hurry up and get their shoes on because they were going to look for Mummy. Her key turned in the lock and there in front of her was her family: Rosie was wearing a cardie over her tutu, George was trying to put his wellies on the wrong feet and Adam was scrabbling round the hall looking for his keys.

They cheered when they saw her.

'Mummy! Mummy's back!' the kids chanted, jumping up at her like puppies.

Adam started fussing round her, telling her to come in, sit down, not to worry because he'd pick up the grape and how sorry they were for whatever it was they'd done.

Lisa surveyed the mess of shoes and school bags and toys and leaves and size 11 workmen's boots scattered over the hallway. He'd said he'd sort the grape – that meant it was still there! Why hadn't he done it already?

She was sick to the back teeth of it all: dishing up, clearing away, wiping surfaces, picking up abandoned clothes, knowing where everything was, being the first port of call even if she was upstairs when the kids were sat next to their dad. She was full of sorrow that it had come to this – she didn't want to do what she was about to do to the people she worshipped most in the world. But she would, because she felt unloved and it cut her to the core. She tried so hard every day to give them the very best – healthy food, cuddles, whatever. She wanted to be a role model for her kids, to give them stability, to be calm, to give them boundaries but still be capable of having fun.

Her chest tightened as she struggled to contain her sense of injustice. Just because she was a mum, a wife, a woman, she was expected to hold the fort all the time.

Well not any more. Not. Any. More.

Her spine straightened, her shoulders went back and her chin lifted.

'Adam, Rosie, George, I've something to tell you,' came a voice so steady she surprised herself.

'I've made a decision. And I won't back down so don't even try to change my mind.

'I'm going on strike.'

10.23p.m.
Tapping away in bed on the laptop, Lisa knew Adam didn't think she was being serious.

She was a softy, always had been; yes, she'd discipline the kids if they were misbehaving but she always offered the first kiss to make up because she hated confrontation. Adam was the same – that was why their marriage worked. A huff here and there never lasted for long. It's not as if she ever got

24

on a soapbox about anything; well, apart from believing in giving her children the best possible start in life and making them feel safe, secure and loved. So she could understand why Adam wouldn't be worrying about her announcement.

For a while, he'd done the predictable attentive husband bit, fussing around her, offering tea and even the remote control. He did bedtime, announcing it as though he was doing her a favour, and she'd kissed the kids goodnight as she ran herself a bath. Had he been paying attention he'd have noticed the click of the bathroom door lock – something she'd never done before as a mum – and he'd have realised she might actually be taking a stand.

But so far he was blissfully unaware and Lisa had shivered with a rush of anticipation as she ate a Wispa in the bubbles, soaking for ages until her fingertips were like Sun-Maid raisins. She felt like she'd strapped herself into a rollercoaster ride which was about to dive and soar around the house, dipping into every room, sending papers flying and knocking over anything that was in its path.

She gave another hint that something was genuinely up when he called from the lounge 'Do you need anything, Lees?' as she got into her M&S pyjamas. 'To be appreciated, love,' she'd shouted down, buzzing with hope and exhilarated by the prospect of her liberation. She'd heard him laugh before he added: 'Be up in a bit, just watching the end of a film.' It was clear he thought the protest was over.

Ha! Lisa's tummy fluttered with the thrill of it all.

Typing up the terms and conditions of her strike, she named the document 'How To Be Me'. She would print it out and stick it on the fridge so Adam had no excuse to fail.

At the top, she wrote 'My Mission' which was that she wanted him to accept that one person doing everything was unfair. He had to understand they needed to split their duties straight down the middle so they were both freed up to actually enjoy one another and the kids. On this, there would be no compromise.

Then her first and foremost point – the kids wouldn't suffer. That didn't mean she'd make their sandwiches if Adam messed them up. Peanut butter instead of ham wasn't going to kill them. In fact it meant the opposite – they'd benefit from all the extra time she'd have by not being chained to the kitchen sink. He could do drop-off but she'd still do pick-up and give them a snack when they got in. But there'd be no cooking, washing, tidying or cleaning.

And second, no matter how tempting it would be to leave her wet towel on the floor or empty mugs in the lounge to give him a taste of his own medicine, she would tidy up after herself. The point of this industrial action was, unfortunately, not to make Adam her slave but to show him how much extra she did. Besides, he would have enough to do without clearing up after her. He was certain to be hacked off with having less time to himself as it was; she didn't want to needle him. She wrinkled her nose in delight as Adam's footsteps came up the stairs.

'What you doing, Lees?' he asked, sitting on the edge of the bed, hoiking his socks off, chucking them in the air and headering them in the direction of the laundry basket. '*Goooooooaaaaaaal!*' he said, imitating a foreign commentator as he then transformed back into the footballer, taking off his T-shirt and whirling it round in the air, dropping it on the floor on his side.

'I'm writing my official notice of strike action,' she said evenly.

'You what?' he laughed, throwing off his combats and bouncing about under the duvet to snuggle up to his wife. 'Are you taking the Michael?' he asked, pulling the laptop round so he could see what she was up to. To prove she most certainly wasn't, she began to read aloud parts of her document, which ran through the daily routine and what he would have to do to run the house properly.

Adam, who had been shifting the pillows around to get comfy, went still.

'My wife has gone mad,' he told the ceiling. 'Send help.'

Then he sat up and turned to her. Slowly, a grin spread across his face.

'Oh I get it, Lees, you had me there. Very funny,' he said, clutching his sides in fake hilarity.

She closed the laptop and placed it on the carpet before burrowing herself under the duvet. 'I mean it, Adam, I told you,' she said.

'Right. Of course, dear,' he replied, yawning, lying down again, shuffling over for a cuddle.

'I'll believe it when I see it. You'll never keep this up, you're too much of a control freak. You'll hate not being in charge and you won't be able to handle the mess. In fact, I put it to you, Mrs Stratton, you love being needed by us three. You. Love. It.'

'Adam, I don't think you understand how fed up I am. I feel like the skivvy. No one tidies up after themselves, you never help out, everything is left to me. Do you know what it says every time you leave your plate in the kitchen without bothering to wash it up or laugh when the kids throw a tantrum because I've asked them to clear away their stuff? It says you don't care about me and it makes me feel like the lowest of the low,' she explained.

Kissing her neck and ignoring everything she said, he said: 'Does this strike extend to the bedroom too?'

'Typical. Never mind what you're going to give the kids for tea tomorrow, it's all about sex. But no, conjugals aren't affected. But if I were you, I'd go to sleep now because you have lots to do in the morning. And every morning until you accept the fact we have to share the housework.'

'You make it sound like you perform rocket science every day. It can't be that hard!' he laughed, as easy-going as ever.

'It isn't rocket science – if only it was, it'd be inter-esting and exciting. I give you two days before you start telling me "not tonight, love, I've got a head-ache",' she said.

'Is this down to that Mo? I bet it is, I always thought she was a bit of a fembo,' Adam said, talking about Lisa's boss at Vintage, where she'd started doing four days a week in September as a shop assistant, her first job since she'd had the kids.

'Yes, because I can't think for myself, my lord and master,' she said.

Then he suggested what she'd been waiting hours for him to suggest. Why don't we just get a cleaner? She'd prepared for this and delivered the rational argument: that's not the point, why should we pay someone to do it just because you don't want to pull your weight? It remains 'not your responsi-bility' if we get a cleaner. Besides, we can't afford one.

Adam had switched off. She could tell by his body twitching towards sleep.

Closing her eyes, then sighing into the darkness,

Lisa was relieved they were still friends, which was something.

But that was because the poor bugger didn't know what was about to hit him.

10.45p.m.
Mandy Rossi heard the door slam and immediately squeezed her eyes shut, willing herself to be asleep before he came upstairs.

Why does he do that? she asked herself, forgetting she was meant to be out cold. He doesn't give a toss if he wakes up the house.

Burying her head under the duvet, she felt her legs ache with tiredness. What a day. Three cleaning jobs as the Housework Fairy, her 'little business' as he called it. Backwards and forwards from the school eight times for drop-off, lunchtime supervisor duty and pick-up, plus the after-school taxiing to Cubs and Rainbows, tea then all the tidying up. She didn't feel twenty-nine. One of the mags she'd read at the doctor's surgery reported on a survey which said women hit their prime at thirty. The rate she was going, she'd kick the bucket when she got there.

Alessandro didn't know the half of it. In fact, he didn't know any of it.

He worked late shifts at Cibo, the local Italian restaurant, which gave him the opportunity to sleep in every morning, lie about all day, finger his

PlayStation then leave the house just before Franco, eight, and six-year-old Lola came home.

And any minute now, once he'd had his ridiculously childish bowl of warm milk with half a packet of cookies dunked in – just like his mum still did for him when they went to visit her in Italy – he'd be up expecting some loving.

That was why she had to pretend to be doggo. But then that didn't always work. His oh-so-subtle hint was to jab her back with his erection, squeeze her boobs and grunt in her ear.

If only he took as long at foreplay as he did with styling his facial hair; those pointed sideburns took hours of his time. She'd often catch him staring at himself in the mirror, examining his chiselled features and flexing his muscles so he could admire his body.

Funny, that was what attracted her in the first place and now she found his appearance a bit of a turn-off. Was this normal? She hoped so: just a phase, it'll come back when I'm less tired, she thought.

He was Italian, born here after his parents escaped the poverty of their post-war homeland. His mum and dad worked their fingers to the bone, setting up an ice cream parlour which grew into a thriving deli café. When Sandro's dad died two years ago, his mum returned to Naples to move in with her elderly sister, who needed looking after. Violetta was a remarkable woman, she'd borne three sons, worked full-time and always had a three-course meal on the table at the end of the day.

Mandy's toes stretched with delight at the memory of being welcomed into her bosom like the daughter Violetta had never had when she and Sandro met, both aged sixteen. When she'd gone into Gelato with her mates one Saturday lunchtime, he was on a shift there. He'd made a beeline for her, making her laugh with his funny Italian waiter act, showing impeccable manners as he pulled out chairs and opened doors – all lovely anyway but irresistible when combined with his devastating good looks.

She'd fallen for him there and then over her pizza and Diet Coke. Violetta was a good person, a great mother, but boy, her legacy had made Mandy's marriage a battle.

Sandro did nothing to help whatsoever around the house. He'd never even changed a nappy and he'd refused to push the pram because it made him look 'gay'. At first, Mandy blamed 'cultural differences' but then her sisters-in-law let it slip that his brothers, to their embarrassment, mucked in at home.

Maybe it was because Sandro was the baby; he'd been treated like one his entire life by a doting mother. Or maybe it was because he was just a lazy so-and-so.

From the sudden silence, Mandy realised the blaring telly had been turned off. He was on his way up.

'Ahhhhhhhhh,' he said, proudly releasing a water-fall of wee as loudly as he could into the toilet bowl.

Dear God, he even needed an audience when he was having a leak, Mandy thought.

She heard him come into the room, sighing as he took off his designer suit. That was another bugbear – he thought nothing of spending his money on labels when his kids were walking round in holey socks. She knew the routine off by heart: dusting down the jacket, placing the trousers with accuracy onto the hanger, whipping his tie straight to put back in the wardrobe.

He pulled back the covers dramatically, exposing her to the cold, with a *'Mamma mia!'* at the sight of her half-exposed backside, which he was obsessed with. Why had she worn a nightie, not her comfy Primark PJs? You silly cow, she said to herself, cross with such a basic error.

Oh no, he wants it, she thought. Not tonight, I'm so tired.

In he got, sending a waft of fags her way. He'd been smoking in the house again. Jesus, she'd asked him so many times not to, what with Franco's asthma. He was just so incredibly selfish.

As predicted, he started grinding himself against her. Then a hand came over her side and . . .

'Muuuuuuum!'

Thank the Lord, Mandy thought as she shot out of

bed into Lola's room, grateful for the excuse to turn Sandro's desire to jelly.

She found their six-year-old daughter sitting on the floor, having rolled out of bed, mid-dream. Lola babbled into the darkness about ponies and trifle while Mandy coaxed her back into bed, smoothing her delicious jet black hair away from her forehead. She waited until her breathing returned to a gentle rise and fall, hypnotised by the sight of her beautiful sleeping beauty.

And she stayed an extra five minutes until she couldn't feel her knees any more just so she could be sure Sandro was out for the count too.

WEEK ONE

Day 1

Cal Hawkins paced the bedroom, willing her baby to stop crying, waiting for the Calpol to take effect.

She'd been up an hour already with Dot, who had woken an hour after her last feed, two hours after the feed before that. Cal was close to tears with worry and exhaustion.

She calculated how much sleep she'd already had, which was fatal because it only made her anxious. Three hours at best so far and possibly another hour before Molly came into her bed at 5.30a.m., which she'd been doing since the baby had arrived, and half an hour more until Ted woke up. How much was that? Not enough.

Oh, come on, Dotty, my love, she whispered, rubbing the baby's back, praying the little mite would just drop off through sheer tiredness. How could Rob not hear any of this? He was only next

37

door, after all. The kids called the spare room 'his bedroom', much to her embarrassment. She couldn't remember the last time they'd shared a bed. But he needed his rest, she was adamant about that, he'd had a promotion at work, head of sales at an IT firm, and if it wasn't for him, they wouldn't be in this wonderful newbuild house and she wouldn't have her own people carrier.

Not that all that meant much at this time of the night.

Dotty's whimpers softened and Cal dared to slow her walk to a meander back to the bed. She tried to put her down in the Moses basket but the howls started up again. Cal would have to sit up with Dotty on her chest all night. She'd just have to nap in the day if she got the chance. Cal tried another feed to settle the baby, visualising her super-powered milk delivering antibodies with a side of sedatives. It was working. Dotty's suckling slowed to a suck now and then with tiny snuffles in between. Bless her, that's all she'd needed.

The tranquilliser effect of feeding soothed them both; Cal shut her eyes and lay back against the headboard. God, she'd had no idea how hard three would be. Two had been easy. Maybe it was her age, she was thirty-seven but feeling older. Not that she could admit this to anyone. Rob had resisted her desperation for a third for a while because he was happy with just Molly and Ted. He'd said she was trying to put off the evil moment when the kids flew the nest, leaving her with a huge empty space of nothing. That wasn't it at all, she'd said, she just didn't feel their family was complete yet. She had a physical ache for another, she thought of nothing else. He'd reluctantly given in then because he wanted her to be happy.

But now Dotty was here he was head over heels, as were the kids; quite simply, she was adored like no other baby on this planet. Her arrival twelve weeks ago was straight out of a midwives' textbook. A home delivery at 3a.m. after a two-hour labour meant the children woke up to their new sister as if the stork herself had been.

Rob had had to go into work; he was going to save his paternity leave for when Dotty was a bit older and 'woke up a bit' because he was a bit rubbish at the baby stage.

So thank goodness for Lisa, who'd treated Dotty like her very own third baby. She'd turned up that morning with a hamper of posh sandwiches, fresh fruit and chocolate so Cal didn't have to get out of bed, took the kids to school, came back an hour later with a home-made lasagne for tea then sat downstairs with the baby while Cal slept for two hours.

She was more than a best friend; like a twin sister really, a soulmate since school. She was part of the family; everyone, including her parents, had known her simply as Cal after Lisa shortened it from Caroline way back when. There was never a time when she hadn't been there.

Thinking of Lisa, she switched on her mobile to see if she'd have the kids after school for tea. Dot had a doctor's appointment at 3.30 and she couldn't be in two places at once.

Ping! A text came through from Lisa and two missed calls. Bums, she hated letting Lisa down. It had become a bit of a trait since Dotty was born. Cal felt guilty even though she knew Lisa understood how stretched she was at the moment – she of all people 'got her', what with all the stuff she had on. She didn't know how Lisa managed everything; well, she did, she was just one of those together people.

Cal opened the text and read it once, twice, three times to make sure she wasn't mistaken.

On strike? What was she on about? Lisa and Adam are rock solid, she thought, she loves George and Rosie more than anything, what on earth is she up to?

She couldn't ask for help now, so she typed a quick reply – 'You nutter! LYL', their long-ago created secret code for 'love you loads', issued whenever one of them needed a virtual hug. She'd have to ask someone else. Rob would never leave work, Mum and Dad were busy with their other grandchildren on Thursdays. Or perhaps she'd have to beg the surgery for a different time. That's what she'd have to do.

Dot was fast asleep now, so Cal carefully scooped her little bundle into the basket, putting the baby's body right up against the side of the wicker weave, which she seemed to find comforting.

Then she settled down herself, willing sleep to come to her quickly, before dawn broke her dreams.

7.45a.m.
Lisa had resorted to hiding upstairs with her tea and toast because she'd had a wearing hour of responding to a million 'Mummy!' requests with 'Ask Daddy'.

It was also the only way to stop herself breaking the strike.

The temptation to abandon it had been there from the second she woke up, when her eyes popped wide open. Usually she tried to doze for as long as she could but this morning, bang, reality was biting. Adrenalin raced through her veins; there was the not knowing what was going to happen, the fear of chaos, the doubting if she was up to it. And the guilt – already, so soon? The 1950s housewife in her head

41

was already up, tying on her pinny, making pancakes for her happy family. She shook the image from her head and braced herself for God knows what, pushing every thought of 'what needs to be done' out of her mind.

'Adam, I'm on strike, remember?' she told the bulk of body next to her when George shouted: 'Get up, Mummy!'

He let out a groan. From his side of the bed, he informed her he wasn't playing and she was being ridiculous.

She refused to budge from beneath the duvet as the children's scurrying feet drum-rolled their stand-off.

Adam sat up and peered into her face, looking genuinely shocked. 'Are you serious?'

This was her last chance. She could say it had all been a joke and now she'd slept on it, she was fine. Or she could give it a go. She decided to test herself: think of the grape and see how you feel. Lisa was just as incensed as last night. There was her answer.

Squeezing her fists for courage, she told her incredulous husband: 'Damn right I am.'

He looked into her eyes, shaking his head in disbelief. She could see he was assessing the situation.

I suspect he thinks I'm just having a funny turn, she thought, and if he treats me with kid gloves then this could all blow over by teatime.

Just as she'd predicted, Adam delivered an understanding 'OK,' then, to himself, 'I mean how hard can this be?' before he threw off the covers and did a zombie walk towards the door. George squealed from the landing when he saw his dad emerge with monster hands and the pair of them went downstairs. Rosie dashed in to her mum and asked if she could have a plait today. Only 6.34a.m. and already she'd been saying no to her precious daughter. She asked her to get her brother so she could have a quick chat before they got up.

George got in on the left, still warm from his own bed, forcing his head into the crook of her neck while Rosie threw her arm over her tummy on the other side. She explained that for a while, Daddy would be doing the things Mummy normally did. It was like a game and they were going to see who won and there was nothing to worry about, they were all going to have lots of fun.

Rosie was desperate to know the official name of the game, asking 'but what's it called?' at every pause her mother took for breath. George simply accepted it as law with an 'OK, Mummy' then announced he needed a wee and off he went.

Well, that was easier than expected, Lisa had thought, marvelling how accepting little minds were.

But breakfast was chaos.

Adam didn't know where anything was and who had what.

The kids thought it was brilliant, shrieking 'cold, freezing, warm, warmer, hotter, BOILING!' when he finally found their Coco Pops and Cheerios. She could hear their cheers as she swiped her eyelashes with mascara. Thank God she was up here, it was so painful listening to Adam bumbling about, pulling out drawer after drawer and opening cupboard after cupboard in search of spoons and glasses and bowls. If she was with them, it would be too tempting to intervene, to feel sorry for her poor babies and clueless husband.

Pulling her 12–14 leggings up underneath her trusty black and white polka dot T-shirt dress, Lisa tried to distract herself with other thoughts. But her ears ignored her and strained to hear her family getting to grips with Daddy being in charge. Rosie wailing as Adam too-violently brushed her long blonde hair. George shouting 'poo' every time he was asked to get his uniform on. Their dad asking them pitiful questions about where he'd find such-and-such or what does Mummy do next. The ten-minute hunt for shoes even though Lisa knew where George had left them – in the dining room, where he'd taken them off after school yesterday because he wanted to make a den under the table. The scrabble for bags. The arduous 'what do you have in your lunch box' conversation to which both kids repeatedly answered 'you know, the usual stuff'. Then howls of derision when Adam sliced granary bread instead of a round of Best of Both.

So many times she drew breath, her mouth open, about to shout down 'don't forget such-and-such'. It was killing her to listen to the confusion. She kept telling herself it was for their own good. This was the twenty-first century – she didn't want her kids growing up thinking mums – women – were responsible for everything. It was for her own good too; she had to remind herself because she felt guilty with a capital REALLY. And anxious. This was not how she'd expected to feel at all. Last night she had been bullish about it. Proud. On a high. Determined.

Now she was practising a smile in the mirror to convince herself and everyone else that she was on top of it. She took the glassy grin downstairs with her when Adam called to say he was about to take the kids to school.

It cracked into little pieces and dropped off her face, joining the rest of the mess on the floor, when she saw the morning's wreckage.

The kitchen was disgusting. Pools of chocolatey milk on the table. A knife resting in jam-streaked butter. Bits of soggy toast in glasses of orange juice. The grill pan dripping with bacon fat. Three tea towels crumpled up, one black with some sort of caffeine-related stain. Her hackles rose as she saw the gaping dishwasher stacked haphazardly – cutlery lying horizontally on the top shelf and mugs perched lopsidedly on the bottom prongs like impaled heads on pikes.

Her footsteps crunched on individual Cheerios, which she imagined threw out spores that would multiply during the day and she'd come home from work to find the house waist deep in cereal like one of those ball pits at soft play.

The children had crazy hair, and toothpaste on their lips. And yet Adam had a look of triumph on his face.

She had to pretend it was all completely fine. He would love it if he was proved right: that secretly, she loved being martyr-in-chief. Lisa battled the urge to wipe their mouths and smooth their heads as she bent down to give George and Rosie a kiss. Slowly it dawned on her she had monumentally high standards. She was going to have to lower them during this strike and she didn't like it one bit.

When they had gone, Lisa was left with fidgety fingers, resisting the instinct – or was it the habit? – to tidy up. Adam had yet to realise there was a full load of wet clothes in the washing machine from yesterday when she'd blown her top. Her hands itched to empty it, knowing they would be musty by the time he sorted it out.

Ten minutes before she had to leave for work. Dear

God, ten minutes to kill in this pit. If I stay here I'll be tempted to jack it all in. Bugger it, she thought, I'm going in early. She grabbed her bag and mac and slammed the door. Every step of her seven-minute walk to Vintage, she tried not to think of her doubt and guilt and the mess that would be there when she got home.

8.57a.m.
Thank the Lord for Mo, Lisa's forty-something boss, who cackled at the news.

'Absolutely marvellous! You go, girl,' she beamed, beneath an immaculate burlesque blonde updo, against a backdrop of gorgeous rococo picture frames, quirky tableware and luxurious cushions and throws.

Right down to her scarlet lipstick and hourglass figure, Mo was 1940s Hollywood glam and had a passion for life, shopping and men, just as long as they didn't want to move in with her. She attributed her happiness and success to her time being her own – she was divorced and her teenage son was away at university. The true love of her life these days was this gift shop, a gem in an ordinary town, whose shopfront always caught the eye of passers-by. This week, it featured a tasteful display of her favourite bits of stock – a fabric fox-printed bag-for-life draped over a distressed wooden chair wedged under an old-fashioned school desk which had been painted white, on top of which sat a lamp shaped like an owl.

'I can't tell you how many times I threatened it when I was married. Just because their mothers did everything for them, they assume we'll do it too. Never again, Lees. And just think what you're teaching the kids. When I left the Slug, I started from scratch and taught my son to cook, clean, iron, everything. I felt it was my civic duty. The last few years, we ended up taking it in turns to cook at the weekends. It was a total joy.'

Babs, the dumpling-shaped café manager and chef, cooeed 'morning!' as she waddled down the fairy-light lit stairs with two lattes; a quick gossip masquerading as her morning ritual. She ran through the lunchtime specials – butternut squash soup with chilli and cumin, three-for-two tapas and roasted veg moussaka – then apologised with delight when she realised she'd interrupted something.

Grateful for the caffeine kick, Lisa gulped her coffee while Mo gave a recap.

'How does Adam feel about it, then? Devastated, I expect,' Babs said, knowing all about Lisa's home life, because she'd grilled her for information from day one.

'He thinks it's a joke, he thinks I'll crack. I mean, if I was him I would too. Look at me, I'm a mumsy mum, I'm not the dungarees type. I try my best, I love my kids and Adam, I'm a home bird. I like having a tidy house and making sure George and Rosie are clean and eating well and all that. But I just don't see why I have to do everything. It's like I had a "eureka" moment,' Lisa said, walking towards the shop door to turn the closed sign to open.

She was aware her voice was getting louder as her blood pumped faster.

'Yes, Adam works full-time but then his job stops when he gets in. I'm on duty from the moment I wake up to the moment I fall asleep – and even then if they wake in the night I get up. I come here after drop-off, go home after pick-up and then I have the kids and the house to look after. To me, they're two different things but Adam sees George, Rosie and the housework as all lumped in together. It makes sense for me to be in charge of the kids because I'm with them more than he is. But that doesn't mean I have to be the only one who decides what we're going to eat, who notices when we've run out of washing-up liquid and who writes the bloody Christmas cards,' she said, her finger jabbing the air as though she was a shop steward.

All the while Mo was nodding in agreement. Having ditched the man who refused to see her as anything other than 'the wife', this was all old ground for her. She'd married too young, Toby had arrived within ten months, and it was only when she'd found out her husband was philandering that she'd pulled herself up by the bra straps as he left and she suffered a huge downsizing of her life. That decision ended up being the making of her. She transformed herself through night school, her lovely mum and dad stepping in to help whenever she needed it, and then she set up Vintage.

Lisa brought up Adam's getting-a-cleaner thing. 'Even if we got one, it would still be down to me to organise and I'd end up cleaning before the cleaner came round anyway. No. This is a point of principle – I won't end my strike until Adam shares the housework equally,' she said.

Then with a final flourish of her head, she was enjoying herself so much, she announced: 'I will not give up until he pegs my knickers on the line!'

A ripple of applause broke out behind her. She spun around to see two middle-aged female customers giving her a clap, a 'quite right' and a 'hear, hear!'

They must've come in when I was talking, she thought. Blimey, I feel like Eva flipping Perón.

Mo added her support with a whistle through her forefingers while Babs whooped and swirled an imaginary lasso in the air.

Lisa gave in to a smidgeon of pride.

I don't know what's got into me, she thought, making her way to the till to start work. But I quite like it.

Day 2

Friday afternoon and Lisa waved goodbye through the window to Mo as she started off on her five-minute walk to school to get George and Rosie.

Ah! The weekend. Lazy mornings, pyjamas, snuggles with the kids, and wine. And it would all kick off tonight with their weekly ritual of a family DVD with crisps and J20s for the kids while she and Adam had a takeaway curry. Not even the hole formerly known as home would bring her down.

In fact she'd seen the funny side of it at lunchtime when she'd popped back in for a bite to eat. She'd never come home during the day before. Usually she'd wolf down a bowl of soup in the café before going on an errand. But today she'd decided to have a leisurely half-hour at home – well, why not?

As she ate her cheese and ham toastie, Lisa had smirked at the stack of unreturned library books in the hall which she'd told Adam he had to return before today in her 'How To Be Me' note. She'd laughed out loud at the overflowing bin and simply screwed up her crisp packet and thrown it on top of the cartons and leftovers that Adam had forgotten to recycle or scrape into the food caddy.

This strike had freed her up so much, she'd even managed to rise above the stress-inducing sight of the kids' clutter all over the lounge last night and watch a soap on catch-up while Adam mopped the kitchen floor. She'd allowed herself a smile, hearing him puffing and panting for her benefit as he washed the vinyl, sticky from George's unfinished ice lolly last night which he'd put down half eaten before wandering off.

'Now he knows how much I have to do' was her mantra of the moment.

What was wrong with her? These things, the mess, usually wound her up. Lisa knew she was in a honeymoon phase. The high of leaving it all to Adam had made her feel light and carefree. The kids seemed remarkably fine too; of course they were. Automatically, they'd asked her for everything, but a gentle redirection to Daddy had left them nonplussed – all they cared about was getting what they were after! She was already spending loads more time with them, helping them with their reading, creating stuff out of Lego, letting Rosie make her up in gaudy green eyeshadow and chasing George around as the Incredible Hulk afterwards.

Adam wasn't coping well, she mused, tramping up the hill. Last night's tea was a disaster because he thought he'd turned on the oven when in fact he'd just switched on the light. The chicken kievs were still frozen when he'd dished up, turning the air blue with swearing. After that, he'd raced up the chippy, fanfaring a tiny tub of mushy peas as one of the kids' five-a-day. Then this morning, when he'd realised there were no clean school shirts, he'd yanked two damp ones from the washing machine, stuck them in the microwave and celebrated his ingenuity when they emerged dry. 'This is easy-peasy,' he'd crowed, holding up the steaming clothes as the kids marvelled at their mad scientist dad. 'I don't know what your mother is moaning about,' he'd declared.

Lisa had initially felt a sickening wave of sadness for the kids, seeing their dad flail about like this. But they were proving resilient and that sadness was probably her own misplaced guilt. At work this morning she'd given herself a talking-to, how it was good for Adam to learn these things because life was unpredictable and you never knew when he might need these skills. She stopped herself going down that maudlin path and decided to just go with it; this was a new experience for her too.

Her mind turned to the family diary. I wonder if

he realises he can't do his Bradley Wiggins act tomorrow at his beloved cycling club, she thought. The kids had two separate birthday parties in the morning. She hadn't mentioned it specifically – she'd written it all down in the note. It was his job to remember everything.

Lisa turned the corner and joined the squeeze to get into the playground, craning her neck to find Cal, her best friend ever since school, amongst the crowd of mums. There she was with little Dot, her three-month-old peering out from the baby carrier on her chest.

'What's this about you being on strike? Have you gone insane?' Cal asked, her perfectly shaped eyebrows angled in a quizzical fashion, framed by a poker-straight blonde bob.

Distracted as she always was by Cal's still beautiful face thanks to her natural 'no worries' outlook despite years of sleepless nights with her three kids, Lisa said: 'Hi, gorgeous, and *hello* Dotty, my darling, how are you, my beautiful baby girl? What? Oh, yes, the strike. I'll tell you about it tomorrow, you should try it, I'd pay money to see Rob changing a nappy while making tea and helping with homework! Not that you'd let him, you domestic goddess, you!'

'Pfffffft, Rob helping? No, thank you!' Cal said, her green eyes sparkling. 'I hope you know what you're doing, Lees.'

The school doors opened and kids came streaming

out, running up to mums, dads, childminders, nursery workers and grandparents.

Cal's two, Molly, who was in reception with George, and Ted in Year 2 with Rosie, bounded towards their mum, and to their baby sister who was kicking her legs with excitement as her siblings covered her in kisses.

Come on, kids, Lisa said to herself, full of anticipation, awaiting their warm hugs. I expect George is dawdling and Rosie is busy talking to her gang of girlies.

Hang on, the deputy headteacher is beckoning me over. What's happened? Lisa said 'see you later' to Cal and then headed over, suddenly seeing her two children beside Mrs Marsh. Oh God, they were both red-eyed and bedraggled.

'Is everything all right, Mrs Marsh? George? Rosie? What's up, my darlings?' she said as she got down on her knees, her arms outstretched to pull her babies in tight.

George burst into tears as he threw himself into her body. Rosie, who crossed her arms and refused to budge from the teacher's side, shouted: 'I hate you. You forgot it was Bring a Bear to School Day so everyone had their teddies for the teddy bears' picnic and we were the only ones without a bear.'

Lisa shut her eyes as her daughter's fury hit her square in the stomach. Was there a worse feeling than letting down your kids? The empathy with their heartbreak, the guilt of getting it wrong, the shame because they'd been humiliated in front of their friends.

A crowd of mums milling around started milling around that little bit closer. She couldn't blame them, they were a nice lot, not a nest of vipers like some schools had, they were intrigued because this scene was really uncharacteristic. Her kids were always happy and no trouble.

'Oh, no, I'm so sorry, love,' Lisa began, looking up at Mrs Marsh, who was giving her a sympathetic smile. She had kids – two boys wasn't it? – she knew what it was like. Lisa recognised it was only a small thing but to her children it meant everything, being left out and feeling unloved; to feel neglected by their mother, regardless of whether she had or hadn't neglected them, was just awful. She knew how they felt. A bubble of worry fluttered in her tummy. She told herself, not now, don't start welling up over your own childhood. Theirs is nothing like yours.

'How didn't I know about that?' she asked aloud, feeling wretched, her voice catching slightly from her daughter's verbal dagger. 'Did a note go out, Mrs Marsh?'

'We put a letter in the school bags yesterday.'

Yesterday . . . yester— Oh no, she felt awful. Even though she'd told Adam he had to check their bags, he either had, and had forgotten, or hadn't at all. Her poor little babies. She didn't want to blame Adam, they were in a transitional stage, things would inevitably fall through the safety net. And this sort of thing happened all the time. And not just to her either – Facebook was full of mums mislaying letters or confessing they'd messed up.

Lisa considered whether she should explain the strike or not. She felt she had to give an explanation because she was usually so on the ball, a regular at PTA meetings, very involved with fundraisers and a volunteer helper at the drop of a hat. But then if she did tell Mrs Marsh, it could end up slipping out and she didn't want the kids to be the subject of tittle-tattle.

'There's been a bit of a change at home, nothing to worry about, Mrs Marsh,' Lisa said, blushing at her white lie, aware the mums had gone quiet and were listening in with bated breath, waiting to hear the words 'divorce' or 'death'.

'I see,' Mrs Marsh said evenly. 'Well, if there's anything further you'd like to discuss, let us know. Now go on, you two, it's Friday and perhaps you can have your own tea party with your bears at home?'

She motioned for Rosie to go to her mother. Professional as ever, no drama; that's why she liked Mrs Marsh, thought Lisa.

The mums melted away as George pulled her hand

across the playground, pleading 'Mummy, hurry up, I need a wee' while Rosie skipped towards the gates, the crime forgotten when she realised it was DVD night and it was her turn to choose.

Damn! With all the kerfuffle, the one person she wanted to talk to, Cal, was already past the gate. Lisa could see the back of her head bobbing away from her. Never mind, she'd catch up with her tomorrow afternoon, they were meeting up at her house for a frequently postponed playdate. She couldn't wait!

3.58p.m.
The plate shattered into tiny pieces as it hit the wall.

Sandro was shouting at the top of his voice, demanding to know why Mandy hadn't woken him.

He was late for work, it was Friday, one of the busiest nights of the week, and he was going to get it in the neck from Tony, the boss.

Her husband looked totally ridiculous, Mandy thought, in his velour tracksuit, which he insisted on wearing in the house 'to save my wardrobe' even though it made him look like he was in a Babygro.

A vein on his neck throbbed as his body, which had been sparko on the sofa minutes before, caught up with his rage.

Mandy, who was also trembling but with fear, knew one thing about dealing with him when he was like this: she had to shout back. Walking away was not an option. She'd learned that the hard way a long time ago.

The kids carried on eating their tea as if nothing was happening. They were having an early one because they had swimming at 5.30 so Fridays were always a rush. With shame, Mandy knew they were used to this kind of scene; that's why they just got on with their food. It was her macaroni cheese which had been hurled across the room – he wouldn't have dared touch theirs. That was one small blessing, Mandy thought, he knew she was like a tiger when it came to her cubs.

'And what the hell are you doing giving them this packet shit? Macaroni cheese, for God's sake! They're Italian!' he added, watching the white pasta slide down the wall, his brown eyes now black.

'Half, actually. And if you made some pasta for them instead of lazing around then they wouldn't be having "packet rubbish",' Mandy punched back.

'I cook all night, why would I cook all day?' he answered, turning his back on her, signalling that the eruption was over. He rang work to say he'd been delayed because one of the kids was sick and Mandy was out.

He was such a liar! How could he say that about them? Making up something to do with the kids was so low, it was like jinxing them, she thought, everyone knows that. Find something else to lie about, anything, just as long as it's not the kids.

He disappeared to get ready. As the kids went off to get changed, Franco gave her a hug of sympathy. Bless him, Mandy thought, rubbing his dark crew cut, he shouldn't be having these sorts of feelings for me, he's only a child. She grabbed the cleaning stuff and got down on her hands and knees. I'm quite an expert at picking up the pieces, she said to herself.

Funny how when I ask him to cook, he says it'd be like a busman's holiday, seeing as he helps out in the kitchen at work. Yet I don't refuse to do any of this even though I've got my cleaning jobs.

Mandy sighed, wondering how it had all come to this. It had started out as young, all-consuming passionate love with her sweet Italian stallion, who was going to take over Gelato, such was his cheffing prowess and charisma. But when he did, it became clear Sandro had no head for business: he lost staff left, right and centre due to his moods, took too long to prepare the food, refused to listen to customers. It ended with his brothers swooping in and taking over to save the place. Was that when he'd allowed the sourness to take over? Thwarted ambition and humiliation meant that for most of their ten-year marriage Mandy was demoted to just the help. What had Sandro brought to it? Apart from his stunning genes, which had given her two amazing children.

God, he hadn't even provided a home. They'd rented forever until Mandy's lovely grandmother, who was known as Granny Glitter for her elegance, had passed away last year. Mandy's equally lovely mum and dad had immediately offered the house to them, knowing how hard-up they were every month. Her sister had been really great about it, but then she didn't need any help because she had a brilliant husband who brought in enough for Sam to have her nails done once a fortnight. The money Mandy and Sandro were supposed to have saved never materialised in their bank account – there was always something he 'needed' like a new phone or, get this, a motorbike which he had his eye on.

Bless Granny Glitter, she thought, looking around at the mess which would have appalled her.

That's why she'd felt such anger; it wasn't the plate that upset her, even though it was from a Debenhams set they'd had as a wedding present. It was the fact that Sandro had chucked it at one of GG's walls; it was as if he'd attacked her memory, it was a show of complete disrespect.

How on earth was she going to get through to him? Every time she tried to bring up the subject of him helping more he gave her a sob story – he was tired, he worked hard, he missed his parents. She was fed up with him sitting on the sidelines, it always felt like it was her and the kids against him. She just wanted him to 'join in', then maybe they could be happy. They had been, once.

Mandy carried the dustpan of china and gooey pasta to the kitchen, trod on the pedal of the bin.

And stopped.

Yes! That was it! Why the hell not?

She recalled a conversation she'd had this morning when she was cleaning that woman's house, the one who owned the gift shop in town. Normally Mandy didn't see her – she was always at work – but today she'd popped back in to get her mobile which she'd forgotten to take with her and the woman had asked her if she was going to join the strike.

Mandy hadn't known what she was on about, which surprised her. Usually she knew most things going on, because people treated her as a confidante. It came back to her now as she hesitated with the broken plate.

Mo had joked that if Mandy was going to go on strike, would she still mind coming to do her house?

Mandy had said she'd never abandon her, nor would she abandon the kids, but if she took action she'd make damn sure she didn't do anything for Sandro.

It was a wisecrack – but now, it wasn't.

That's exactly what she would do.

So she walked back into the lounge-diner and as she silently asked Granny Glitter to bear with her, she dropped the shards of macaroni-cheesy china back onto the carpet.

Day 3

2.24p.m., Saturday, 17 May

Once the kids had devoured slabs of Cal's home-made chocolate cake and squash, the two mums were pretty much free to have a chat.

There was the occasional 'Mu-uumm' from upstairs or a request for sweets or a random question but it was easy compared to what it used to be like. Cal and Lisa, who had been side by side since primary school, had come upon motherhood at the same time so their bond had survived the constant interruptions and the starting to say something but forgetting what. They were lucky too because their approach to raising kids was pretty similar: you can't give them too much love, mind your manners and strict bedtimes, but if they want to come in during the night, let them in because they obviously need a cuddle.

'So. What do you reckon?' Lisa asked, rubbing her for-once nail-varnished hands together and smiling at Cal, awaiting her verdict, which was always supportive. That was a given amongst mates.

'About what, hun?' Cal said as she settled down at her huge oak kitchen table with a decaf cuppa after putting the baby down for a nap.

'The strike! I thought you'd be dying to know the details!'

'Oh, that. Well,' her friend said, wiping away an imaginary crumb.

Lisa gasped. 'You don't disapprove, do you? Oh my God, you do, don't you!'

'It's not that I disapprove, it's just a bit . . . extreme, isn't it?' Cal said diplomatically, tilting her head to the side, her kind eyes lit up by the sunshine flowing in through immaculately clean windows.

Lisa saw something flicker on her face. She'd seen the same look when someone made a pointed comment about her kids or asked her why she didn't go to work. Anyone else wouldn't have noticed but Lisa knew Cal of old so she could tell there was a defensiveness about her.

Flushing with panic because she had counted on Cal's backing, Lisa ran a middle finger round her Cath Kidston mug as if trying to round off the edge of hurt and disappointment and embarrassment and – yes – a prick of anger that she felt. What's going on? They had a tacit agreement to back each other up no matter what. Both women had been on the catty end of comments from other women – Cal, who had been accused of being 'greedy' for having a third child, and Lisa, who was considered 'perfect' for having a clean house – and they always, always stood up for each other.

But they were on new ground here.

'Um. Yes. It is extreme but it's got to be. Before we had kids, Adam was really good, wasn't he? He used to do half the cooking and hoover and think about stuff but now he expects me to do it as if I'm his mother.'

'But he's the breadwinner, Lees,' Cal butted in. 'Things are different now. We've always said, haven't we, that whoever does the bulk of the childcare should be the one who does the house too. It makes sense. It doesn't mean "man walks in and expects tea on the table", it's completely not the same as how it was for our parents. It's . . . different. If I was the breadwinner, I'd want a clean house to come back to, wouldn't you?'

'Sort of, yes. But no. What I mean is, I accept I am the main carer and sorting out the kids is my job, absolutely. But I don't understand how this means I have to be responsible for the running of everything as an extension of that. Adam works full-time. But I work even fuller time, with my job, the house and the kids, say if one is sick and I have to leave Vintage straight away, and it doesn't stop until I go to sleep, you know that.'

Cal sighed. 'I understand your point. Rob is useless on so many levels. And it's not as if he's here much anyway what with the ridiculous hours he works, particularly since we had Dot. Don't take this the wrong way, but what about George and Rosie? It's like . . .'

'What about them?' Lisa squeaked, her heart in her mouth.

'It's like they're caught up in it all. Don't you think you should tackle this stuff without involving them? They're only little, this is about you and Ad. I just wonder if you've really thought it through.'

Lisa stood up, her head reeling with Cal's accusation. It was OK for her, she loved being a stay-at-home mum, she was an earth mother, never happier than when she was immersed in Babygros. It was all she'd ever wanted whereas Lisa was somewhere entirely different – she'd earned a new chapter for herself at Vintage after the years at home looking after the kids. Her job as a mother wasn't done, far from it, but she felt a person again, a human being – she wanted to be somebody. This was all part of the strike. Why couldn't Cal see this?

'If you mean that scene at school yesterday.'

'No, well, yes, a bit, poor things, but that's just a blip, Lees. You're pulling the rug from under their feet.'

'I'm not! I'm just trying to educate them and make

them realise it's not automatically Mummy's job to wipe their bottoms and make their lunch boxes.'

'But what about when they've run out of clean pants? Are you going to let them go to school in dirty ones to make your point? Because I know you – before this, you'd have called that neglectful.'

Stung, Lisa's voice whispered low: 'Jesus, Cal, do you really think I'd go that far?'

Cal cross-examined her: 'I didn't think you would but isn't that one of your rules? Not to lift a finger until Adam agrees to do half. Would you leave them in dirty pants?'

Lisa was stunned. Because they'd only fallen out once, and that was when they were seventeen and Cal who was paralytic on 20/20 had snogged a boy at a party when Lisa had been plotting to pull him. And because Lisa realised she hadn't considered the dirty pants question.

Shit. Adam wasn't on top of the laundry. The basket was already overflowing with their clothes – there'd been hilarity that morning because George had had to wear swimming trunks as pants because he had no clean ones.

It was crunch time. Grubby drawers or not?

Lisa drew breath then threw her palms out, laying her cards down. 'Cal, I'm going to be honest. I hadn't actually thought of that. Really stupidly. But this strike is going to take me out of my comfort zone.

My bum is clenching at the prospect of my two babies not having clean clothes. I feel sick thinking of them asking Adam for some.

'But all I can do is grit my teeth. If I tell Adam what he needs to do around the house then I'll change nothing – I'll still be responsible for the thinking of all the stuff that needs doing. I have to make him think for himself or I might as well give up now.'

Cal exhaled slowly as she shook her head from side to side. The tension seemed to have subsided. They'd both said their piece. Lisa sat back down and felt awash with tiredness, which Cal sensed.

'I'm sure you know what you're doing, hun. And you can always change your mind, you know, no one will think badly if you do,' Cal said gently. 'I'm just worried, that's all. What with how you feel about your mum.'

A shout brought them back to the room before Lisa had a chance to dwell on the past.

'Mum! George has wet himself! He was dressed up as Spider-Man and he couldn't get the costume off in time.'

Cal jumped up, gesturing to Lisa to stay put.

'I'll sort it, Ted's got some shorts which'll do as trousers for George. And,' she said, with a wicked glint in her eyes, 'luckily for you, I can spare a pair of clean pants!'

Phew, at least they were laughing about it. They

were fine again. Just like normal. Cal walked back in with a howling baby Dot, who'd been woken by the kids.

Lisa went weak-kneed at the sight of the chubby cherub in Cal's arms. She adored Dotty as if she was her own. She had finished her family after two kids, she felt complete, Adam did too. But when Cal had managed to persuade Rob to have another, Lisa had been ecstatic. Cal had been desperate for one last baby when her youngest had been on the verge of starting school and Dot was like a little present not just to her mum but to Lisa too. Having Dot to cuddle and change and sing to was blissful for Lisa; it was probably the last time she'd get to hold a baby she truly loved until she became a grandmother. Cal looked tired, she noticed. She had mentioned something about trips to the doctor but Lisa knew her best friend was more than capable of dealing with it; it was her third, she was an amazing mum and she could cope. Rob wasn't around much, true, but he was doing really well – he was some sort of sales whizz and they had all the trappings that came with that. They'd moved to this beautiful newbuild, they had a VW Transporter van, he drove a BMW. And they had Bonnie their lovely black Labrador as well as the three gorgeous children.

'Come to Aunty Lees, come here, darling,' she said, taking Dot from Cal and walking her round the room, managing to stop her crying. Covering her with kisses, she breathed in the smell of baby and savoured the touch of her lips on flushed cheeks.

'So when's the christening, Cal? I can't wait to be godmum,' Lisa said, feeling a wave of love for her unofficial third baby. Cal's sisters, their husbands and the in-laws had taken priority for the first two kids so Lisa had been thrilled when she and Adam had been asked to do the honours for Dotty.

'It's on my to-do list, along with a million other things,' Cal said, taking a slab of meat out of the fridge and clattering around the drawers for a knife. 'Rob's family are coming round tonight. I promised I'd do a pulled pork thing and now I wish I'd said we'd get a takeaway.'

Taking the cue, Lisa gathered the troops. On the way home, Rosie and George bounced all the way because it was pizza night.

Lisa wondered what state Adam would be in. Probably on his back with a can of lager on the sofa watching Sky Sports News on the telly. Fair enough. Lisa had enjoyed a rare Saturday morning off – she'd done her nails and put on a face mask – while Adam missed his cycling session to take the kids to the two separate birthday parties. Hats off to him, he'd managed it, even remembering to buy presents – albeit on the way there – but probably because his tail was between his legs after the kids had reprimanded him for forgetting their teddy bears. Lisa had mentioned it to him, gently reminding him he needed to check their bags, which hadn't gone down well.

He'd accused her of rubbing his nose in it, said he was trying his best and that the strike was 'bloody stupid'. She'd thought she'd been really reasonable, actually, but she hadn't fought back because she knew things would get worse.

Tonight she was just going to collapse onto the sofa and drink wine and not think about anything. Not the mess, the unidentifiable dried blobs of food on the surfaces, the dustballs, the dwindling milk supply, or Rosie's homework.

And she was absolutely not going to think about that unsettled feeling in her stomach. The worrying about what would happen next week once the novelty of the strike wore off. When reality kicked in. When her resolve and his ability to cope were really tested.

And she was definitely not going to think about visiting her mum on Monday.

Day 4

Lisa sat at the dining table, inwardly flinching as Adam cleared away the plates.

This, the first 'public screening' of the strike, was toe-curlingly awkward.

Her mother-in-law, Lesley, watched in bemusement while her darling boy performed what she called 'women's work'. He'd refused her persistent offers of help because he was enjoying making his wife squirm. Lisa cringed with every clatter of cutlery that he collected, deliberately taking his time for emphasis. Bastard, Lisa thought. I've done this a million times while he's let me do the 'back-and-forth to the kitchen' marathon by myself, him sat there jabbering away, cracking crap jokes and talking football with his dad. Adam's excuse then was that he didn't want to make his father feel inadequate because he couldn't lift things these days after his stroke. But now he's doing the Joan of Arc act, performing as if he's after an Oscar.

All he'd done was make a roast, admittedly his first ever one, and he'd gone online to find out how to do it – and then he'd belittled her weekly Sunday dinner by claiming it was just a 'glorified fry-up'. Worse, the kids were playing up, enjoying the never-witnessed-before sight of Daddy wiping away gravy stains from their place mats, picking up on and confused by an atmosphere they couldn't understand.

Adam was hamming it up because he wanted to make her pay. That morning they'd had a row when he announced he was off to play golf; after all, he'd missed cycling yesterday so he needed a break.

As it dawned on her that he was getting changed to go out she'd felt a total bitch, especially after they'd managed a quickie before the kids had woken up, and they were both on a post-coital cloud of contentment.

The thunder came when he said he'd be back by one o'clock 'in time for when you dish up'.

He was expecting her to cook for his parents when they came over for Sunday lunch!

Then lightning when she'd reminded him she was on strike and he'd accused her of taking things too far; she'd proved her point, he said, and couldn't they just get back to normal?

It was then she'd produced a sheet of paper she'd

printed off the internet which was a housework contract. It listed chores in columns and the aim was to divide the tasks into two. This was what she wanted him to agree to in practical terms. But at the moment her initials were beside every one – apart from 'exterior painting', which was marked with Adam's because he'd said he'd do it two years ago and he still hadn't.

He accused her of being 'hurdy bloody gurdy ridiculous'. What on earth did she want from him? He was doing it, wasn't he? He was doing her work without complaining. Wasn't that enough?

'My work?' she'd spat. Oh dear, she said, he hadn't 'got it' at all, had he?

So she directed a bolt below the belt when she informed him he'd have to cancel his mum and dad – which she knew he'd never ever do. His mum would kick up an enormous fuss and he couldn't face the emotional fallout which would last forever, just as it had when he couldn't pick her up from the station three years ago because of a work thing. His sister had just moved away so there was no back-up and his mother still went on about it.

The storm had been interrupted by Rosie yelling for loo roll because they'd run out.

Lisa delivered the fatal blow: 'Daddy will get you some kitchen roll.'

Followed by a suggestion that he should get some Andrex at Tesco when he was buying a joint of beef, potatoes, a pudding because she wasn't going to make one and, while you're at it, milk for breakfast tomorrow and bread and ham for lunch boxes plus whatever else he thought he needed for the week's meals. Oh, and did he realise the uniforms needed washing, he had to organise all the stuff for their looming annual spring bank holiday camping trip with his sister who never lifted a finger, the carpets need hoovering and it was about time Mickey was wormed?

As Adam went round the table asking who wanted pudding, his mother oohed and aahed at his shop-bought blackberry and apple crumble. 'My favourite,' she simpered, tucking into the steaming bowl with gusto.

Oh. My. God. She doesn't even like 'hot fruit' and she *knows* I know that because every time I do an apple pie or whatever she always insists on waiting for hers to cool right down before she eats it. The front of her!

She's not normally like this, we get on, we always have, we both love Adam. Sometimes her views are a bit dated but she's always been diplomatic with me. Yes, we've disagreed about things but that's because we're from different generations. I mean, I like the woman, I admire her for keeping it together when Roy was poorly; we both think family is the most important thing in the world.

Just because her son is doing 'women's work', she thinks I'm irresponsible and lazy! Well, well, well.

Lesley's surprised amusement at Adam's revelation that he was running the house had given way to defiance. At that moment, Lesley looked up and caught Lisa's eye. The glance the two women exchanged said 'I've got your number'. Lesley obviously wasn't going to let her son go down without a fight.

Lisa could understand why; the strike was like a personal attack on Lesley, who'd never let her son do a thing when he was growing up. It was a critique of her way of doing things. Of everything she believed in. Lesley would often say how happy she was when the kids were small, hanging up 'napkins' on the washing line, loving the squares of terry towelling fluttering in the sun. That had been her job, fair enough, she'd never gone out to work after she got married. But Lisa didn't want that for herself or her children. It was time to stop doubting if she was doing the right thing. It was time to build the barricades.

Right, thought Lisa, that's it, picturing herself tying the strap of an imaginary camouflage helmet under her chin. Scraping her chair back, she cleared her throat and announced: 'I'm off for a sit down to watch some telly and I might even have a nap.'

3.44p.m.
Looking around what the brochure for the newbuild estate had called 'the day room', Cal took in the scene of destruction. It was a far cry from the glossy show home she'd fallen in love with.

There were breakfast crumbs on the oak worktop, half-empty *Toy Story* and *Brave* cups and brightly coloured plastic plates uncleared from lunch, her plate had hardly been touched because she hadn't had a chance to eat as she'd gone back and forth to get this and that for the kids. The floor was under there somewhere, beneath crayons, headless dolls, comics, books, cars and bits of Yorkshire pudding Bonnie was yet to find. The hob was host to stacks of baking trays and saucepans from their roast and someone had graffitied the fridge with felt tip. She'd only just tidied up this morning when Dotty was asleep. It was becoming harder to keep things shipshape.

It was no good: she was going to have to get a cleaner.

She bristled at the thought of it; a stay-at-home mum with three kids, two of whom were at school all day, and she didn't have the time to stick the hoover round.

But she was struggling to fit it all in and the

housework was the first thing to go. Mum had always said 'Don't bother with the dusting when you can be playing with the kids.' That was so true. Cal's childhood home had always been a bit of a wreck. Two sisters plus Lisa, a menagerie of animals and Dad tramping mud in from his beloved veg patch but it never seemed to bother Mum.

She indulged in the warm memories of growing up; all of them like sardines, the sisters sharing a bedroom in the terrace up the road, where Mum and Dad still lived. Cal considered what was important in life: happy kids and a good marriage were joint first. Shiny integrated kitchens were way down the list.

So why did it bother her having a messy house? To appear as if she had everything under control when really she was floundering. Take yesterday, she'd tidied up manically before Lisa had come round. Silly, really, because Lees was there to see her, not her house. But Cal had pride. And she had wanted three kids and she needed for it to look like she was thriving – not because she wanted to deceive anyone; more to convince herself she wasn't a failure.

The question of a cleaner was harder now there was Lisa's strike. It gave off a terrible vibe – that she didn't care about Lisa's plight and, worse, she couldn't relate to it.

'A strike, dear? How uncouth, I've got a cleaner, darling,' was how she imagined it would sound.

But she couldn't carry on picking up after everyone in the state she was in – if she stopped to pluck a hairball from the floor she could see herself making a little cushion out of it and lying down for a nap.

She was obsessed with sleep. Desperate for it, wishing away the hours of daylight so she could collapse into bed. If she didn't have to do any house-work then she would save some energy and be able to make it up to the kids, who were going through a bit of a patch. In hindsight, a new baby came too quickly after the move. But it was done now and she just hoped things would improve once she found her feet again.

At the moment she felt she was walking in treacle with no one there to pull her free. Not even Rob. He was in the office today, another Sunday taken over by his job. She couldn't ring Lees, she knew Adam's family were over, and her parents were at one of her sisters'; besides, she'd used them loads of late.

She could hear Rob's voice in her head. 'I told you so,' it said, 'you're the one who wanted three, not me!'

Not that he would really say that, he was too much of a nice guy. But he'd definitely think it.

Quickly, before Dotty woke up and the kids' film ended in the front room, she went online and googled the Housework Fairy, a local cleaner who'd been recommended by a mum at the school gates a few weeks ago. Cal clicked Thursday AM and was relieved the slot was free so she gave her details, feeling pure relief. She convinced herself it was the right thing to do – it was employment, it would put money into someone's pocket and they could more than afford it.

The monitor flared into life: a line of green dots scaling a semicircle indicated the baby was awake and yelling.

Only three more hours then it's bedtime, thank God, Cal thought.

Day 5

What a lovely INSET day that was, Lisa thought as she looked into the grubby mirror to inspect her Jolen bleach moustache.

The strike had freed her up to take the kids to a local castle for a knights and ladies dress-up day. Adam had been working, this was his busy time of year as people fussed about getting their gardens ready for summer. So instead of fobbing the children off with a quick trip to the park then a DVD while she did the housework, as she usually did on a bank holiday, she'd seized the bull by the horns and taken them out. Rosie and George had loved it – all that fresh air, foam swords and 'forsooths!' had fired their imagination all right. Their 'picnic' had been hot dogs which Lisa had happily bought. The day had cost her a few quid but now she was earning, she didn't have to worry about treating them now and again.

Normally she would've insisted on taking sandwiches, but downing tools had meant she wasn't going to pack a picnic.

Not even Adam's grump had ruined their lovely day. He'd got in at 6p.m., knackered from ten hours of physical work. Lisa didn't ask what's for dinner? She knew he was smarting from having the short straw while they were having fun. She'd pre-empted it anyway. The kids had had tea at Nanny Angie's – God, why did she have to insist on being called that? – and, when she'd got in, Lisa had attempted to make herself a tuna salad out of a flaccid lettuce and two furry tomatoes in the fridge's bottom drawer.

He'd asked if there was anything going and she felt guilty as hell saying no. She'd had to cast her mind back to all those times when he'd made a cuppa and not asked if she wanted one or moaned at the 'boring' sandwiches in his lunch box. All small things, yes, but together they were one big smack in the face. This, she told herself, was why she was on strike but it didn't stop her pang of conscience as he clattered around the kitchen in his dirties, making beans on toast with grated cheese, muttering to himself about the injustice of it all.

Tapping the side of the bath, she wondered how long she'd had the bleach on. She checked her watch: a bit more to go.

If only Mum could see me now, she snorted. She

painted her top lip because she knew her au naturel mother wouldn't approve.

Tea at hers hadn't gone well. Her mother had been completely thrilled, which was a really bad sign.

'Oooh, it reminds me of Greenham, love,' she'd said as she launched into a narrative about the time she went to Embrace the Base in 1982 to join thousands of women in a protest over the Government allowing American nuclear missiles onto British soil.

Not Greenham. Again. The thought of her hippy mum in dungarees, sporting hairy armpits, made her shudder. Everyone else thought she was the coolest mum in the world. But Lisa had spent her teenage years being mortified at her tub-thumping crusades. Why couldn't she have been normal like Cal's mum? Baking cakes, making dens, playing hide-and-seek. But no, her mum was an embarrassing cliché. During Lisa's childhood, Mum smoked roll-ups, drank pints, laughed too loudly, banned bathroom locks, paraded around naked because 'wimmin' should be proud of their bodies and rang the aunties to inform them her baby had started her periods or had snogged someone. Lisa had been dreading telling her because she knew that Angie, as she asked to be addressed, would come to the conclusion they were the same, that her political-animal activity had inspired her daughter's strike.

It was nothing to do with her, Lisa told her reflection, worrying she was turning into Angie. My strike is about feeling unloved and about self-respect and making my children responsible grown-ups. I'm completely different to her and I consciously raised my two in the way I wanted to be brought up: crafts, games, hugs and lots of selfless love. And I make damn sure I wear a bra while doing it. Mum had thrown her into adulthood before she was ready, leaving her with a key and kiss every time she had a 'meeting' to go to. She often made her own dinner and put herself to bed. Her mum mocked her interests of pop music and clothes, calling her a square. Lisa had felt such a disappointment.

Dad – nicknamed Wolfie after Citizen Smith by her mum because she found his real name Derek too boring – worked shifts so he was hardly around. When he was, he was in the shed. With no siblings or cousins to keep her company, she always ended up round Cal's. The joy of walking into her house felt like cuddling up on a soft maternal bosom. This was the family she wanted; this was the family she created with Adam.

Angie's excitement almost put her off the strike. Yes, she could see why her mum drew comparisons with her decision to take industrial action. But she was getting the wrong end of the stick. Lisa didn't want to change the world – she just wanted her husband to chuck the empty milk carton into the recycling rather than put it back in the fridge.

A knock at the door.

Please, please, please let it not be Mum. Lisa had left behind the wooden shields George and Rosie had painted in the crafts tent at the castle – please don't let it be her returning them. She'd never get rid of her, she thought as she went downstairs. Or maybe Adam had forgotten his key and he was back early from the pub. That, she doubted.

Stepping over the unruly pile of takeaway flyers posted through the letter box which Adam hadn't picked up, Lisa pulled open the door with her hand covering the white stripe underneath her nose.

There perched on the step was a school mum she recognised because of her beauty. A tiny body, bar her boobs, with beautiful chocolatey brown eyes, little nose, perfectly plump lips, she peered up from beneath her luxurious brunette hair.

'Hi, it's Lisa, isn't it?' she said, looking a bit awkward, her hands fiddling in the pockets of her pink hoodie, her legs jiggling inside skinny blue jeans.

'Yes, hi, I've seen you in the playground,' Lisa mumbled from behind her palm. Then realising she must look a total idiot, she invited her in with a 'Quick,' flashing her lip in explanation.

With a nervous smile which exposed her bright white teeth, Mandy Rossi introduced herself with a 100m.p.h. gabble: 'I live round the corner, got two at the school in Year 2 and Year 4, and I'm a lunchtime supervisor. I'm sorry to come over like this but I've heard about what you're doing – I've also got a cleaning business, called the Housework Fairy and I do your boss's house. And, well, this is going to sound so stupid but I think you're amazing and you probably think I'm a stalker, which I'm not, I swear, I just really wanted to tell you that because of what you're doing, I'm doing it too.'

Lisa's eyebrows jumped.

'What? Oh my God. I can't believe it! Really?' she said, beckoning her in and up the stairs so she could take off her tache.

In the bathroom, Mandy put the lid down, sat on the loo and began to explain. Mo had told her what Lisa was up to. 'It's not as though people are talking behind your back,' she added, which told Lisa that was exactly what was happening. But the fact that Mandy had gone to the trouble to say that revealed she was self-aware, trying to be truthful without looking like a stirrer.

Her other half, she said, was a male chauvinist pig through and through. She hadn't realised how bad he really was until they were married; they'd met young and hadn't lived together before they tied the knot. He was of Italian stock and his mother had cosseted him all his life and he expected the same from his wife.

'He even expects me to cut his toenails for him, just

like his mamma did until he left home!' Mandy hooted. 'His brothers descend en masse and I'm expected to knock up a quick three-course meal while they talk macho bollocks about motorbikes and football, then he gets up and leaves with them, saying he's off to do some "family business" – and have I washed and ironed that shirt he left on the floor this morning yet – leaving me to tidy up.'

For Lisa, it rang so many bells; feeling worthless and taken for granted by the one person who said he would walk to the ends of the earth for her but couldn't be arsed to swish out the sink when he'd had a shave.

Excitedly they exchanged tales of being put-upon – at last there was someone who understood.

But Lisa felt responsible. If it wasn't for her, Mandy wouldn't be embarking on this; she had to see for herself the consequences. So Lisa set off on a tour of the house to make sure Mandy knew what she was letting herself in for.

Starting in the bathroom, she excused the smell of wee and pointed out gobs of spat-out toothpaste in the sink, hairs in the plugholes, wet towels and filthy footprints on the mat. The landing, featuring a bursting laundry basket and trails of clothes dumped and left as though it was a crime scene cordoned off by the police. The master bedroom with its unmade bed, half-open drawers spewing pants and socks and seven pint glasses of water on Adam's side. Tip toeing into the kids' rooms so as not to wake them, Lisa whispered there were carpets under there somewhere, covered in toys and books scattered like lily pads.

Downstairs, with air stewardess arms pointing out chaos 'here, here and here', Lisa took her into the hall, which was littered with mud, abandoned coats and twiggy bits from outdoors.

The kitchen, where the worktop was stained with half-dissolved coffee granules and tea bag drips, the fruit bowl sticky from seeping mouldy apples and oranges, the table buried beneath breakfast things and the stinking bin, its lid yawning open from a mountain of unrecycled cat food tins and milk cartons.

The lounge with half-open curtains, its carpet covered in hundreds of Lego pieces, cups of green fur, felt tips missing their lids, empty crisp packets and pieces of crumpled paper on the sofa.

In the downstairs loo, which also reeked because Adam was oblivious to Bloo block, seven cardboard toilet roll tubes lay by the radiator and the soap was filthy. The dining room table was covered in a sheet to make a tent and stuffed toys were on blankets left over from when the kids had been playing hospitals on Sunday night. There were still crumpled serviettes on the floor from their roast with Lesley.

Lisa spelled out in excruciating detail how the

sight of it made her feel sick. How it pricked her conscience. How on the edge she felt. Forget child-birth, this was far harder; it was like being on a reality TV show, an endurance test to see how long she could cope in a rats' nest. While the kids were doing fine, so far, her mutiny was creating tensions with Adam.

Leading Mandy back to the kitchen, Lisa told her how Adam had asked for some help with the kids' lunch boxes this morning because he was running behind. She'd refused, reminding him he'd waltzed out every morning for a bacon butty without consid-ering if she needed a hand. He'd shouted at her, calling her petty in front of the kids. She wasn't afraid to admit she was frightened of where they were heading – her dream of Adam accepting her terms seemed further away than ever.

All the while, Mandy nodded silently, responding to the worst examples of mayhem by sucking in air as though she was about to have a contraction.

'So, are you still sure you want to join me?' Lisa asked her. 'Because you have to be committed and it has to come from you.'

Mandy closed her eyes and bit her lip, weighing it up. Lisa felt a tingle of anticipation – it felt just like *The X Factor*.

Then, boom.

'YES! Bring. It. On. I've had it up to here,' Mandy

said, gesturing a mile above her forehead, which came to Lisa's chin.

Quite spontaneously, the two women hugged. Then Mandy set off on a delirious solo conga, singing 'We're not doing housework, we're not doing housework, la, la, la, la, ooh, la, la, la, la', as she weaved around clots of curdled yogurt and splodges of pasta sauce cemented on the kitchen floor.

Day 6

4.59p.m., Tuesday, 20 May

Adam crashed into the house, grunting from the effort of carrying nine shopping bags in each hand, and kicked the door shut with a giant slam.

Lisa wondered if he'd popped into the BBC Sound Effects Department on his way back. Why do men always treat it like a performance when they do something?

She shouted 'hiya!' from the kitchen where she was helping the kids with their homework. 'You OK, love?' George and Lisa were playing word bingo, where he had to match the words she drew with those on his card, while Rosie was writing a story, the brief of which was 'a fairy tale based on your family'.

Adam stomped in, dropped the bags heavily and something shattered. He kissed George and Rosie, told them it was pizza for tea because it was his rules and then switched on the oven, cursing a lime green goo, which looked like washing-up liquid, seeping out of one of the carriers.

'That,' he said, grabbing a grimy tea towel to mop it up and dipping his knee by accident into the spillage 'just about tops it off.'

Being too small to know that now was not the time to start picking holes in their desperately tired dad, Rosie and George began berating him for the state of their lunch boxes. The crusts weren't cut off, the bread had bits in it, he'd forgotten their fruit juice cartons and they'd had to have water and Rosie had George's Fruit Club and George had Rosie's Mint Club and they were really cross with him.

Lisa tried to distract them with a 'whoop, pizza!' and 'isn't Daddy the best, kids!' in a desperate damage limitation exercise.

Adam made an exaggerated play of cupping his ear, asking the room: 'Did someone say something?'

'Oh, Ad, don't be like that, they don't mean it,' Lisa replied, thinking his beef was with the kids.

'Is somebody talking? Because all I can hear is blah, blah, blah,' he sneered, and Lisa realised his vitriol was actually aimed at her.

'You're mad at me, Adam?' she asked, genuinely surprised she was the bullseye. 'Kids, why don't you go and finish your stuff in the lounge and Daddy will call you when tea is ready. Go on, off you go.'

Then Lisa gently asked Adam what was going on.

On all fours, he bent his head down then raised it like a lion and roared.

'What's going on? WHAT'S GOING ON? You need to ask me? You have no idea what it's like, the worry, being responsible for paying the mortgage and the bills. It's tough enough out there without having all this shit to deal with – my work's starting to slide because I'm knackered and preoccupied and the business is built on word of mouth so if I don't come up with the goods, there'll be no jobs. I didn't have time for lunch because I had to pick up some materials and then go to the post office to pick up a parcel that you could easily have got. Then I went to the supermarket. Then on the way back the van started making these spluttering noises and I'm going to have to take it to the garage tomorrow so that's half a day's work gone. Do you realise what you've done, Lisa?'

She should've held back and allowed him to calm down. But she wanted him to know this was how she felt – that her job of raising two kids to be decent human beings was just as important as his paid job, plus she had work on top of that and then she was expected to do all the other stuff.

'Tired? Stressed? Fed up with the overwhelming relentless monotony of it all? A list as long as an elephant's whatsit?' she said. 'Now you know how

I've felt every day for the last God knows how many years. And you've not even been doing it a week.'

Adam changed tack, hoping the shame would get to her.

'I'm not the only one who thinks you're being a selfish cow, do you know that?' he said.

'Oh, really,' Lisa hissed back. 'Well, I couldn't care less what people think. What matters to me is this family, chores being divided equally, the kids getting more time with both of us. Do you remember before we had the kids when we shared the housework, we even did it together so we could hang out? You used to cook, you used to clean, you used to be an adult. And then, bit by bit, as soon as I was at home with the kids, you sat back, you started to see me as a mum rather than a wife, even when I went back to work to my "little pocket money job". The trouble is you've had it too good for too long.'

'I don't know why you had to go back to work in the first place. We were happy as we were – we'd manage on my wage. I never put you under any pressure to find a job.'

'Adam! You've completely missed the point. Haven't you been listening to anything I've said? I've been at home for almost seven years, I waited until both of the kids were at school and I can't sit around playing the housewife all day, I need to do something for myself. I'm doing this because you've never once said thank you for anything I've done. You've just assumed I'd do it.'

'But look at me now, eh, covering your arse so you can swan about being all bloody women's lib,' he jeered.

This was the problem – this was the hurdle she had to get him to jump. Couldn't he see those jobs weren't hers by right? They were *theirs*. This wasn't a feminist crusade; it was about teamwork, about two adults who loved one another splitting the jobs around the house so they could spend more quality time together with their kids. But he just couldn't or wouldn't see her point.

'Do you know who you sound like?' Adam said, lunging right at her Achilles heel.

Lisa fought for breath. Their simmering silence was interrupted by the dinger. The pizza was ready.

She pulled herself together while Adam dealt the plates in anger.

Lisa went to tell the kids. She wasn't hungry; her stomach was full already with frustration and ire.

In the lounge, she sat down and put her head in her hands, ashamed that George and Rosie had heard their row. We hardly ever argue – well, we hardly used to, anyway, she thought. Bedtime would be painfully drawn out now, with George and Rosie messing about because that was how their anxiety came out. God, I feel awful. She'd expected upheaval, yes, but not such venom from Adam; he knew her mum was off limits.

Lisa gave herself a talking-to: things have to hit rock bottom before they get better, so just go with it. Adam has to realise that although he is the main earner, not everything can be calculated with a monetary value. Raising kids is priceless yet he seems to think his day job is worth more than my 24 hours a day on duty. Think of Mandy. You're not behaving like a madwoman, she's the proof of that. Hunker down, Lees, keep going. This is important.

She picked up Rosie's exercise book, filled with pride at the sight of her beautiful handwriting and delicate illustrations.

'Once upon a time,' Lisa read, 'there was a mummy fairy and a daddy fairy and they had two baby fairies who lived in a mushroom at the bottom of a garden. Their house was nice because the mummy fairy had a magic tidying up wand but one day it broke into two and the mummy fairy went off to the super-market in the woods to see if she could get a new one.'

She tittered at the next line: 'The daddy fairy was left doing the cleaning and he was very angry.'

Ha! I bet he was, she thought.

'The mummy fairy couldn't find another wand, they were all sold out so she had an idea. At home she gave one half to the daddy fairy and saved the other half for herself and then they both made a wish and then suddenly they could do it together and they finished it dead quickly. The end.'

Lisa was ecstatic! Her six-year-old daughter had a better grasp of what was going on than her idiot of a father. How could a grown man fail where a child hadn't?

Day 7

12.15p.m., Wednesday, 21 May

That's weird, Lisa thought, as she drove past home on her way back from the warehouse to pick up stock for Vintage.

The curtains of the lounge were still drawn this morning when I left and now they're open, she realised.

So she parked up and walked to the front door. Well, there was no point not going in – it wouldn't be burglars, she reasoned, unless they were house-proud ones.

She let herself in and was instantly assaulted in the nostrils by an alien scent, one she hadn't smelt in yonks. Mr Sheen. Surely Adam hasn't taken an early lunch to tidy up? The hallway was immaculate, shoes paired on the rack and not a grain of dirt on the mat.

There was a soft breeze too and the house felt cooler

than normal; someone had opened the windows to give the place an airing. Lisa trod softly towards the lounge where she heard the TV blasting out.

She tiptoed through the door – and caught her mother-in-law red-handed, cooing over David Dickinson as she stood in front of the ironing board, beautifully pressed shirts and skirts, tops and trousers hanging from every available high point. Funnily enough, Lesley did have a hint of Widow Twankey about her, what with her golden bouffant-set hairdo and gaudy green eyeshadow. Lisa had the urge to shout: 'Oh no you don't!'

'Lesley! What's going on?' she announced.

'Oh, oh, oh, oh! Lisa! You gave me such a shock, dear!' Lesley said, her hands on her chest, in a tone suggesting her daughter-in-law shouldn't go creeping around like that – in her own bloody house!

'Er, snap,' said Lisa. 'What on earth are you doing here? Doing that? You haven't moved in, have you?'

It turned out 'poor Adam' had asked her to help out because he was struggling. 'A man can't be expected to do the housework can he, dear,' Lesley stated as fact rather than as a subject for discussion.

Apparently not. Lisa couldn't believe it. Actually, she could. It was completely feasible he'd rope in his mother. He did it that time I had a hen weekend a couple of years back, she recalled. He was all 'you go, we'll be fine' and ended up taking the kids to Lesley's half an hour after she'd gone and stayed there overnight, making the most of his willing accomplice offering to babysit so he and his dad could go to the pub. It turned out he'd had a longer lie-in than Lisa did in her paper-walled Brighton B&B, plus a bacon sandwich in bed.

Lesley went off on one, saying how sorry she felt for Adam, he was working so hard, he needed a hand. And she wasn't trying to interfere, she really wasn't, but she couldn't stand by and let her boy suffer alone when she had the time to do it. She enjoyed house-work, she felt a real achievement and she'd been dying to get things straight in here since she'd seen the way things had fallen apart when she and Roy had visited on Sunday.

'How long have you been here?' Lisa asked, trying hard not to show her anger. It wasn't Lesley's fault.

'Since first thing. I've got my key, haven't I, so I let myself in and got to work!' her mother-in-law answered in triumph.

Lisa went round the house on an inspection. It was singing with tidiness. No dust, no bits on the floor; sparkling photo frames, gleaming handles, chairs tucked under the kitchen table, throws precision-thrown and no tidemark in the bath. The windows and cupboards and mirrors had been scrubbed

clean of fingerprints and all the beds had been
changed.

The sheets were on the line outside, there was a
wash on and a pot bubbling on the hob: 'mash for
the cottage pie for your tea tonight, dear.'

It was blissful, Lisa thought, privately grateful for
Lesley's housekeeping services. The lived-in look had
been really getting to her, making her angry and
resentful that Adam wasn't up to scratch. The physical
mess frightened her too; so much could go missing if
things weren't returned to their rightful place. Looking
around, she felt a weight off her shoulders, it was as
if Adam had a clean slate now, a second chance. If he
could only keep things like this.

'Well, thank you, Lesley, I really mean that, it's very
kind but Adam shouldn't have asked you,' she said,
cursing the flaming cheating so-and-so for going
behind her back.

'I've enjoyed it, dear. I'd come in every week if
you'd let me,' she said, which Lisa could interpret
several ways. If she was being mean-spirited, Lisa
could translate that as a dig at the way she kept
house. But probably Lesley meant it in a clucking
hen way or perhaps she felt left out of her son's
life, a bit surplus to requirements, even
redundant.

'I wish you would,' Lesley added, confirming to
Lisa her mother-in-law wanted to be more involved.

Lisa was genuinely touched by the offer. She reached out to Lesley, took her hand and tried to spell it out.

'Look, Lesley, you can come over whenever you like, you know that, you don't need to come here and clean as an excuse,' she said.

A watery film appeared in Lesley's blue eyes and she scrabbled around in a sleeve for a hanky, which she daintily dabbed in the corners of her eyes before blowing her nose like a foghorn.

Lesley sat down and explained that she liked to feel useful. She couldn't bear doing nothing and she wanted to get out of the house because she needed a break from Roy, who was irritable these days, frustrated by the after-effects of his stroke.

Lisa's heart went out to her. She must feel her empty nest so acutely. She probably feels like an observer, watching us all rush around, stopping briefly for the odd lunch here and there, always knowing we're trying to get off the phone when she rings because we've got stuff to do.

God, this strike was bringing all sorts of things she'd never expected to the surface.

Lisa decided now was not the time to bang on about Adam's limitations. She stayed for a few more minutes, making sure Lesley was feeling chipper, telling her a stack of pillowcases in the cupboard needed ironing, which cheered her up.

Then she got back into the van and texted Adam to let him know she was on to him.

'We've had a break-in,' she typed. 'Nothing taken, they couldn't find anything to nick in the mess. Suspect apprehended behind an ironing board.'

1p.m.
Back at the shop, Mo whistled through postbox-red lips as Lisa revealed she'd tackled a 5-foot-2-inch duster-wielding burglar.

'You've got balls the size of space hoppers,' she said, laughing, knocking back an espresso at her desk.

Lisa was eating a sandwich in the office while keeping an eye on the till, working through lunch because of her earlier crime-fighting diversion. 'I actually felt sorry for her.'

'Whaaaat? Are you mad? Most women would be furious about their mother-in-law breaking and entering, particularly when Adam was supposed to be doing the housework,' Mo argued.

Well, yes, there was that, Lisa said, but she was having a wobble.

Was she being selfish? she wondered. Had she bitten off more than she could chew? The timing of her strike was, on reflection, not great; this was Adam's busy season and the time of year when they saved hard to cover for the quieter months. The summer holidays would be even more expensive this year, what with having to pay for kids' clubs for the weeks she, her mum and Lesley couldn't cover due to other commitments. Adam never took time off then, that's why their spring bank holiday camping trip was such a big deal. Their 'main' holiday was a week away in the October half-term, usually a cottage in Cornwall or, if they stretched themselves, an eye-wateringly expensive four days at Center Parcs.

She tried to jolly herself along with a well-rehearsed pep talk she'd prepared earlier, having known there would be moments like this.

So far, the strike had given her loads of time with the kids. She had more energy – she even felt up for it 'in bed'. Adam however was unusually tired, going up before her and falling fast asleep, whacked by all the extra thinking and doing. He had spent less time down the Red Lion, claiming he didn't feel like it, but she suspected it was because he didn't want his mates to find out he was wearing not the trousers but an apron.

'So what are you doing with all this time on your hands then?' Mo asked.

'Mainly kids' stuff. Helping with schoolwork, playing games, that sort of thing. A bit of swimming, too. Then when they're asleep, I'll watch some telly, read, have a bath, do my nails, or go online, do a bit of research about stuff,' she said.

'Oooh, planning a revolution, are we?' Mo asked, narrowing her twinkling grey eyes.

'No! I've just got a finger in a few pies, that's all. Talking of which, your cleaner, Mandy, that mum who's gone on strike, has invited me round tonight,' Lisa told her.

Mo performed a silent comb-over with her hand, swiping the air above her blonde head.

'What are you doing?' Lisa asked, worriedly looking around her as if Mo was secretly summoning for men in white coats to appear with a syringe and straitjacket.

'Sounds like you're going to give Arthur Scargill a run for his money!' her boss honked, slapping her thigh in delight.

'Very funny. You make it sound like I'm plotting to overthrow mankind. It's nothing of the sort, it's just a chat, a chance to swap stories and support each other because this is one of the hardest things I've ever done.'

She was excited about seeing Mandy – she was like a breath of fresh air. Maybe it was her age – she was seven years younger than Lisa – or perhaps it was because it was a new friendship with a difference; not made through their kids, like most of her circle. Whatever it was, Mandy was vivacious and beguiling and determined. Lisa needed that at the moment; Cal's negative vibes had unsettled her. But right now she wanted a positive influence in her life. And possibly, it occurred to her, it was a validation that she was doing the right thing.

As if reading her mind, Mo told Lisa: 'Listen, you have my complete support. I think what you're doing is marvellous and I'm just annoyed I can't join in! I'd never live with a man again after the Slug so my job is to be cheerleader-in-chief. You should feel proud, Lees, you've hit a nerve and I don't think you realise it.'

With that, Mo clacked off on her stilettos and disappeared upstairs, leaving Lisa feeling she was on the brink of something but not sure quite what.

10.38p.m.
Blimey, Lisa hadn't meant to stay this late, she had work in the morning, a really busy day because Mo wanted to dress the window for summer. For the first time, Lisa would be 'in charge' on the shop floor. Mind you, she was so nervous about it, she wouldn't have gone to sleep even if she was at home now. It was silly, really, considering she could run the house with her hands tied behind her back: and the 'corporation' she ran was much harder, with two, no, three children – if you counted Adam – needing her every five seconds! But Lisa had never been the boss at work, she'd always been the reliable back-up, ready to catch any dropped balls but never the one to be doing the actual juggling.

Mandy went to top up Lisa's glass.

'God, no, I've got to go, I didn't realise it was this

late! I feel a bit tiddly anyway. This is really unusual for me, being out on a school night!' she said, waving away the bottle.

The evening had been a real laugh. The two mums had talked so much they'd been breathing through their ears, making the most of having the house to themselves, what with Sandro at work and the kids asleep. Mandy was a live wire, and Lisa had no idea how she'd ended up with her husband – they'd only just met so there was no way she could ask that most personal of questions. But then there were loads of couples like that. She and Adam were one of the few who had seemed to grow in the same direction rather than apart; until now that was.

Mandy's strike was slightly different: she was only refusing to do Sandro's washing or cooking or shopping or whatever.

'If I left him to look after the children's stuff then they would be a social services case,' she had explained. 'I just don't trust him like you trust Adam. Sandro wouldn't step in out of duty because he has no sense of duty. I wish I could leave him to it but he's so self-obsessed. And his hours mean the kids wouldn't get a packed lunch or clean clothes so I just couldn't bear that. No, my strike is about getting him to realise how much I do for him.'

Lisa had completely understood; she was lucky having Adam – to a point. She could see what Mandy was up against. Dotted around the lounge-diner were his cups of yesterday's coffee, empty crisp packets and last night's beer bottles. A smashed plate of congealed pasta remained on the carpet, which Mandy had squared with masking tape on which she'd written HAZARD and covered with an upside-down transparent Tupperware container so the children didn't hurt their feet. The space where he sat on the sofa was sunken and dishevelled, peppered with biscuit crumbs, and a PlayStation console and a stack of game sleeves were scattered where his feet had been. Already some had been cracked by the children who'd accidentally trodden on them.

His mess in the kitchen hadn't been cleared away – Mandy pointed out gaps in the cupboards where his favourite treats such as his 'bloody baby biscuits' had gone unreplaced.

In the bathroom, his gel remained cap off and oozing onto the cold tap of the sink, his wet towel lay scrunched on the floor, along with filings of his black stubble.

Sandro's side of the bed was littered with luxurious socks, Calvin Klein jockey pants and toothpicks, which revealed his 'revolting wake-up ritual', Mandy said, and falling out of the laundry basket like entrails were flashy shirts which gave off a strong sweet smell of aftershave.

Back downstairs, Lisa had studied the photos on the wall when Mandy nipped off for a wee.

She recognised him as one of the staff at Cibo. There he was, bronzed and muscular on the beach in a pair of orange trunks which revealed too much of his privates; a snarling Sandro posing on top of a motorbike, his fingers in a V for Victory sign; a laughing Sandro with Franco and Lola on his knees – his legs ludicrously wide – their faces turned to his, kissing his cheeks; and a pouting suited Sandro with his arms draped protectively round Mandy's shoulders, making her seem even more petite.

'How's he taking it?' Lisa had asked once Mandy reappeared.

'He's doing what he always does when he doesn't like something – he's sulking,' Mandy said. 'He's muttering Italian under his breath as he goes around the house and he's stamping like a giant. This is the calm before the next storm, which he's definitely building up to. We had a huge row the day I told him he had to look after himself. He threatened to leave, which I said was absolutely fine by me. Then he tried to slobber all over me as if that was going to make me change my mind! But now he's getting angry, I can feel it.'

Lisa was full of admiration for her. She'd crack if the tension at home had an edge of violence to it.

Clearly, Mandy coped by laughing at it; her small

frame jiggled with glee as she explained how Sandro had rung his mother in disgust to complain about his wife's antics. He'd put her on speakerphone so Mandy could hear her mother-in-law's anger – not that she could speak Italian but you didn't have to be able to understand any to detect her flashing rage. Her husband continued to consult his mamma whenever he came across a domestic problem, funnily enough whenever Mandy was in earshot. Long protracted discussions were held at top volume and then she'd find him minutes later, trying to work out the correct washing machine cycle.

'He shrunk his favourite cashmere jumper yesterday,' Mandy had said, clapping her hands in delight. 'Oh you should've seen him, he was purple!'

The ultimate challenge was yet to materialise, Mandy had explained. He had yet to cook anything for himself because he ate at work, but surely a day off would force his hand. This was her dream: to come back from one of her cleaning jobs to find her man tapping into his proud Italian heritage, creating a delicious pasta dish for the family from a recipe which had been passed down the generations.

As Lisa put on her cardie, they agreed that the evening had been a therapeutic godsend.

'It's like we've set up our very own trade union,' Mandy laughed.

Lisa didn't feel the chill of the night as she walked

home, glowing inside at the thought of the women creating the National Union of Mothers.

Ha! Perhaps Mo was right after all: maybe she would need to buy herself a donkey jacket.

WEEK TWO

Day 8

5.02a.m., Thursday, 22 May

To Lisa's shame, her first thought when George started throwing up at 4a.m. was how it would affect her strike.

Sitting in the darkness, her back supported by pillows while her boiling hot son fitfully slept across her lap, she wrestled with her biggest dilemma yet.

Adam had gone up into the loft conversion, which he used as his office but which doubled up as the spare room owing to an ancient sofa bed from his bachelor days.

It was what they always did when the kids were ill. She took over and he got to shut the door on them. It was a given that he needed to be fresh for work whatever happened at home.

But she was on new territory now. Should Adam be the one to take the day off now that she was working? This was the first time one of the kids had been poorly since she'd started working and ever since she'd been dreading making the inevitable call, which would leave Mo in the mire. Why was it assumed she would be the one in the doghouse?

And she was on the picket line.

Staring into the night, Lisa reminded herself of her first rule – the children would not suffer. Then there was the fact that her stand was about housework. Technically, and erring towards relief because she couldn't bear the thought of abandoning George, she should be the one staying at home.

But this wasn't clear cut. While the principal role in this instance was childcare, there was a huge domestic element involved in having a day off with an ill child – washing vomit-covered pyjamas and sheets then hanging them out to dry, remaking beds, disinfecting sick bowls, cleaning the bathroom or scrubbing carpets if they'd missed the bowl, and bringing squash and toast or whatever the little one could stomach.

Over and over, she asked herself should she stay or should she go? It was a tormenting battle of head versus heart but she didn't know which was which.

If she was going to work, she'd have to wake Adam right now because she needed to get some rest. There'd be a whispered argument and nobody would be able to go back to sleep for both she and Adam would be silently fuming.

If she was staying at home, she'd have to break her strike and that would mean everything she'd been through would be for nothing.

And yet she couldn't leave George – he needed her and she needed to be with him. It was as simple as that. She couldn't imagine walking out on him, probably in tears, and leaving him looking so little and wan, his bed hair needing smoothing.

As the red digital numbers flicked to 5:32a.m., she finally came up with a solution. She'd take the day off work because her strike was not about neglecting her maternal responsibilities. But she wouldn't touch the washing machine and if George recovered enough to eat before Adam came home, he'd only want biscuits or jam sandwiches before then anyway. Pleased with the compromise, and so grateful she wouldn't be turning her back on George, she sent Mo an apologetic text – she was so sorry because she'd been looking forward to being in charge today – then dozed off.

9.12a.m.

Cal had beads of sweat on her lip as she power-walked back home after taking Ted and Molly to school.

It was a gorgeous day, the first she could remember this year in which the sun shone with real warmth. Her mind flickered back to last spring when they'd had the most perfect half-term week of weather and

119

family time by the seaside in Cornwall. Ted and Molly had finally seen each other as playmates rather than rivals so they spent their days squealing in the sand, needing less supervision than ever before, giving Cal time to read, sunbathe and reacquaint herself with Rob; their marriage had been about the children for so long. Lisa, Adam, Rosie and George had driven down for a couple of nights to join them on the spur of the moment because the rental cottage was huge – much bigger than it had looked in the brochure. The idea of inviting them down was Rob's, devised one minute and an invitation issued the next. It had been such good fun: the men barbecuing, the kids absorbed in their own games, and precious time for Cal and Lisa to chat, get tiddly and reminisce about their friendship. They spent two days unable to believe their luck – the cottage swimming pool which Rob and Cal had suspected would be manky and freezing was sparklingly clean and warm. The kids splashed around in their water wings for hours and hours, emerging only for a burger or an ice pop. The break had gone down as one of the best ever, Cal was sure it would be part of the kids' memories for years to come. Just like the year Lisa had joined her family on a camping holiday to the South of France. Although that was because both of them had had their first ever snogs – they still hooted with laughter about their dreamy French boys Pascal and Xavier.

That Thursday night in Cornwall was when she and Rob had conceived Dotty: she was born out of sheer joy and Cal had sailed through her third pregnancy.

It was a far cry from how she felt now. Fat, sweaty, tired and weighed down. Not least because Dot was in her sling, finally curled up fast asleep after a screaming session in the playground, and radiating heat like a hot-water bottle.

Cal had to get back to meet the cleaner, who was coming round for the first time. But she wouldn't be there yet. Not for half an hour, that was the stupid thing. No. Cal was steaming home to give the place a quick tidy before the woman arrived. She was completely aware how ridiculous that was, but she didn't want first impressions of how she kept her house to be bad ones. Why was she bothering?

It was because she was desperate to keep up the illusion she was OK. In truth, of late, Cal had been snorkelling through a bog, always running late, always forgetting stuff on the list and always shattered.

At least when the cleaner started, she'd have more time to enjoy the baby. She'd get there, she knew it, it was just taking a little longer than she'd expected. Dotty was a dreadful sleeper, not like the other two, and maybe it was because Cal was older and wearier now. Not that anyone had noticed because no one had asked – everyone assumed she was coping just like she had before. Lisa called her an 'earth mother', a label Cal secretly liked because yes, she was a relaxed kind of person and a natural at motherhood. Well, she *was*. Now she wasn't so sure.

Letting herself in, she went around picking up breakfast bowls and pyjamas, not daring to put Dot down in case she woke up before she'd put away the cereal and peanut butter.

She stuck the kettle on to make a coffee, then while she waited for it to boil she sat down on the day room sofa and closed her eyes. Just five minutes then I'll put a wash on, she thought; she'd forgotten how many clothes babies got through. Especially this one. She'd been back and forth to the doctor about Dot's vomiting; it was possibly reflux but as she was putting on weight there was 'nothing to worry about'. Famous last words, Cal said to herself before zonking out on the spot.

She was woken by a shout at the door.

'Hello?' came a woman's voice through the letterbox. 'Anyone there? It's the Housework Fairy,' she said, which had the effect of sticking a rocket up Cal's backside.

'Oh God, I'm so sorry. What time is it?' Cal said, opening up, welcoming her in, as Dotty started to bawl at being so rudely awoken.

'Quarter-to,' the cleaner said. 'That is the right time, isn't it? You're Caroline, aren't you? I'm Amanda, have I got the wrong house?'

'Yes. No,' Cal said through a fuzzy, disorientated head. She'd been sparko for fifteen minutes, that was all, but it felt like hours.

The cleaner was full of apologies, offering to come back, she knew how hard it was with a little one.

Dear God, there was no way Cal was going to let her escape!

'No, come in, come in, tea?' she said.

'No, ta, got to get on,' she replied, giving a wave with one hand as she picked up her bag of cleaning stuff with the other. 'Where do you want me to start? You just get on, forget I'm here. You must have your hands full, she's gorgeous.'

'Oh, thanks, yes, she is. Erm, well, the kitchen day room thing needs a good going over, and the lounge, plus the bedrooms, oh, and the bathrooms and . . .'

The woman held her eye then burst out laughing. 'The whole place, then?'

Cal's face broke out into a smile and she nodded, warming to this funny lady.

'No problem,' the cleaner said, darting off to start work, waving her bottle of Dettox like it was a wand, 'I'm the Housework Fairy, aren't I?'

6p.m.
It was one of those quirks of life, Lisa thought as all four of them cuddled up on the sofa to watch a film in the dark.

Once you'd stopped worrying that it was something serious, a one-off day at home with a not-too-poorly child was, in actual fact, quite lovely. Having them close while they let you fuss over them unleashed the full majesty of your maternal instinct. Anything else of concern melted away on days like these, she reflected, taking in her nearest and dearests' faces lit up by the flickering TV, the closed curtains and a bag of popcorn at the ready as they played 'cinemas'.

Her day had started properly when Adam woke her with a cup of tea, the first time he'd done that since Rosie was a baby, before he'd left to take their daughter to school on his way to work. He'd given her and their still-sleeping son the tenderest look she'd seen since her crusade had begun, dropping kisses on their foreheads; he'd always said the sight of her and the kids made his heart melt.

As the morning went on, Adam had sent a flood of texts asking for updates on his 'brave little man' which included gushing affirmations of love for her and their family.

Then something had occurred to her. Of course he was genuinely concerned, of course he was. But could his response to this situation be tied up with what had happened over the last eight days? Was Adam ever so slightly thrilled because his wife was behaving as a Neanderthal man thought she should?

And was he expecting this to be the end of her silly little game?

Lisa had felt awful, doubting her husband's motives. She berated herself for even thinking that of him. Lisa put it out of her mind as George slowly perked up during the day, which they spent reading books and watching telly, still in their pyjamas, the cat purring on their laps covered by a duvet.

Still the texts came in from Adam. It was their eighth wedding anniversary in a week or so and would she like to go out for a meal, just the two of them? Leave it to him, he'd book a table somewhere. What's more, he'd get his mum to have the kids for a sleepover. He loved her so much and he wanted to make her happy. Plus he'd get fish and chips for tea once he'd picked Rosie up from after-school club.

God, it had felt good to be communicating again without snapping; maybe they'd get through this a better couple, she had thought. Maybe he was beginning to see her point. Yes, that was why he had been so lovely – he'd never normally arrange a sitter. He was thinking ahead, he was acting of his own accord. Bloody hell, she'd thought, this experiment is working!

Just before Adam and Rosie were due back, she'd run a bath for her and George; it was so nice having some alone time with him, splashing in bubbles and feeling his warm body next to hers. Even better because the bathroom was still sparkling from Lesley's visit. She'd missed having a clean house, really missed it. In truth, she couldn't wait for her strike to be over, it was exhausting trying to stay calm about discarded undies, dirty dishes and skid marks. She knew she had great expectations but at last Adam was going some way to meeting them. She felt like Supernanny! A little bit of pain had definitely been worth it.

Teatime was brilliant. Adam was attentive, George was almost back to his normal self and Rosie was full of sweet concern for her brother. There was no doubt this strike had brought Adam closer to the kids and they had their own little jokes going on as a result. This was how family life should be, Lisa thought, watching her gorgeous tribe chit-chatting away, making jokes and laughing, getting excited about their camping trip, which was only two days away.

And then it got even better. Adam cleared away the plates and poured her a glass of wine as Lisa turned the lounge into the cinema.

Yes, it turned out he was after a pass to go to the pub for a cheeky one later but fair play to him, without even a prompting he said he'd go once he'd put the kids to bed and tidied up.

As the family film rolled, Lisa thought it was all too good to be true. But then again, she reasoned, we all deserve a slice of domestic bliss from time to time, don't we? Her chest rippling with happiness, Lisa decided she would call off her strike tomorrow.

11.34p.m.
A sack of drunk potatoes collapsed onto the duvet, sending shock waves across the bed.

Lisa jolted awake with a sudden 'huh' and scanned the pitch-blackness for clues.

A groan, then the stench of lager and spirits and sweat and kebab.

'Adam, you stink. You're drunk, aren't you?' she sighed as the crash test dummy slumped in the recovery position.

A huge fart, a belch, another groan, this time longer and deeper, followed by 'I love you so much, Lees, why are you doing this to me?'

She rolled her eyes in the darkness then relaxed back into her favourite position and told him to go to sleep.

Lisa felt a deadweight on her hip as Adam hoiked his right arm onto her in an attempt to stop her drifting off.

'No, I bloody well won't,' he said, slurring, catching some dribble, his face half buried in the covers.

Suddenly he lurched up and reached out with his left arm to put the bedside lamp on. Oh my God, he looks like one of the extras from *Thriller*, Lisa thought, as her vision adjusted to the light.

Inches from her face, he was on all fours with

bloodshot googly eyes, a trace of chilli sauce on his chin, a speck of dried lettuce spiked on some stubble and a cider-and-black Joker smile.

'Have you seen yourself?' she asked, instantly wishing she hadn't engaged in conversation with him. The first rule of talking at this time of night to a steaming drunk – or a toddler, in fact – was to not talk to them.

Adam burst into tears, belly-flopping onto her chest, sobbing into her pyjama top, telling her over and over how much he loved her and the kids. Lisa patted his back, trying not to breathe in his noxious fumes, and realised the window to go back to sleep was not only shut but locked and bolted.

'What's up?' she asked, stroking his hair and kissing his forehead, expecting a fuss about nothing. The last time he was in this state it was over his football team losing in the FA Cup final years ago.

Another erratic jerk; he sat up, started pulling his clothes off, and slobbered his way through an explanation, jumping from one detail to another, going backwards and forwards in time like Doctor Who. As Lisa pieced together the jigsaw of soggy beer mats, her sleepiness was replaced by wide-awake fury.

A bloke in the Red Lion had asked him outside 'for a word' about Lisa's strike because his wife had been roped into it. He accused Adam of being 'a pussy' because he should be the gaffer at home.

A scuffle broke out, a bit of shoving at the bar, until Ginger Steve stepped in to drag the men off one another as the landlord waded in to calm things down. Adam said he'd been humiliated in front of everyone, Lisa had gone behind his back to recruit his drinking mates' wives, he didn't feel like a man any more and she had betrayed him.

Reliving the story, he became angry all over again, which Lisa met with crossed arms and thin lips.

How dare he come in here this wasted, wake me up, vent his spleen and not once – not once – suggest it was this other man at fault, she thought. Especially after today, when he's been so amazing. Well, he can stuff it.

But she didn't want a screaming row; she didn't want the kids to be disturbed. So she told him: 'As the responsible half of this marriage, I'm not going to get into an argument about this now. You'll wake George and Rosie. I'm surprised you haven't already.'

'Oh, what's that on my head? It's a thumb, that's where you want me, isn't it?' he spat, spraying her face with flecks of saliva.

Lisa felt a surge of indignation and repulsion. He had learned nothing. He was even more of a pig than she'd thought.

'Excuse me but didn't it occur to you to defend what I'm doing, what we're doing as a family? To tell that bloke how you've actually got to know your children rather than just sharing the same

129

breathing space? Oh, I'm sorry if you aren't interested in knowing the quirks and the delights and the small things that make them tick,' she said with disgust.

'George's obsession with superhero socks. How he always wees in the bath. His fifty-five goodbye kisses in the playground. Did you notice how happy George was when you knew which one was his favourite water bottle when you made him a drink tonight? And Rosie was chuffed to bits when you actually asked her about her reading level when you went through her bag earlier. What about when she asks every morning if she can have the crusts cut off her sandwiches? Her sudden love of nail varnish and French plaits and make-up? Or does this mean nothing? Or maybe, just maybe – and it hurts to admit it – maybe you're embarrassed to admit you have enjoyed getting closer to your children because it doesn't fit your macho image. Yeah, Adam, you're such a man. I was going to call off my strike tomorrow but after this . . .'

He pulled a face like a panto Ugly Sister, picked up his pillow, then flounced out, announcing: 'I'll be in the loft until further notice, Pam bloody Grier.'

'Good,' she said in a shouty whisper to his back. 'And it's Germaine, you thick sod,' she said, before slamming her body down on the bed in a huge huff, tossing and turning, trying to get the covers right.

130

She'd never get to sleep now, not after the row she wasn't supposed to have had. Why hadn't she just left it? They could've talked about it tomorrow. Adam would probably have had time to mull it over and he'd have apologised and they would be well on their way to harmony by the end of breakfast.

But she'd jabbed at the fire when she knew specifically not to. Why? Because this mattered to her, far more than she'd admitted to herself before.

Lisa's head and heart throbbed with grief at the loss of her new man. His inner caveman had been in there all along. What was it they said about *in vino veritas*? This was how he really felt, and it was so disappointing.

Being let down is worse than the anger, she thought, particularly when it's accompanied by a soundtrack of rip-roaring snoring rattling down from the loft.

Day 9

11.04a.m., Friday, 23 May

Ping. A light bulb went on in Lisa's head as she priced up some beautiful teal art deco vases at work.

She stopped and laughed, berating herself for not seeing the wood for the trees.

Being angry with Adam had distracted her from the real story of last night – another mum had joined the strike, making it three so far. It was someone she didn't know, which meant not only was word spreading but so was support.

Why hadn't she thought of that before? She called over to Mo, who was in the shop window doing the display, up to her eyebrows in boxes and bits of polystyrene, and told her the latest.

'I told you so,' Mo purred, peering over the tops of her trendy NHS-style black-rimmed glasses. 'You're on to a winner here, having the guts to do what so many of us have dreamed of doing. By the

132

way,' she added, returning to her work, 'someone's rung from the paper, the number's in the office, might as well call now as we're quiet.'

It was probably something to do with the school quiz night, Lisa thought, she'd given the Vintage number on the email she'd sent to *The Herald* when she'd asked for a short piece to go in advertising the event.

As soon as she said her name to the receptionist, she was transferred to the editor, an Alex Baxter, which was odd. Why would he want to talk to her?

He (who turned out to be a she) wanted to run a story on Lisa's strike. Flushed with excitement, Lisa explained the situation so far and agreed to pose for some photos at lunchtime. Well, what harm could it do?

'I wonder what Adam will say,' Mo said when Lisa returned, flustered, to the shop.

'I don't care, after what he did last night,' she said, picking up the pricing gun and blowing the end as if she was Calamity Jane.

And there was more to come, she muttered to herself, louder than she intended.

'That sounds ominous,' her boss replied. 'Come on, spill.'

Suddenly, Lisa was full of self-doubt; bringing her private thoughts to life made them sound whimsical.

It was the first time she'd admitted to anyone apart from Cal that she wanted to do something with her life. She wanted fulfilment beyond her role as 'mum', to improve herself and her kids' lot and make everyone proud of her.

'I want to do a course or something,' she said, nervously, her eyes searching Mo's for a sign she wasn't being ridiculous. 'I left school with my GCSEs then went to college and spent years temping until I became a PA, which I really enjoyed. Then I met Adam and fell in love and got sidetracked, not that I ever had plans for a career or anything. Then I became a mum and that's been all, until now. It's not that I'm not happy at home or here, you know I love it, and it's probably ridiculous of me to think I could ever do anything more but I'd love my own business . . .'

Mo leapt in with a bollocking.

'Now listen here, you're a natural organiser, you've got great ideas, huge potential and I don't think you realise how good you are. This shop has benefited so much from you working here. I've never been able to rely on someone as much as I do on you. You've reorganised the stocktake, there's far less waste than before and your input into the café has been brilliant – even Babs has told me she thinks you're a diamond and she doesn't like anyone sticking their nose into her kitchen. I can't tell you how impressed I am. You have no confidence, that's your trouble. Of course you can do it, lady, whatever you set your mind on. Just go for it and if I can help, I will.'

'Cal says I should wait till the kids are older. I know what she means, Mo, and she says Adam needs to be fully on board, which is right, but I feel like he won't ever do that because he knows how much he'll lose out, if I'm studying or working at night or whatever. This strike has confirmed that to me, that's for sure.'

Mo nodded and mulled it over. 'Cal is right to an extent but there's never the right time. There will always be an adjustment period, a resistance to change. You just have to be prepared for a bit of an initial backlash, that's all.'

A 'TA-DAAA!' interrupted their chat.

There stood Lisa's mum, beaming wildly, breathing hard, wearing a camo onesie and patent Doc Martens, as if she was Ms Rambo. On one side, she splayed a *Strictly Come Dancing* jazz hand, in the other she held a wooden placard which read WOMAN AT WAR.

Dear God, Lisa thought, she looks ecstatic.

'Look what I've made you,' Angie said. 'Thought it might come in handy if you're going to do a march or something. Oh, I'm so proud of you. I've even joined you – won't hurt Dad to clear up after himself, will it!'

'Oh. Thanks. Not staying, are you? We're very busy,' Lisa hinted, faintly offended that her mum had chosen to deliver her first ever words of praise about this, rather than the fact that Lisa had given her two grandchildren, which she considered to be her greatest ever achievement.

Angie told her she couldn't stop anyway, she was on her way to a meeting but would she like her to write to the MP or get some of her groups involved, in fact would she like her to organise a demo or – oh, look who's here, how lovely, it's Lesley!

Oh, Lord, I'm surrounded, Lisa thought.

'Lesley!'

'Angie!'

This is like a bloody sitcom, Lisa realised, as her mother-in-law swept in to suffocate them in a fog of perfume.

The two elders air-kissed and exchanged pleasantries, completely unaware Lisa was thinking Hellooo? I'm at work.

'Lisa, I won't beat about the bush, dear,' Lesley finally started, her purple-eyeshadowed lids fluttering half closed half open to both underline the importance of her words and signal she had no intention of listening to anyone who might interrupt her. 'I've come to appeal to you, woman to woman. I'm very disappointed in all of this, you know.'

'Right. O-Kaaay . . .' Lisa said, wondering what

the hell she was supposed to say to that when she wasn't the one who'd gone into another woman's house and started doing her ironing behind her back.

'I'm of a different generation to you so it's natural I find this charade confusing, but that's by the by because the issue here is how you're going about it. Can't you try to be a bit less confrontational and undignified?' she whined.

'Just look at me and Roy, forty-five years we've been together and all that time he's thought he's in charge. But he isn't. I am. I let him believe he is, though, and we rub along very nicely, thank you. Anything I've wanted changing, I've planted the seed in his head and then let him think it was his idea and *voilà*, I get my own way,' she said with a grisly smile which revealed peach lipstick on her teeth.

'Call me old-fashioned but this is how it works, 'twas ever thus. You're going about it all the wrong way. The children, Adam, they're all suffering. Let me give you a tip,' she said, tapping her powdered nose: 'you need to be, how shall I put it, more wily, more coquettish. If you want someone to take their coat off, you make the sun shine, dear. You don't rip it off them, do you?'

This was not the time or the place, Lisa thought, watching her mother with dread; Angie was at boiling point, hands on hips, shaking her mass of hennaed hair emphatically, ready to deliver a right-on sermon of drivel.

'Now hang on a minute,' Angie said, thrilled to be sticking her oar in, 'this is an act, not of heroism but she-roism, by one woman, my daughter, on behalf of every downtrodden woman in the world and the truth of it is this—'

Stepping in as though she was Lisa's minder, Mo absolutely agreed that all three of them needed a discussion but it was out of the question at this moment because they had an urgent shop matter to attend to in the office.

Glory be, thought Lisa, Mo is my guardian angel.

Lesley harrumphed, heaving her bosom skywards, while Angie stamped her foot and declared 'the revolution is coming, Lesley, you mark my words' before Mo escorted them to the door, pointing at little trinkets here and there to defuse the tension, which miraculously worked as if they were two brawling toddlers diverted by a packet of sweeties.

The open door tinkling, the women mwah-ed once again as though their spat had never happened and went on their way, one left, one right.

Lisa applauded her 8-stone-something boss for having the physical presence to remove the silly old battleaxes from the shop with a dose of Lesley's recommended cunning.

'Tell me, Mo,' she said, 'what was that you were saying about a backlash?'

2.59p.m.

A waft of something delicious hit Mandy as she entered the house.

Glory be! Had Sandro finally got the message? Dropping her cleaning stuff in the narrow hall, she called out for him and checked her appearance in the mirror. If he was here, she wanted to make sure she looked nice, considering he'd gone to so much effort in the kitchen. A blob of dirt from her last job was on her left cheekbone, a quick lick of her finger sorted that, she puffed up her hair, took off her overall and smoothed her vest top.

No answer. He'd probably gone to work already, she mused, surprising herself with the sense of disappointment she felt. Perhaps their 'chat' this morning, when she'd popped back in to get the keys for one of her clients' houses she'd forgotten, had hit home. There'd been fireworks, there always were, but looking back, had there been a glimmer of comprehension in his eyes when she'd said she wanted them all on the same side, as if they were Juventus? It had been a masterstroke, Mandy realised, bringing in his beloved football team. Perhaps the penny, or more aptly the penne, had dropped. And telling him she'd be more likely to sleep with him if he did more must've helped too! Ha! Men are so one-dimensional, she thought, the way to their heart was definitely not via their stomach.

In the kitchen she found two enormous dishes of lasagne, both covered and cooling on top of the hob. The oven, wall and floor were smattered with sauce, small chunks of chopped onion and mushroom were on the floor, used saucepans were stacked in the sink and there were a few bits of stringy mozzarella on the worktop. Never mind, she didn't mind sorting that out, she thought as she filled the washing-up bowl with Fairy Liquid. She might as well tidy up because he'd met her halfway.

She hugged herself with joy, her heart filling with gladness. It hadn't been as hard as she'd expected: a few days and he'd come to his senses.

Mandy inhaled deeply and felt disproportionate relief – yes, he'd only cooked, but when she was the one with that responsibility on her shoulders day in, day out, her mind always ticking over wondering what she was going to feed the kids tonight, it gave her a thrill.

How funny, she thought, this is all it takes to make me happy! Two bloody lasagnes! I'm so easily pleased, she laughed, but that's ten years of marriage for you. With a smile, she decided she'd stay up for Sandro when he got in tonight, give him a bit of loving to show how much she appreciated it.

She put the kettle on; she wasn't in any rush this afternoon. Mum was taking the kids to their swimming lessons. I think I'll have a bath, she thought, I can shave my legs and then when I collect Franco and Lola, we can pop into the restaurant to see Sandro on our way home. They sometimes went in for tea on a Friday but tonight there was lasagne! They could stop for a quick drink, though. The kids love that, seeing their dad at work, Mandy thought, he always makes such a fuss of them in there, more so than at home, probably to do with being amongst 'his own', feeling part of a bigger family.

This was a turning point in their marriage, Mandy realised. The kids were growing up and often she'd worried how it would affect her and Sandro; whether they'd grow apart and have little in common as the children needed them less. But now with a bit of luck they would come back together and find happiness again, just like they had when they met.

She considered how lucky she was. She didn't need a big house or possessions. Blimey, she saw enough grand homes to know that – never did she clean a place and wish she lived there. Yes, she sometimes imagined herself all glammed up and living the dream in a marbled kitchen with an island but then lots of her clients had told her they were trapped by the size of the mortgage. Take that lady she cleaned for yesterday. OK, she had a new baby so she was bound to be tired but there was something deeper about her unhappiness. The way she'd trailed around after her as she worked. She wasn't inspecting what I was doing, thought Mandy, I knew that by the gratitude she kept expressing when I was scrubbing away. She seemed lovely, but distracted too, nattering about the lovely weather. What was it she said about the price of having such a nice home? For someone who had it all, her new lady certainly didn't look as if she was enjoying it. She'd said she never saw her husband and she felt she was bringing up the kids alone. Mandy had nodded, she knew what that felt like, but at least Sandro was showing he could change and she was sure she could get him more involved with the kids. She'd managed to get him to do some cooking after all so she could definitely work on them having more family time.

She nipped upstairs to start the bath running, adding a splosh of the designer bubbles Sandro had got her for Christmas. Sandro loved the musky smell it left on her skin and it had become one of 'their' things: if she'd had a soak, it was a sign she wanted him, like the first step of foreplay. Not that she'd been up for it much of late, but now perhaps they could reignite their love life. The thought of it made her tingle as she trotted downstairs to find her hairbrush.

Mandy went into the lounge-diner, humming 'Here Comes the Sun', noticing the room was a bit of a tip, but Rome wasn't built in a day, was it? Oooh, what's that? she thought, as she saw a note on the dining table, with her name at the top in Sandro's handwriting.

Probably a love letter, she joked to herself, *my dearest Mandy, I'll always love you, you'll never have to wash my pants ever again.* Yeah, right. He wasn't that amazing!

Lifting it, she began to read: 'Mand, don't touch those lasagnes, spoke to Mum and she told me to make them, then divide them into separate portions for the freezer so I DON'T STARVE. Will do it when I get in. S.'

The colour drained from her face as she scrunched the paper into a tight ball. The little . . . what a . . . I can't believe he's done this. He's cooked for himself, not us, he's actually gone to all that effort and won't share them. Unbelievable. Feeling winded, Mandy gulped for breath as she tried to digest his selfishness. He didn't even say the kids could have some.

Her mood tumbled, pulling her shoulders down and making her cry. She felt foolish now, berating herself for being so naïve. Embarrassed too – how could she have thought she was capable of turning his head when she was so thick and clueless?

She picked up a photo of Granny Glitter from the sideboard and touched her face. All she could feel was cold glass, not the lovely soft and wrinkled skin she remembered cuddling up to right up to her death.

'Oh, what am I going to do?' she asked out loud.

A wicked thought came to her as if it had been a gift from her grandmother's ghostly spirit, which had observed the whole thing.

That's it. Don't get mad, get even, Mandy thought as she went up to get in the bath, sniffing away the tears, pulling herself together, thinking she would play the long game.

She'd divide the dishes up herself for freezing, claiming she'd cracked because she couldn't stand the mess, making sure the kids had some tonight; well, why the hell not? Not enough so he'd notice.

Then she'd have a bit of fun.

Revenge is a dish best served tampered with, she thought, as she submerged her body then head under the water like a crocodile.

6.34p.m.
Lisa was just drying her wet bits in the swimming pool changing room when a tap on her shoulder made her drop her towel.

A complete stranger, who was just as starkers as she was, reached out and pumped her hand.

'Hi, I'm Mel, I just wanted to let you know I'm on strike too. Isn't it brilliant being able to come up here at this time on a Friday night while they're at home with the kids!'

Momentarily, Lisa was in the headlights, undecided what to cover first with her spare palm – boobs or down below? The nethers, it was. Thirty-blimming-six and her default position when faced with nudity was shame. Thanks, Mum.

Never mind that! Smile and keep eye contact, she instructed herself.

'I work at the chemist's, got twin girls at the school, it's brilliant because they're well into equal rights, they did something about it at school, so their dad has his work cut out with them bossing him about!' Mel said, delivering a cackle which made her boobs dance.

Lisa laughed, then asked how she'd found out about it – was she a friend of Mandy's?

No, Mel said, she'd just heard about it in The Grapevine wine bar in town on a girls' night out and a gang of them had made a pact there and then!

'Well I never,' Lisa said, marvelling at the budding movement in her town. 'That's incredbile!' She threw her hands up in the air before remembering she was in the altogether.

'I better, you know, get dressed really . . .' She laughed.

'Course!' Mel guffawed, turning away to get her stuff out of the locker.

Still buzzing, Lisa enthusiastically got to work on

145

drying in between her toes. She felt refreshed from that swim after a twenty-four-hour rollercoaster of downs and ups.

It was also her way of staying clean. Or, more accurately, staying away from the cleaning things. How long did they say it took to break a habit? A week, a fortnight? Forever? She'd never considered herself an addict before. She'd never smoked or touched drugs and though she liked a drink, she wasn't one to get trolleyed every night of the week. But cleaning, well, not doing any was really getting to her. God, you're so sad, she told herself. Look, she reasoned, it's not that I'm addicted, it's more like I can only relax once everything is in its place. I've been conditioned to do it to make sure I keep on top of everything; it's just part of who I am. I don't particularly enjoy doing it, but once it's done, I feel I've achieved something.

Why was she talking in the present tense? You are on strike, Lisa Stratton, she thought sternly.

If only she could think like a man: 'Oh, look, there's a dried pea on the floor, I wonder what the football score is?' And that's only if they actually notice it.

Instead of 'there's a dried pea on the floor, I must pick it up, even though I'm chopping carrots, emptying the dishwasher and helping George with learning his sounds, blimey, the floor needs a mop too, I'll do that in a sec.'

146

She'd tried to distract herself with books and TV, face masks and painting her nails but dread was everywhere she looked. Over the top of her book, she'd see an empty packet of sweets that needed binning. The telly was smudged with fingerprints. And beautifying herself meant having to stay still and wait for things to set or dry, which meant her eyes wandered to dirty skirting boards and dusty shelves.

Watching Adam working away was painful because she tried to stop herself giving him tips or reminders – he had 'How To Be Me' and mistakes were all part of learning. Sometimes, the sight of him all cack-handed made her feel physically ill. Particularly when he cooked things like shepherd's pie, which meant pans piling up, none of which were swooshed out with water to make them easier to clean. By the time he'd stuck the dish in the oven, the floor resembled a pigsty with potato peelings. He wouldn't start tidying up at this point, oh no. He'd walk off and start another task which he would then abandon when something else crossed his mind; he was incapable of multitasking. Jobs took hours, everything was done on the back hoof and he'd go from chilled out to flustered in five seconds.

It made Lisa panic.

And that made her think about her life. She had left the land of feeling proud of being able to run a house. She wanted more than that now. It's not that she pitied anyone else who enjoyed being a home-maker, it was to do with feeling ready to do something for herself. Crucially, though, only something that would benefit her family too. But what? She was bobbing about in the ocean, having only just got her 10-metre badge.

That's why she'd started coming to the pool to take herself out of the danger zone.

She had to stay strong after last night. There would be no reconciliation until Adam was happy to admit he would do half of everything and be pleased to do it. Ha, she thought, doing up her bra, I can't see that ever happening. Which was why she had to make it happen.

He'd been in a foul mood at breakfast, barking orders at George and Rosie through his hangover.

Stupid Adam. If he'd come home last night and told her he'd defended their honour then she'd have called it a day. Even if he'd apologised at breakfast, she might have done it.

But he didn't and that's why she'd agreed to the interview and photos today. Had Alex Baxter asked her yesterday, it would've been a firm no.

Adam wasn't going to like it one bit. But he hadn't learned a single thing in the last nine days so she had no other option. She'd given Alex his number so she could ask him for a quote in the interest of balance; he was bound to go mad at that but it served him right.

Flushed from both the latest mum coming forward and the struggle of wiggling her trousers up her resisting wet legs, Lisa pulled a brush through her hair then grabbed her bag and walked out into the car park, planning on dropping Adam right in it by asking how he was getting on with the packing for their camping trip tomorrow. He hadn't done a thing about it, despite a few hints here and there from Lisa; he just didn't have a clue about the preparation involved.

He would think she was being spiteful because of his hangover. Damn right, she was.

It was time to turn the screw.

8.48p.m.

Lisa waited until Adam had flopped down on the sofa next to her and informed her he would be going up to bed in a minute.

'Ad,' she said, staring straight at *Corrie*, to make it look like it wasn't anything to be worried about.

'Mmmm,' he replied, rubbing his eyes with the heels of his hands, beginning his evening routine of 'getting ready to go up' movements.

'Camping tomorrow,' she said, leaving a pause before she dropped the bomb. 'Everything packed?'

5 . . . 4 . . . 3 . . . 2 . . . 1, boom.

He sat up straight and jerked his head towards her face like a meercat.

'What do you mean "everything packed?" You do that, not me,' he said, believing it.

Lisa had had plenty of time to prepare herself for this. So she began a list of all the things that needed doing before they set off after lunch.

'Tent, sleeping bags, extra blankets, pillows, warm pyjamas, socks, pants, warm weather gear, wet weather gear, cold weather gear,' she said, as Adam repeated 'what?', standing up, sitting down then standing up again.

'Wellies, flip-flops, trainers, towels, shower gel, kid's shower gel, shampoo, conditioner, camping chairs, the plastic camping crockery set, barbecue, coal, firelighters, towels, gas stove, gas cylinders, swingball, badminton racquets, shuttlecocks . . .'

'You're not serious?' Adam said.

'Yes, deadly,' Lisa replied. 'Then there's the shopping list: bacon, eggs, cereal, tea bags, coffee, milk, cheese, sausages, pasta, pasta sauce, crisps, butter, bread, wine, beer, fruit, squash, no need for dinner stuff because we go out to eat at the pub at night. But make sure there's enough for eight of us, seeing as your sister expects us to cook breakfast and lunch for three days for them as well . . .'

Adam was refusing to believe his ears, telling her

'but, but, but you do all of this' as her memo continued out loud. Naturally, he accused her of being spiteful, another thing she'd expected to hear, so she was able to bat it back, telling him they could cancel – the kids would be disappointed but they'd get over it.

'Oh and don't forget the quiz we do every year round the campfire and the little treasure hunt for the kids, they love that,' Lisa said, delivering her final piece of advice like a parsley garnish.

Adam looked crushed and crumpled, as if someone had taken away his favourite toy.

Lisa softened, knowing full well how daunting the task was – she'd had to do it for the last four years on the trot. He considered his job to be putting the easy-peasy tent up then opening a bottle of beer.

'It's not as bad as it sounds, love, all the stuff is in the garage, the sleeping bags are in the loft, you just need to do the shop tomorrow. I'll take George to football so you can do the rest, Rosie'll help, she's really good at this sort of thing now.'

Adam opened his mouth as a flash of anger crossed his face. Then he stopped, realising he had no choice. He wouldn't be able to bear letting down the kids so he'd just have to get it done.

'You know, Adam, if you just accepted the terms of the strike then we could do it together,' Lisa said seductively, sensing this might be the time when he'd back down and agree to do his share. 'We can work out a rota of housework duties which can start when we get back next week. You don't have to put yourself through this.'

Adam nodded silently, puffing the air out of his cheeks. He was mulling it over, she could tell. Would he bite?

He leaned over to give her a warm kiss on the lips.

'Not a bloody chance, Lees,' he said, shocking Lisa to the core. 'I'm the breadwinner, I work my balls off to feed this family and I think you've gone completely over the top with all of this. I do all the dirty jobs round here, the trips to the tip, the unblocking of the drains, the painting inside and out, and you don't lift a finger with those so why should I help with the housework?'

He told her it'd be a cinch sorting out the camping stuff and he didn't know why she made it seem such a big deal. Then he said goodnight and left her to chew the cud.

Bugger. This hadn't gone quite as well as she'd hoped. She was the one in free fall now. He had a point, she didn't share those jobs, but they were few and far between, she told herself, they hardly added up to the toil of running a home and the kids and working. But she hadn't even considered 'his' dirty jobs.

They'd reached stalemate.

Lisa shuffled awkwardly in her seat, wondering how long before she could go up and not risk bumping into him on the landing. This camping trip would be interesting.

Day 10

Lisa couldn't believe her ears.

So that was why Cal hadn't been in touch, why she hadn't replied to her texts and why she hadn't answered her emails – she was obviously avoiding her because of what she was up to.

The bloody cheek of her, she thought, as she hid her real feelings with a big smile and an 'ah, that's nice' to Rob, Cal's husband, in the main hall in the leisure centre.

The pair were sitting together on a wooden bench in the dead centre of the room, which was divided by a huge curtain to separate Molly's gymnastics and George's football, so they could watch their own kids but have a conversation at the same time.

Lisa had taken George because Adam had gone shopping with Rosie; he'd got up at the crack of dawn and made enough banging and crashing for Lisa to think he wanted her to know he was packing for their

154

break. By the time she'd come downstairs, there was a jumble of bedding by the front door and he was whistling with what seemed like forced cheeriness. While shifting boxes and bags into the hall, he delivered an ominous 'You wanted me to do it my way, Lees, and that's what you're going to get.'

She'd beamed to show she was fine – absolutely fine – with him being at the helm. But Adam taking it on board as happily as he did worried her; he knew how much she loved having a 'perfect' bank holiday expedition, it was 'golden family time'; she'd banged on about it enough over the years.

Was that why he'd been so bright and breezy? He'd rabbited on in a jolly manner about heading into town to stock up and said that he and Rosie would stop off for a McDonald's brekkie while they were out.

George was gutted when Lisa insisted he had to go to football. It felt very odd being the bad cop for once. Usually Adam was the one who put his foot down if something serious needed saying with the kids. It hurt him less to do it than Lisa and he didn't mind if George and Rosie 'hated' him for five minutes. It was a silent agreement he and Lisa shared; she would always dish it out if necessary, of course she would, but there was something about being a mum that meant you were unable to bear their unhappiness even if they'd done something wrong.

But today he'd forced her into his position. And he was loving it.

On the drive to football, she told herself it was good to hand over the reins. Adam was bound to surrender after this weekend when he realised how hard it was to make camping look effortless.

He hadn't even remembered to rebook George's football lessons, which she'd discovered at the start of the class and which had led to an anxious fumble for her chequebook while her son cried sorry tears because he was convinced he'd been red-carded.

She'd almost calmed herself down when Rob plonked his backside down next to her and teased her about Adam being a bigamist.

Unwittingly, he'd dumped Cal and Adam right in it – she'd only been helping him out on the quiet.

Lisa felt as if she'd been punched in the guts; her friend, the one who'd always been on her side, was betraying her. Rob explained his wife had helped by 'picking up a few bits and pieces for Adam when she was in the supermarket, well, she was there and it was no bother'. She'd also ironed some of the kids' clothes because she was doing some anyway – Adam was there doing their patio with Ginger Steve so it made sense for him to bring them with him – and she'd delivered a few meals to Adam because she'd made a big batch for the freezer so there was plenty to share.

And it was so hilarious, he continued, when Adam

called Cal in a panic yesterday after he'd put a dishwasher tablet in the washing machine and 'would the red powerball turn everything pink?'

Rob couldn't see the blood draining from Lisa's face because his eyes were watching Molly on the beam. If he had, he would've stopped then and there.

But no, on he went, digging the hole ever deeper with his sniggers of derision at the thought of Adam with a feather duster. Rob wasn't angry at Lisa at all for bringing his missus into it, he wasn't that sort of bloke. Cal loved helping out and he could see the funny side of it all.

Hysterical, isn't it, he said with a nudge, his words joining the jumble of echoing noise in the hall, which whirled around Lisa's head, making her dizzy.

Lisa noticed her foot was tapping at 100m.p.h. It was like Mickey flicking his tail in anger when he was being manhandled by the kids but still Rob didn't notice.

Then, with self-congratulatory delight at his punchline, Rob told her he drew the line at having the kids for tea because Adam wanted to go for a bike ride and Lisa was too busy training for the Olympics swimming squad.

That did it. Not only had Adam roped in someone else to have George and Rosie without mentioning it to Lisa, but they'd been laughing at her.

Lisa felt wounded and judged and stupid. As if

their dirty washing had been aired in public, even though it was only in front of Cal and Rob.

She changed the subject swiftly, cruelly, to ask how Dot was doing. She knew he wouldn't have a clue because he was out of the house by 7a.m. and not home until the kids were in bed.

He flustered and blustered when she asked which medication Dot was on for the reflux. She wanted him to feel judged like she did now.

Lisa instantly felt bad, she'd delved into their laundry basket this time just because she was upset with Adam and Cal. What was happening to her? She was ashamed to have been spiteful and tried to reassure him she'd never seen such a healthy baby.

A protracted blow of the whistle signalled the end of the football class and Lisa leapt up too eagerly, desperate to get away. But to what? She had a sense of dread about the camping trip.

What she needed was a positive mental attitude. The sun was shining, the forecast was amazing for once and they were going to have a brilliant time. Of course they were.

3.13p.m.
Adam had done a fantastic job, she had to give him that, Lisa thought as she cursed under her breath, wrestling with a bundle of poles, trying to work out which bendy bit went where.

Dazzled by the glorious sunshine she was completely flummoxed, but had to pretend she wasn't since she'd proclaimed that tent erection was a fuss over nothing on the three-hour drive to the Welsh campsite.

It had started off as a bit of banter; he was teasing her from the passenger seat, having insisted she drive to see how she liked it, saying the preparations were actually really easy. It was true, damn him, he'd organised everything they needed and they'd left on time after he made a quick sandwich. Mind you, she usually had to do it with the kids hanging off her. Why did they do as they were told with him and not her?

He'd made a compilation playlist for the journey, full of the kids' favourites, declaring it 'a new tradition'. She'd always made them listen to a talking book on the way in years gone by.

As Rosie and George bopped in the back to the truly awful 'Gangnam Style', she made the mistake of biting back with 'well, you make such a song and dance about putting up the tent, you only do that so you can justify spending the rest of the holiday drinking beer from your chair.'

So that was why she'd ended up scratching her head, unfolding poles, trying to feed them through the openings of their super-duper orange tent, which had two bedrooms and a living area. Grrrr, she said. Yet again she'd fed the wrong one through the awning bit.

Adam had taken the kids off to the play area, which was beside reception, so they could spot his sister Sarah and family when they got here. Lisa had to get this done before they arrived or she'd never hear the end of it.

She would definitely have a glass from that box of wine which was on ice in a coolbag Adam had packed. That was another good idea. She always froze things before their departure so they'd be defrosted but cold when they got there. He hadn't had the chance so, all credit to him, he'd come up with a solution. Not just that, he'd gone through the menu for their holiday – fry-ups every morning for the adults and brioches and yogurts for the kids ('no boring cereal because they're on holiday' received a huge cheer), croissants for elevenses (nice touch, Lisa thought), a snacky lunch of crisps, cheese, pâté and fruit (Lisa's favourite), a BBQ in case they fancied a change, then bags of booze, J20s and juice once they'd had their pub tea every night. He'd remembered to get his mother in to feed the cat, charge the iPad so the kids could watch a film every night (genius) and – his *pièce de résistance* – he'd upgraded them all to blow-up beds because the roll-up mats had been chewed by something in the garage.

She couldn't fault him. Annoyingly enough. Still, she shouldn't moan, she thought, Rosie and George are delirious with excitement. This was for them, and any improvements Adam made to their experience was a good thing. She shouldn't let her nose be out of joint; it wasn't about her.

Once the tent was standing, Lisa set about pegging the ropes and when that was done, she stood back to admire her work. There, she said, wiping her forehead with her wrist, that wasn't so hard. She inhaled the fresh country smell – it was a beautiful day, the sky was blue, not a cloud was in sight and the grass was a perfect green. Her first sip of chilled white wine – in a proper glass, not a plastic one, thanks to Adam – was heavenly.

Running footsteps thundered up behind her. George was squealing with excitement, his cousins were here and Daddy said he could have some sweets.

Squinting, she saw Adam and Co. approaching and waved enthusiastically with both arms. Was that her sister-in-law in skinny jeans and breaking into a run? Blimey, she's lost a shedload of weight, Lisa noticed, as, quite out of character, Sarah gave her a bear hug.

'You've started early!' she said, gesturing with delight at the booze in Lisa's hand. 'Glad to see it, Lees. Pour me one!'

A walking pile of sleeping bags revealed itself to be Dave, Sarah's husband, who announced with a serious face: 'No drinking for me. Until I've unpacked the car. Wahey!'

Adam opened two bottles of lager and the four of them shared a 'cheers!' then discussed their journeys from opposite ends of the country. Sarah and Dave lived up north, thanks to Dave's job in the Lakes as an outdoor pursuits instructor. The kids were beyond happy: Rosie and George played tag with Matthew, who was in the same year as Rosie, and Rebecca, just three months older than George. Wow, Sarah's in a good mood, Lisa thought, I wonder what's up with her? Normally she's a bit of a misery guts, always finding something to complain about but in a funny way. But today she seems happy. Dear God, does that mean she'll help out for once?

Usually Sarah saw their camping trip as an opportunity to put her feet up, always 'I was just about to do that' when Lisa started cooking or clearing up. Adam had never noticed his sister's laziness, of course he hadn't, he was too busy jabbering away to Dave about music, beer and football. 'Oh you love being the mother hen anyway,' he said every time Lisa brought it up. That was kind of true, but only because she wanted to make the holiday perfect for the kids. She had more invested in it emotionally than Sarah, she presumed, as they wouldn't get away in the summer like them. It was a long way until the October half-term. That's why she didn't let it bother her too much that Sarah wasn't her ideal companion; she was diluted by Adam and Dave, who was your archetypal Nice Guy. Always fun, always hands-on, Dave was easy to get on with.

Testing the water with Sarah to see if she'd grumble as she normally did, even when she was paid a compliment, Lisa told her she looked amazing, really fantastic, bright-eyed and healthy and how had she done it?

'Bit of a midlife crisis, I think, Lees, turning forty made me think a bit so I joined the gym and started paying attention to what I was eating and . . . yes, this,' Sarah said, smiling, pointing at her slimmed-down thighs and waist.

'Your hair too! That style really suits you, you're like a new woman,' Lisa said.

'Yeah, I still can't believe it either, I just decided to have it shorter, it's ideal for the gym too,' she said, stroking the dark brown strands of her pixie 'do on her neck. 'Ha! Listen to me, I sound like a loony. Dave is still getting used to the "new me", aren't you, Dave?'

'It's like waking up with a different woman, which suits me after twelve years with her!' he said, gazing in admiration at his wife. 'Now it's my turn to lose "this",' he said patting his paunch, at which Adam sucked in his stomach and pulled a bodybuilder pose to show he was happy with his physique.

Then he called Rosie and George and told them: 'Come on, kids, time to do The Secret Thing Mummy Doesn't Know About!'

Taking their cousins with them, they all piled in the tent. Several zips went up and down to seal off the area from prying eyes, accompanied by sniggering, loud whispering and orders to 'take this' and 'hold that'.

Sarah looked quizzically at Lisa, her mouth an 'O'.

'We've had a few changes too since we last saw you,' Lisa said, trying to explain; 'you'll see.'

Adam's voice commanded Lisa to shut her eyes and she felt his hands on her shoulders, twisting her round and guiding her to the front of the tent.

'You can open them now,' he instructed.

'Oh my God! That's so sweet,' Lisa gasped as she took in a wonky blow-up inflatable palm tree tied to one of the ropes by the door, balloons hanging off various hooks in the 'ceiling' and Rosie and George dressed in hula skirts with garlands round their necks.

That wasn't all – Adam had made up a mini 'beach bar' area out of a cardboard box on which Rosie had written in felt tip 'The Beach Hut'. On top of it was a cocktail shaker and a cup of Del Boy umbrellas.

Seriously, she couldn't have been more shocked by the way everything was turning out.

'Mummy, which is your bestest bit?' George asked her, whirling his arms around his head in sheer delight. 'Mine's the cocynut with googly eyes. Daddy got it for me today, it's not a real cocynut so we won't eat him, it was my idea to give him eyes.'

Adam and Rosie were now swaying, their hands simulating waves, as Sarah and Dave peeked inside in wonder at the Hawaiian theme.

'Come on, Mummy!' Adam shouted, dragging her by the hand to join in the ridiculous scene.

Then a group hug while Lisa praised them all for such a lovely idea, talking into their hair and ears and kissing them all over.

Well! She'd never have predicted all of this – there she was expecting bedlam and Adam had pulled this out of the bag.

She was on a high: nothing would go wrong this weekend. Normal life was suspended until they went home on Monday. And they were going to have a ball.

10.05p.m.
Lisa chucked off the blanket which was keeping her lap warm and only just missed the burning embers of the barbecue Adam had lit not just for toasting marshmallows but to keep out the chill of the evening.

'Careful, Lees,' Adam said, tutting as she heaved herself out of her chair, announcing she needed a wee.

But her legs had seized up since the sun had gone down and her thighs couldn't support her, so she fell backwards, too heavily, and her chair rocked back, throwing her upside down on the grass so she was lying with her knees in her face.

'Haaahahhahahaha!' Sarah cackled from her chair, waving the men to go and pick her up because she was too weak from laughing to help.

'Thank God the kids didn't see that,' Adam said over his shoulder to Sarah and Dave as he escorted his weaving wife to the campsite loos across the way.

'I don't think you should have any more to drink, Lees,' he told her, 'you're quite pissed.'

'I am not bloody drunk enough, Ad,' she giggled, holding on to his arm. 'This is your fault, anyway, all those bloody cocktails, I need food, what snacks have you got? Can you make me a cuppa?'

On the walk back from the toilets, Lisa realised how squiffy she was – her line of vision was jumpy, as if she was in some edgy drama with shaky cameras, and she was so thirsty.

'Sarah's so funny,' Lisa said, 'it's like she's had a personality transplant.'

'She's always been like that, you've just never really taken the opportunity to get to know her,' Adam said a little defensively.

'Pfffff,' she raspberried, 'haven't had the chance to sit down in her company before, more like. Do you know what, I'm having a brilliant time, Ad. And the kids, they're loving it, I think they're at the right age for all of this now, don't you? Here we are, Adam's making tea, anyone want a brew?'

Sarah nodded as Dave went into their tent to check on Matthew and Rebecca while Adam went to fill the kettle.

It was the chance Sarah had apparently been waiting for, to grill Lisa on a few things she'd obviously noticed about Adam's behaviour.

It was all down to the strike, Lisa explained, wrapping the blanket round her shoulders as she brought her up to speed on the story so far. Sarah was full of admiration but confessed she was lucky because Dave was far more houseproud than her, thanks to his stint in the army years back. Encouraged by the melting of ice, Lisa seized the moment, tentatively telling Sarah things felt 'better' between the two women and it was as if something had clicked into place after all these years.

'Yeah, you're right,' Sarah said, 'it was when I saw you today and you had a drink in your hand and I thought "finally, she's chilled out a bit".'

There was a jumble of 'don't take this the wrong way' and 'I'm not slagging you off' from her sister-in-law as she tried to soften the blow of her well-meaning words.

Lisa knew what she meant. She had always retained a distant edge on these camping trips, having her head full of what needed doing next, tinged with a speck of resentment that Sarah didn't do anything. But perhaps all this time she'd never properly relaxed.

Seeing as they were straight-talking, Lisa said she'd taken a leaf out of Sarah's book, letting the kids run a bit more free, stopping the helicopter parenting and allowing someone else to take the strain.

'Are you calling me a lazy cow?' Sarah asked, with faux horror.

'Well it did always feel like I was doing everything, if I'm honest,' Lisa said.

'But I could never get near the blimming kitchen,' Sarah said, 'you were always there, saying you could do it, you liked doing it and turning down help. Every year I've gone back with a load of food we've never got round to eating because I assumed you liked to do it all!'

Adam reappeared to spark up the stove as the two women laughed with relief at having cleared up their misunderstanding.

'Looks like you've got work cut out, bro,' Sarah said. 'There are two lazy cows to wait on now!'

Suddenly, an ooooof came from the side of the Stratton tent. Dave had tripped over a guy rope. Adam inspected the scene and condemned it as 'a schoolgirl error, Lees, a schoolgirl error'.

It was as if he'd been waiting for the chance to criticise her tent erection skills, Lisa thought, the way he went on about it. He was shaking his head, muttering 'dear, oh dear' as he got on his hands and knees with a torch in his mouth to adjust the toggles of every single rope to make them shorter. He had to make his feelings known, didn't he. What a shit, she thought. She never humiliated him in front of anyone; well, not before this strike anyway. Who did he think he was? Survival expert Ray bloody Mears?

A whistle sounded in the night. Lisa pushed her bottom even more firmly into her chair.

'Oh, Adam,' she sang, 'the kettle's boiled.'

Day 11

9.14a.m., Sunday, 25 May

'Just toast for me,' Rob said to the waitress at The Busy Teapot.

Cal pretended she was about to faint. 'No Mega Full English?' she said. 'Are you on a diet?'

Her husband gave a small, embarrassed laugh, waiting until Cal had ordered then instructing the kids to share a fry-up because they never finished a whole one anyway before claiming he wasn't that hungry.

'Suit yourself,' she said, licking her lips at the prospect of bacon, sausage, eggs and beans. She'd been up since 5.30 with Dotty, so needed refuelling.

She looked fondly around the table and took in her brood: Dotty was napping in the pram, Molly was colouring while Ted played on Rob's phone. This was their Sunday morning ritual, breakfast in their favourite café followed by a trip to the park; weather permitting, of course. Today was lovely. The sun was

170

warming up nicely and the kids were in shorts and T-shirts. Even Rob had his legs out! Cal wasn't brave enough yet to bare hers because she still felt a bit blobby. But beneath her flared linen trousers she had flip-flops on and painted toenails.

'Ahhhh,' she said, smiling at Rob's balding head as he read his paper.

'Ten weeks till our holiday, not that I'm counting!' Cal said, mouthing a silent 'yeah' and waving her hands as Rob cleared his throat. They were going all-inclusive to a hotel on a Greek island for a fortnight. It was costing a bomb but what was the point of Rob working so hard if they couldn't reap the benefits?

The resort looked amazing in the brochure – three pools, a kids' club, seven restaurants with early sittings for families, a private beach and a spa, which Cal hoped to visit several times in the fortnight. She wanted to try one of those hot stone massages; she could see herself lying on her front in a darkened perfumed room, with gentle music playing, every aching muscle in her body soothed into submission.

It was going to be bliss. No cooking, no tidying, no washing – their villa was serviced daily, she'd checked this several times now online, getting a quick kick on each occasion. Best of all, the kids would be barefoot and free for a whole fortnight, their skin would turn brown and their blond hair would turn white. The oldest two were just at the right age now for a holiday like this, Cal thought, and Dot was young enough to be content to splash in the baby pool and then sleep – if Cal was lucky – while she read a book.

'I feel a bit smug, Rob,' she said as her plate appeared under her nose. 'Not in a horrible way. We're just so lucky, aren't we?'

He nodded slowly, reaching out for a piece of her bacon to slip on a piece of his toast.

'I knew you'd be hungry when it arrived!' she said, pretending to tell him off but letting him get away with it. Besides, she needed to start thinking about being a bit more sensible food-wise if she was going to be in a swimsuit.

Rob was quiet, she noticed. 'You OK, love?'

He said he was just 'chillaxing', enjoying the rare quiet of his family's company. Which obviously set the kids off chattering. 'Typical,' he said, winking at Molly whose latest obsession was spelling out whatever things were around her. 'Sausage, s-o-s-i-j,' she said, looking pleased with herself as Ted laughed with his mouth full, splattering the table with bits of food, then corrected her with glee.

Cal tutted at his manners and started to wipe up the chewed bits and pieces.

Her gliding hand must have triggered something in Rob's mind, because out of the blue he said he'd noticed something different at home.

'Like what?' Cal asked.

'Dunno,' Rob said, scratching his weekend stubble. 'Like, things seem tidier – are the kids helping?'

'Wow, you've noticed,' Cal teased. 'I didn't think men saw mess.'

'No, we don't usually, but when Dot was born, everything went to pot, quite rightly, you had other things on your mind, but this last week you seem to be on top of things.'

'Well, I do feel a bit better, a bit more adjusted to having three kids, I think,' Cal said, feeling buoyed by his kindness. 'And the cleaner has helped.'

'Cleaner? Since when did we have a cleaner?' Rob said, choking on his toast.

Ted piped up with a 'don't talk with your—' only to be spoken over by his father, who had gone from 'chillaxed' to cross in one bite.

Cal said yes, she started last week and she didn't think Rob would be interested, the house was 'her business', he had his job, she had hers, that's the way it had always been.

But Rob was angry, Cal could see by the deep furrow halving his forehead. Why on earth was he worrying about it?

'Why do we need a cleaner?' he said, almost spitting out the words. 'You're at home all day, you don't work, Molly and Ted are at school and Dot, well, she doesn't need much entertaining at the moment – what

173

are you doing with yourself all day if you aren't doing housework?'

Cal was crestfallen. 'But it's only once a week, I'm still doing loads round the house, like the cooking and washing. The cleaner is brilliant, she scrubs the loos, dusts, hoovers and changes the sheets, all the stuff that only needs doing once a week. It's a massive help, Rob, and Dotty has me up every night.'

Rob wasn't listening. 'How much does she charge?' he asked, his blue eyes cold.

'Fifteen pounds an hour, she comes for two, it's worth every penny,' Cal said.

Apparently Rob didn't think so – he quickly totted it up and considered £1,500 a year a waste of money, especially with all the expenses with the new house and Dotty.

'But you just said you appreciated a tidier house, you're benefiting too, you know, and the kids get more time with me. I think you're over-reacting, Rob,' Cal said, feeling bruised and confused.

He just shook his head at her then screeched his chair back, got up and barked at the kids to hurry up, he was going to pay and then they were going to the park.

1.59p.m.
Adam had started the barbecue two hours ago but it still wasn't hot enough. Not that he'd admit it.

He hadn't bought any firelighters because he was a man and only girls used them, he'd said, blowing and wafting and probably racking his brains for memories of Boy Scout tips to get his coals to turn white.

The kids were complaining of starvation, whining at the adults, draping themselves over Sarah's and Lisa's laps as Dave offered Adam tips here and there.

'Piss off, Bear Grylls,' Adam said to every suggestion in a tone the children knew meant they'd be on a hiding to nothing if they pointed out his bad language.

'Just go and play, it'll be ready soon, take some crisps and go and play,' Lisa said, rolling her eyes at Sarah over her brother's stubbornness.

'Ad, we could just go to the clubhouse,' Sarah suggested, bravely.

'No need, it'll be ready in five,' he shot back as though his manhood depended on it.

He'd been saying that for the last hour, Lisa thought, poor thing. But why didn't he buy any firelighters? Men are so ridiculous, they cannot be told. It had all been going swimmingly.

They'd all slept until 6.30a.m. which wasn't bad considering the sun was up so early, no one had been cold and the weather was all sun, sun, sun.

But little problems were starting to rear their heads. Adam had forgotten ketchup and brown sauce for the bacon sandwiches. George only had one pair of pants so he was wearing them inside out because he refused point blank to wear a pair of knickers and Matthew's were too big. They only had kids' toothpaste. The suncream was not a 30 SPF but an ancient factor 8 from Adam's bachelor days. Rosie's DS wasn't charged.

Each time an issue cropped up, Adam became increasingly ratty, offering a sarcastic 'boo-hoo' at a moan or a 'well, in my day, we didn't have x, y or z'.

This must be why he's being so pig-headed about the barbecue, Lisa thought. He probably feels he's losing his grip on it all when it had gone so well yesterday.

Still, Sarah and her were getting on like never before. Lisa had never sat down properly with her at length, to get to know her. She'd always considered her as a mini Lesley, a bit judgmental and set in her ways. But she could see this was because she'd never taken the time to find out about her. It was like that with in-laws, you would spend time with them, thinking 'we're family, we don't need to make that much of an effort', but then realise you knew very little about them and their lives.

So that morning they'd parked their bums in their camping chairs and chatted away, letting Adam do all the hard work while Dave played with the kids.

Sarah was training for a 10-kilometre run, she

wanted to do a half-marathon after that and one day she hoped she could do the London Marathon. Her job was under threat at the council, where she worked in the environmental health department. She was hoping for redundancy so she could work with animals, something she'd always dreamed of doing, perhaps at a charity for rescued donkeys or a farm-yard visitors' attraction. Did Lisa know Lesley had never let them have pets 'because of the furniture'? That was where she thought it stemmed from. What else? Oh yes, Sarah and Dave were planning how to celebrate his 45th in the summer. He wanted a barn dance and a hog roast but she was trying to persuade him to spend the money on hiring a huge cottage and getting just a few close friends and family to go along – 'you and Adam and the kids are definitely invited,' she added.

Then it was Lisa's turn to tell all – how much she loved working, how after temping for years she finally felt she'd found her niche, how much she admired her boss, how she had plans for the future.

'Plans?' Adam said, earwigging, as the hiss of flicked water on the coals revealed they were ready for the meat to go on.

'Yeah, I've got plans,' she said, not entirely convinced now was the right time but bolstered up by the presence of Sarah, who would definitely support her.

'Go on then,' Adam said, flipping a burger and rolling a sausage.

'You'll probably think this is really stupid of me,' she began, fiddling with her fingers, peering out of the corners of her eyes to see his reaction. 'But I've been thinking about this for a while, well, before I met you even, and then things happened.'

'I whisked you off your feet with my good looks, amazing charm and considerable dancing talents,' Adam cut in, putting down the tongs to do his best dreadful Wham! moves, closing his eyes and pouting, banging an imaginary tambourine on his left leg.

'Yes, George Michael. Anyway, I want to do a course or maybe even a degree.'

Sarah clapped her hands but Adam stopped mid-jig, exhaled, ruffled his hair and rubbed his face with his hands.

Was that disapproval? Probably, but she had committed herself now and she couldn't and wouldn't stop. She started gabbling: it was her ambition to have her own business, she wanted to learn, maybe do an adult education thing or a long-distance-learning qualification, better herself, set an example to the kids, bring money in, because before she knew it the kids would've moved out and she'd be stuck at home too scared to take a chance, she loved working at Vintage and Mo had been really supportive.

Adam returned to the barbecue and silently went back to work.

'Love?' Lisa asked in a small voice, knowing this was his seething stage, fearing what was going to happen next.

He slammed the tongs on a plate. Then he detonated.

'I just don't understand what's got into you. First the strike and now this. We're only just coping now with this "statement" of yours, your job and the kids finally both being in school and now you want to go on *Dragons'* bloody *Den*,' he jeered.

'Are you actually living on the same planet as the rest of us? Have you seen the state of the economy – the cuts, the job losses – I wasn't going to tell you because I didn't want to worry you but I've lost that big council contract that pays for our holiday every year, "no longer viable" they said, blah blah bloody blah, these are hard times, Lees.

'I'm under enough pressure as it is and now . . . now, you want to "make something of yourself",' he said, in a high-pitched imitation of her voice.

'Aren't your kids the proof you've made something of yourself already? Are you even thinking about your kids? If you do a degree, you'll be in the dining room, studying all hours, missing out on them and I don't know how you think we're going to pay for it.'

Frustrated, bewildered by her husband's reaction, Lisa stood up, delivering a shouted, strangled cry: 'All I want to do is make you all proud of me, that's bloody all.'

No one said a word for a good minute as everyone tried to calm down. Sarah busied herself putting out coleslaw and rolls as Lisa bit her lip so she wouldn't cry.

Then Adam shouted 'Burgers are ready!' at the kids before turning to tell his wife that once they'd all eaten, he was going down the pub and he didn't give a bollocks if she didn't like it.

Day 12

8.59a.m., Monday, 26 May

Mandy had been up all night because of Sandro's stomach but it had been worth it.

'Mummy, what's wrong with Daddy?' Lola asked, at the sound of her father groaning from the loo.

'Just a tummy bug,' Mandy said, brushing her daughter's hair before weaving it into plaits.

Franco finished off his cereal and announced that from now on he'd call Papa by the new name of Poopoo, which Mandy pretended to disapprove of, belying her inner snigger at Sandro's misfortune.

Well, it wasn't really misfortune, she thought, it was the price he was paying for being so selfish with the lasagne.

On Friday, after she'd stewed in the bath, she'd rifled through the first aid cupboard in the bathroom and found what she'd been looking for right at the back: an ancient crusty bottle of liquid paraffin dating from one of Granny Glitter's episodes of constipation.

The label had said 10–30ml daily in divided doses at breakfast and bedtime so she'd stuck to that for fear of the warning on the back about some rather nasty side effects. Taking one of the kiddy medicine syringes, she filled it over and over and plunged it into the lasagne at regular intervals, lacing it with the laxative.

Judging by the dirty dishes in the sink on Saturday and Sunday morning, Mandy saw he'd enjoyed two huge plates. All she had to do then was wait.

And bingo, in the early hours of this morning, he was backwards and forwards to the bathroom, complaining of gurgling insides and nausea.

Full of mock concern, Mandy sympathised and asked if he'd eaten anything unusual? He knew what she was getting at but he refused to entertain the possibility that it could be his own cooking – not that he knew she'd tampered with it. That was the thing with Sandro, Mandy thought, that was why this had worked so well: he hated losing face. It was the worst thing that could happen to him, which was why he was obsessed with his appearance and why he made such a fuss of the kids in public.

But at breakfast, when she was checking what there was in the freezer for tea, she noticed a gap where there'd been his divided-up portions of lasagne. They had been transferred to the bin in the night, probably when he'd come down for a glass of water.

Ha! This would be hurting his pride more than his bowels.

As Mandy ushered the kids to the front door, she had a flashback to a scene from when was it, eleven or twelve years ago? They'd gone bowling on a date, the place was heaving and they were both aware they were the best-looking couple in there. She'd spent ages getting ready and had worn a white vest with jeans to show off her tan; Sandro was also in a designer white T-shirt. They felt like celebrities, known as a perfect couple, both gorgeous and stylish, with some calling them the Posh and Becks of the town. They were deeply besotted then, hearts palpitating at the sight and touch and smell of each other, wrapped up in lust and the headiness of first love. He was familiar yet exotic with his Italian background and she would imagine them raising beautiful babies together.

It happened earlier than she'd expected, that was why she'd got married at nineteen: she'd fallen pregnant and they'd rushed their big day. None of the family minded really, there was a harrumph from his side and her mum had wept when she'd told them but once they'd got over that and the families had arranged the shotgun wedding, pulling a few favours with the priest, they were pleased they could 'do' something to make it better, and delighted there'd be a baby. Mandy miscarried before the first scan, something she'd never got over. Sandro had blamed her – there was nothing wrong with him. He saw it as a failure, a stain on his public persona. It hadn't occurred to her at the time, not until now really, that when bad things happened he saw them as a personal slight.

That's why her mind had taken her back to their date in the Hollywood Bowl. He loved an audience and so when it was his turn, he would strut around as if he was about to go onstage, psyching himself up for a strike. But that night, his run-up had been too energetic, and as he released the ball he slipped over onto his white-jeaned bottom. The people playing on the alleys either side and beyond had burst out laughing, which set off Mandy. Sandro wasn't happy, he'd raged at her and declared the game over, dragging her out by the wrist, ending their night prematurely. She'd tried to talk to him about it in the car on the way home but he accused her of humiliating him so she'd never brought it up again.

Only now could she acknowledge it, seeing it as a pattern of behaviour. At the time, she'd felt sorry for him, blamed herself, thought it just a flash in the pan. Only now did she wonder if she could handle it for the rest of her life. But if she thought like that, then what did it mean? Was she prepared to split up with him? That was a deeply uncomfortable prospect for her, with the kids so young. She couldn't put them through it. Divorce would be the ultimate slap in the face for Sandro – and he'd make it so difficult.

Franco's 'earth calling Mummy' brought her back to the present. How long had she been staring into space in the hall? He had opened the front door and she felt a warm breeze on her bare shoulders and the hem of her maxi dress wafting around her ankles.

'Sorry, lovely,' she said, sticking her sunglasses on, 'I was miles away. Got your scooters, you two?'

She shouted up to tell Sandro they were off to the skate park and could he bleach the toilet, which of course he didn't bother to answer, and slam, they were gone.

11a.m.

'What? We're going?' Rosie asked, her eyes pleading with Lisa to tell them it was some kind of joke.

'But we always go home in the dark after camping,' she said, her bottom lip jutting out of her sun-kissed freckled face. Lisa felt her daughter's sense of injustice but she knew there would be no changing Adam's mind.

He had had enough. For the first time in Lisa's memory, he wanted to go home early. He was always the last to leave, a lover of life and parties, and she was the boring one.

But not today. As he packed the car, probably nursing a slight hangover after what he called his 'lunch break' when he escaped to the pub yesterday, Lisa told Rosie and George to have one last play with their cousins. Adam had insisted he wanted to beat the traffic but he wouldn't look at her as he said it when he was tidying up after breakfast. His humour had disappeared, replaced by few words and a tired look on his face. He hadn't had much of a chance to sit down and relax, being the one who was cooking and cleaning and making tea and acting as the first port of call not just for Rosie and George but for Matthew and Rebecca, who'd taken their cousins' lead to 'ask Daddy'. They always wanted something, a drink or the swingball, and he was always trying to catch up with the conversation, asking Lisa, Sarah and Dave, 'what's that you're on about?'

Lisa was gutted to be leaving early. The tables had turned; she'd really enjoyed herself, much more than on any other camping trip, which she'd dreaded every year. She'd sat there amazed while she watched Adam work, thinking, wow, I used to do so much on this supposed holiday. And her conversations with Sarah had made her think about her pre-strike self. Watching Adam in action, there was definitely a hint of martyr about him – she must've given off the same scent. He looked uptight and harassed and she could definitely identify with that feeling.

What was she going to do about Adam's mood? He wasn't even budging when Lisa tried praising him out of his mood: the inflatable palm trees had been such a lovely idea and the blow-up beds were so much better than the mats.

And what was she going to do about his attitude to the strike? Why, when he was clearly so miserable, wasn't he agreeing to her conditions of splitting the work right down the middle?

A moment of clarity: Adam still thought it was her job to be the housewife. Even after all of this! It was a depressing thought for Lisa, who wondered when on earth this would all end. She couldn't back down, no way, but she was alarmed by how much deeper they could sink.

Suit yourself, then, she'd thought, as she took the tent down, helped by Sarah who shared her disappointment at their departure. They were going to stick around until the evening.

After they'd waved goodbye and their in-laws had disappeared from view, Lisa asked everyone if they'd had a good time.

'Yeah! It was the best ever although Daddy forgot the quiz and the treasure hunt,' said the kids, who asked for their playlist.

Adam simply said 'not really' then told Rosie and George the battery on his MP3 had run out so they'd have to play I Spy instead. Lisa, who was driving because Adam wanted a nap, gave her husband a look, knowing full well he had a car charger which would sort that out.

His stubborn stare out of his window told her to keep quiet. Then he leaned his head back, shut his eyes and told her: 'I can't wait to go back to work tomorrow. I need a rest.'

Lisa reminded him that all he had to do was say the word and she'd end the strike. But he was having none of it.

'I'm not budging, Lees, you haven't suffered enough yet,' he murmured before dropping off.

What did he mean by that? It was obvious she found his lackadaisical approach troubling, he often teased her when she got up and left a room at the sight of his inept ironing or vacuuming. What could be worse than that?

She considered the cruellest thing he could do to her. He'd never walk out or leave the kids hungry – he loved them too much. They'd always said in jest that if they were ever to divorce they'd still share the house because neither of them could cope with the thought of not seeing the kids every day. So what was he planning?

Oh lord, no. Of course. He knew her inside out; her weaknesses, her fears, the lot. She knew exactly what he was going to do – he was going to put his heart and soul into the house. That would mean he'd go up in the kids' estimation and where would that leave her in the pecking order of their affections?

They'd already started seeking him out for practical needs – George did it yesterday when he scraped his knee and asked Adam for a plaster. What if they turned to him for emotional stuff too?

Things would come to a head soon, she was pretty sure of it.

The kids occupied with counting red cars, Lisa scrolled through her mind for something less troubling to think of. But she could only come up with another issue which was worrying her: her friendship with Cal.

Day 13

8.56a.m., Tuesday, 27 May

'Oooh, look who it is!' Mo said, waving a newspaper from across the shop at Lisa, who'd just walked through the door at Vintage. 'You're famous!'

Lisa had completely forgotten that her interview was running in *The Herald* today.

She took the paper from Mo and saw herself on the front page. Oh my God! A bold headline declared 'Mum's On Strike' and a photo of her clutching her mother's placard smiled out from the right-hand side of the page. It was astonishing, a shock even, because it looked official in black and white; not the little protest she thought she was undertaking.

She scanned the words for Adam's name – not here, not here, where is he? There he was. 'Despite repeated attempts to contact Lisa's husband Adam Stratton, he was unavailable for comment.'

Lisa retraced their steps over the weekend and

realised he'd left his phone at home – last night he said he'd had five missed calls from a blocked number and he was stressing about missing out on a job. Oh dear. He wasn't going to be happy when he realised it'd been Alex Baxter after a quote.

She pushed the dread from her mind and read on. The editor had really gone to town on it, with another two pages inside. The main spread pitted two opinion pieces against one another: Alex Baxter was the pro-strike voice – she really understands what I'm standing for, Lisa thought, as she read the article. Alex ended by revealing she was joining Lisa for a week. She had two teenage sons, one thirteen, the other fifteen, so her motive was to prepare them for adult life; men couldn't live on Pot Noodles alone, she reasoned. Her husband had agreed to the experiment and was sceptical about how much his wife really did. The other side of the argument, the anti-strike piece, was by David John, captain of the golf club and a well-known local businessman who owned a huge construction firm. He declared the strikers 'selfish', intent on bettering their own lives rather than those of their families. He said mums should take pride in all the duties which keep an economy's workforce fed, clean and happy. He said hard-working fathers were role models in themselves and expecting them to clean the loo was like asking a Premier League footballer to clean his own boots. The reason men didn't 'see' mess was because they had weightier things on their mind, which included paying the bills.

What was he on about? Lisa thought, it's as if he's from last century – he seemed to have missed the point of modern mums going out to work and feeling overwhelmed by all these so-called responsibilities imposed on them for generations. His poor wife. Imagine being married to somebody like that.

Then she realised with a churn of her stomach that Adam and any man who objected to sharing the domestic duties fundamentally agreed with him. They might not admit it, they might dress up their excuses with 'new man' phraseology but fundamentally, they didn't consider it their job to scrub the toilet. It was very depressing.

Mo must've seen her face drop, so she chimed in just at the right moment.

'Listen, lady,' she said firmly but kindly, 'you're doing really well. The paper has effectively come out on your side. You're bound to get criticism so don't let the Slug get you down.'

Lisa looked up from the paper to Mo, looked down at his photograph, taking in his oily portly face, lilac Pringle V-neck jumper and his receding grey hair, then looked back at her stunning boss.

'Him? He's the Slug?'

'Yes,' Mo said, making fake sick noises. 'Toby's father, never paid a penny of maintenance, left me with a young child when he found another piece of skirt and then became a multimillionaire while I was scrabbling around for pennies to buy his son a pair of shoes. I'm actually delighted to see him take the opposing view – it confirms how miserable I'd be if we were still together. He's on his third wife now.'

Lisa just couldn't picture her with that. 'But look at him,' she said.

'I know, dreadful, isn't he? He was quite a looker when he was young, very charming and a real go-getter compared to the rest of the men around then. Do you know something? Last year he sent an enormous bunch of red roses to the shop – typical of him, to want everyone to see his generosity – and the card asked me out for dinner. It was addressed to "The One I've Always Loved". He was in between wives. I never replied. Six months later he was engaged to number three, a woman twenty-five years his junior.'

'Never!' Lisa gasped, wondering how it was possible he could think he was worthy of Mo.

The door tinged as their first customers, an elderly couple, came in. Mo welcomed them with a bright 'morning!' Then she advised them of today's special offer: Lisa's autograph was free with every purchase.

193

9.21a.m.

Cal jumped on the bus, marvelling at how easy it was to get on, pay, find a seat and sit down when she wasn't struggling with the pram.

She'd left Dot with her mum for the morning so she could go to the big out-of-town shopping centre to get some bits for their holiday.

It was the first time she'd been alone for three months and it felt glorious. Luxurious, even. There had been a little lump in her throat as she'd kissed her baby goodbye but it was only for two hours, she'd have to be back for her feed. Ha, with her first she wouldn't have dared be apart from Ted for a second until he was properly weaned – what if he'd choked on something when she wasn't there? Only she could protect him. Then when Molly came, Cal had had to be different with her new baby, leaving her in the pram far more frequently than she had first time round because she had to be there for a toddling Ted. It changed again with Dotty; her longed-for third and last was a violent mixture of all of that. Not putting her down because she wanted to enjoy every moment but then organising a date to go shopping with Lisa at the first available opportunity she had for some precious girly time. It hadn't worked out – her best friend had forgotten to ask for the morning off and by the time she did it was too late.

Cal registered her disappointment as she stared out of the grimy window. It had been ages since they'd gone for one of their expeditions to wander the shops and then have coffee and cake. She pictured them traipsing round Topshop, holding up tops and trousers, asking each other 'is this a bit too, you know, young for me?' or, 'can I get away with this, do you reckon?' while the other stifled a laugh. They always ended up in M&S and bought something there because the sizes were more generous and it made them feel better about their post-kids tyres. If they had time they'd try on the most outrageous shoes they could find and see if they could walk in them; the last time, about six months ago, a pregnant Cal had tried on five-inch-heeled leopardskin shoe boots and had to be held up by Lisa to stop herself collapsing on the floor. It was something they'd always done, since the first time they'd been allowed to get the number 12 by themselves, when they were thirteen. In those days it was Miss Selfridge and Dorothy Perkins, searching for the coolest things they could afford with their clothes allowance. Which wasn't much, usually a crop top or a pair of ripped jeans. But shoes, their secret passion, were too expensive, which was why they loved them, yearned for them. Biker boots or patent studded stilettos, like they'd seen on the Spice Girls – they'd try them all on as if they were practising to be grown-ups, like

Cal's three older sisters who would glam up for a party as if they had been at the Boots make-up testers.

Yes, it was a shame Lisa couldn't come, they'd seen little of each other of late, too little, and she was probably being paranoid but things felt weird between them.

The bus stopped and Cal speed-walked straight to M&S, there was no time to mess about today. Up the escalator to the children's department where she was looking for UV suits for the baby and Ted. Molly could use his old one but the eldest two needed new shorts and T-shirts too. Oh and beach shoes, plus beach towels because their others were beginning to look a bit threadbare. And look at those sundresses, so cute – she had to get Molly a couple, they'd be worn again when Dot was bigger; and Ted was desperate for some skinny chinos like the big boys wore. While she was there, she thought she'd have a look downstairs. Cal saw a beautiful striped maxi dress which she tried on and cheered when it hid her tummy, then a perfect pair of wedge sandals to go with it. Well, she deserved it, she'd pushed out three babies and Rob was on good money and it'd been so long since she'd treated herself. She didn't want Rob to feel left out so she bought him a pair of beige linen trousers, which would look fantastic with that black shirt of his. She could see them now, walking along a Greek island's promenade at sunset, looking like they were the perfect family, the kids chasing one another on the sand, Rob with his arm round Cal as she pushed the buggy.

Standing in line, she picked up two pairs of sunglasses, which were a bargain at a fiver each, she was bound to break one of them, she always did. She was next up. She handed her basket to the assistant, who oohed and aahed at her collection of goodies. Not even hearing how much it all came to, Cal tapped in her PIN and looked at her watch to see if she would have to run for the bus. No, plenty of time. She was glad she hadn't driven, she'd wanted a complete break from concentrating, just for a couple of hours, and the car was so big it always difficult to park.

'I'm sorry, madam, your card seems to have been refused,' the assistant said, bringing Cal back down to earth with a bump.

'What?' she said, calculating the date. Rob had only put the month's housekeeping in on the 15th. She couldn't have spent it all. Racking her brains, she tried to think of anything she'd forgotten she'd bought: nope, nothing untoward. I wonder what that's all about then, she thought.

'I can try again, sometimes the chip can be scratched,' the lady said, giving her an understanding smile.

'Oh, don't worry, no point messing about, that card

has played up before. Here, stick it on my M&S account, that's fine,' Cal said, relieved when it went through and she wouldn't be holding up the queue any longer.

God it felt good, walking to the bus stop with two heavy bags of shopping; this had been the break she'd needed, a little escape, a little indulgence. And she was missing Dot. She'd wondered if she would, being so knackered, but she was, there was that undeniable pull on her heart, a sign they had bonded. She hadn't admitted it before because it was too scary a prospect, but it had taken longer than with the other two. Thank goodness.

Life was on the up and Cal felt as if she was finally on an even keel.

11.49a.m.
Just as Lisa had finished wrapping a beautiful art deco lamp, her phone rang from beneath the till. Lesley's and Roy's names appeared on the screen. Oh no, Lesley was bound to be calling to give her an earful about the piece in the paper. She thought about ignoring it but that was rude, better to face up to things.

'Hi Lesley,' Lisa said cheerily.

'Lisa?' came a voice. 'How do you know it's me, dear?'

Lisa groaned – she couldn't recall how many times

she'd had to explain to Lesley about modern technology revealing a caller's identity.

'Are you OK?' Lisa replied. 'I'm in work.'

It was a blatant hint. She felt bad for doing it, but if she didn't say it, Lesley would be on the phone for ages.

'Yes, I'm so sorry, I know, I'll be quick,' Lesley said, surprising Lisa with an uncharacteristic line of self-awareness. She must be dying to get this reprimand off her chest.

'Go on,' Lisa said, mouthing 'Lesley' to Mo, who immediately pushed her into the office and took over with a hand-signed OK.

It was nothing to worry about, Lesley said, but she'd broken her right arm, she'd fallen yesterday morning when she was doing her spring clean. She'd been on the stepladder, reaching with her feather duster to get an awkward cobweb. She hadn't rung because she didn't want them to cut short their holiday, she was fine, she'd been to the hospital, a neighbour had driven her, Roy had got them a cab home after her X-ray and plaster-casting. And what she was wondering – it was a bit delicate and she was awfully embarrassed to ask – but she needed help washing her hair and she couldn't ask anyone else because, cough, well, you know, Roy and Adam were men and Sarah wasn't local and she didn't want 'just anyone' seeing her in her brassiere and slip.

Lisa was overwhelmed by sympathy for her; she knew how proper Lesley was and understood how much she valued her dignity. So she said an immediate yes, she'd pop over after work because the kids were going to friends for tea so she had plenty of time. Lesley couldn't tell her how grateful she was. Then her second surprise of the day. Lesley told her she'd read *The Herald* and she thought it was 'very informative'.

It wasn't praise, Lisa knew that, but it was as far as Lesley could go; not approval, but an acknowledgement of what she was doing, and that was good enough.

She sent a quick text to Adam to tell him about his mother's broken arm, with a PS about *The Herald*. She wanted to flag it up so he had time to cool down before she saw him in the evening.

Then she returned to work, realising it was the first time Lesley had asked her for help – blimey, she must be desperate, she thought. But it felt like a small step towards rebuilding their relationship, which had suffered since the start of the strike.

2.12p.m.
Mandy was on the final house of the day.

She'd done three so far, two grand back-breaking three-storey ones and a flat belonging to a widower who seemed to hire her for the company, because his place was spick and span and there was always a fresh brew waiting for her. She'd suggested umpteen times that perhaps he'd be better off saving the money he paid her but he wouldn't have any of it, bless him. An hour to do this one and then she would get the kids from school.

She'd never met the guy who lived here. She didn't even know his name. He'd pushed a key through her door in an envelope bearing just his address after one of his mates' wives recommended her and he was always at work when she called round. He left the cash on the side with a scrawled 'Cheers' and that was that. When she hadn't met clients, she liked to imagine who they were and what they did.

This one was easy – he was a family man because of the photos of kids on the wall, but with no feminine stuff about he was clearly separated or divorced. Would this be how it would end up with Sandro? If they did ever split up, would he live in a small place like this, a two-up, two-down, a room for him and a room for the kids? Stop it, Mand, she told herself, you're being maudlin.

Whoever lived here was a bit of a lad, she could see that. His recycling bin was full of cans of lager and pizza boxes and his fridge was home to a few jars of curry paste, three manky mushrooms and a tube of Anusol. Oh yuck! But he had asked her to clean the fridge so he obviously wasn't bothered about her knowing he was prone to piles.

His lounge was very 'male' too – a big black cord sofa, a massive TV, hundreds of DVDs stacked haphazardly in columns by a sound system and a huge framed poster for a film, one she'd never heard of but which looked arty.

But when you took a closer look, there was obviously something more to this man, because his dishes had the remains of tasty-looking noodles and one of his recipe books was open at Thai chilli seabass. His shelves were full of travel books and there were some amazing photographs on the wall from exotic places she guessed he'd been to. The headboard of his bed was a surfboard and his wardrobe, which was open, revealed a load of really nice casual T-shirts and shirts.

The house smelt good too, sort of earthy and masculine but with a lemony scent mixed in with it. Why was he single? she wondered. He looked a bit of a catch to Mandy, judging by the photo of a man she presumed was him taken on a beach with a mate. He was tall, had a shaved head, was brown with freckles and sported a gorgeous tattoo of an eagle on his left pec. His face was lovely too, not particularly good-looking but he seemed open and warm giving a thumbs-up for the camera.

Mind you, appearances could be deceptive. Just look at Sandro: immaculately dressed and puppy dog eyes, particularly if there was the prospect of a tip coming his way. Dig deeper and you found a boy who'd never grown up. She realised she'd been waiting for him to become a man over the last decade and it hadn't happened.

Mandy knew she was entering 'what if' territory. What if she left him? What if she was happier alone? What if the kids were better off without the daily arguments?

She became aware she'd been dusting the same spot over and over for the last minute or so. God, she really must stop this fantasy – life wasn't easy, you had to work at marriage, Granny Glitter said so, and she'd had fifty-one years under her belt with Gramps. Divorce wasn't an option. This was just a phase, things would improve, the strike had just magnified all of it. OK, he was sticking his shirts in to be washed and ironed at the launderette for a tenner a time but at least he was taking responsibility for it. Not that he was doing any more for the kids. She felt like a single parent. Maybe they needed an outing together, perhaps a trip to the zoo or something? Yes, that was it: a bonding exercise, they called it.

With a plan, Mandy felt better, more positive about life, ignoring the voice in her head that asked why was she always the one making an effort? She packed up her bottles and dusters and went down the path to the car, the trusty little yellow Fiat Panda that she'd had for years and years. She opened the boot and chucked all the stuff in. Then she got in the driving seat, switched on the engine and . . . nothing.

Oh shit. She tried again, then again, but it was flooded, wheezing each time she tried the ignition.

What was she going to do? It was ten minutes until pick-up. She hadn't time to sort this out now.

So she locked up and started running towards school. She could be there in five if she jogged.

She'd have to come back later to get the car.

3.45p.m.

Lesley's face was etched with pain when she opened the door to Lisa. Minus her usual warpaint and bouffant crown, she looked vulnerable and tired. The only time Lisa had seen her like this was on the day Roy had had a stroke.

Poor love, Lisa thought, kissing her soft cheek and telling her she wasn't to lift a finger, that she was here to help.

Lesley, who winced as she adjusted her sling, insisted she was doing well, she hadn't slept much, that was the problem, she couldn't get comfy. Roy had gone down the club for his afternoon pint, she said, which told Lisa everything she needed to know – he hadn't altered his routine and he would still expect his dinner on the table when he got in later.

'Has Adam been round?' Lisa asked, taking her shoes off as it was a slippers-only zone.

'No, I told him not to. He said he would, but then when he heard you were coming over he said he had a lot on and he was no good at girly chats,' Lesley said, putting a positive spin on her son's no-show. Lisa could see a flicker of hurt in Lesley's eyes – she knew that feeling all right.

Her mother-in-law gave an embarrassed little cough, one of those signals people give when they want to change the subject.

What was wrong with him, Lisa thought, she's his mother, why wouldn't he want to check she was OK? Why did he consider it good enough that she went along? It was that thing again about responsibility, about caring and sharing; the thick end of that wedge that men used to justify leaving their wives to send birthday cards and buy presents for their family. It was a lazy response, a reliance on 'women are better at this sort of thing'. But it would be cruel to dwell on it so Lisa slapped on a smile, clapped her hands and told Lesley to go through into the front room and she'd bring in a cup of tea.

As the kettle boiled, Lisa took out a load of shopping she'd picked up on her way over. She found a casserole dish then began furiously chopping chicken breasts, an onion and some mushrooms, added water to the chasseur packet then mixed up all the ingredients and popped it into the oven with two potatoes. She cut up some green beans and carrots, plopped them in a saucepan of water and put it on the hob. Then she stacked a quiche, salad, milk, cheese, eggs and a steak and ale pie in the fridge, hoping this would be enough for a couple of days until Lesley got her strength back.

With the tea brewing in the pot – it had to be in the pot at Lesley's – Lisa bleached the downstairs loo and swept the floor. Then, when she took a cup in to her mother-in-law, she told her she was going to hoover and dust and she was not to argue.

Lisa knew how houseproud Lesley was; she did the housework every day so that it wasn't a big job, just a cursory wipe of the surfaces and a quick whizz round with the vacuum.

As she went round with the Pledge, she told herself this didn't count – it wasn't her housework so she wasn't a scab. Her strike applied at home, not here. She felt a frisson of adrenalin as she worked, enjoying the illicit process of making everything shine which would make Lesley happy. She found herself thinking 'ooh, I've missed this' then berated at herself for being so old-fashioned – it wasn't the cleaning she missed in actual fact, she realised, but the sense of achievement. There, she'd said it: housework was a boring menial job but you couldn't deny the feeling of satisfaction when it all looked nice. Although it would be even more satisfying if it was Adam doing half of it.

Twenty minutes later, she asked Lesley if she was ready to do her hair.

'I thought you were on strike, dear,' Lesley said, confused.

'I am. Just not here. Don't tell Adam, whatever you do, it'll ruin my image.' She winked, helping Lesley up the swirling-patterned carpeted stairs because her knees weren't so good these days.

In the bathroom, Lesley knelt over the bath while Lisa washed her hair. It was bizarre – Lesley was half-naked, Lisa could see every curve and wobble, yet she didn't see it with a critical eye. She saw the mother of her husband, a wife who'd devoted herself to her family and who couldn't ask for help from those she most loved. Then she filled the sink and helped her mother-in-law with a stand-up wash. There was no embarrassment as Lisa chatted away about the camping trip, filling her in on what Sarah was up to and updating her on her other two grandchildren. Eyes were averted as a flannel and then a towel went to work and it was only when she'd helped Lesley get dressed that they shared a moment of intimacy; just a brief look, the merest of smiles, but it was there.

Afterwards, while Lisa blow-dried her hair in the master bedroom, Lesley made herself 'presentable' as she spoke the poem of her youth, 'a little bit of powder, a little bit of paint, makes a girl what she ain't'.

Then Lisa sprayed what seemed like an entire can of Elnett to hold everything in place.

It was approaching five o'clock and Lisa wanted to go before Roy returned. She could imagine Lesley wincing as she explained Lisa had come to her rescue; it would be an admission of being 'in a tizz' and Lesley was not that sort of woman. Besides, her father-in-law was the epitome of 'you can't teach an old dog new tricks'. If Lisa was there when he got back, she'd have to bite her tongue not to say something as innocent as 'look after her, Roy' and that would just make things worse for Lesley.

'You're a wonder, Lisa, you really are,' Lesley said, her voice rich with appreciation.

'It's nothing, honestly,' Lisa said, opening the front door to go. 'Don't forget the chicken and jacket potatoes will be ready at 5.30. I've topped and tailed some veggies so all you have to do is switch the gas on. I'll be over tomorrow after work again. And remember, not a word to anyone.'

9.05p.m.
Lesley's broken arm had taken the sting out of the front-page story, Lisa admitted to herself, with a twinge of guilt as she closed down the laptop on the kitchen table.

Rubbing her tired eyes, she reflected that it had been a good day to bury bad news – a tasteless saying, yes, but it was pretty accurate in her case. When he'd got home from work, Adam hadn't been that bothered by it because he was more concerned about his mother.

Not that he was bothered enough to visit her, which Lisa didn't say because it suited her to be demure and heroic today.

He'd simply said he was glad he hadn't answered 'that woman's' phone calls because he didn't think she'd have printed his response in a family newspaper. Anyway, it was tomorrow's chip paper, he said, and he just thought Lisa had shown herself up. At least he'd maintained a dignified silence, he said pointedly.

On her way home from Lesley's, she'd been stopped several times by strangers, recognised as 'the one in *The Herald*'. They wanted to know how it was going so she thought a Facebook page might provide a few answers; she could do updates and find out who else had joined her.

Her first post was a link to the newspaper's online site, with the slogan 'Like if you're on strike!' And by the time she'd finished faffing around, asking friends to 'share' it, she'd had five already, two from friends of hers who weren't 'out' but told her she was 'amazing' and three from women she didn't even know. How thrilling!

She got up from the table and opened the fridge,

looking for something to nibble on. It was virtually empty save for a piece of Parmesan and some jars of this and that – God knows what Adam was going to put in their sandwiches tomorrow. It made her feel anxious – how can anyone live like this? Then she astonished herself by correcting herself, thinking 'Marmite or peanut butter is fine', as if she'd had a personality transplant.

I'm changing, she thought, then to see if that was really true, she paced round the house looking for trouble spots which had always made her cross. The washing machine, where a clean set of clothes was lying unloaded inside. The bottom of the stairs where Adam put stuff to go up but always forgot to take with him. The downstairs loo with its dripping tap and wonky mirror. The kitchen floor with bits of bits all over it.

Each time she closed her eyes, opened them as if she was seeing it for the first time and waited for a physical reaction, like a phobic confronted with a tarantula. But whereas before the sight had induced a rage like a dose of PMT, now it irked her less. Was this because she'd got used to it or found a new focus? Probably both. Adam had certainly improved of late; not dramatically, but at least the washing was being done. He seemed to have found a rhythm, doing a load every day rather than waiting for it to accumulate and then panicking.

This was a breakthrough, it showed intention, thought, consideration. He wouldn't know it yet, Lisa knew, because he was still beating a path through the overgrown jungle around him. But there were shoots of hope.

She decided to have an apple; she'd been munching too many goodies on the sofa of late. But there weren't any. One of her earliest memories resurfaced. She'd gone to school and instead of a Granny Smith apple, the clean taste of which she adored, there was a British Cox's orange pippin, which was earthy and sour. She'd gone home and moaned at her mum, who told her about apartheid and her boycott of South African goods. Lisa remembered being so cross about it, she drew a picture of her mum the next day with an apple for her head! Now, though, she had a moment of understanding, of how her mum had wanted to make a difference, no matter how small her contribution.

God, Lisa thought, that's what I'm doing, and she realised perhaps she'd been rather harsh on her mum. She went back to the table where the newspaper was lying and looked at her own face, smiling with the placard. The story was better because of that placard, because of her mum: the image summed up her intent, the placard said it all. Lisa felt bad and tears sprang to her eyes, she'd been so hard on her mum, she'd tried to educate her in the ways of the world but all this time

Lisa had only thought of herself. Angie might not have been the baking wonderwoman she'd wanted as a mum but she had values. Lisa had never gone hungry, she'd always had clean clothes and her mum had always shown an interest in her studies. Looking back, that had been just as good, even better, than a plate of fairy cakes. She recalled Cal moaning about her mother 'trying to get her fat' when she was a teenager – mums just couldn't win! Lisa ran through her mind, seeking her own mother's achievements: she'd been a keen letter-writer for Amnesty International, writing on behalf of victims of human rights abuses in far-flung places. She'd traipsed round the town in the cold collecting money to build schools for children in developing countries who were sent to work at the age of seven. And she'd campaigned on behalf of a hostel for battered women, which was still standing today.

An unfamiliar feeling washed over her as she wiped her eyes: that of pride in her mum. She had to make amends, Lisa knew that. But how?

'Lees,' came Adam's voice from the lounge, interrupting her thoughts, 'can you come in here a sec?'

She went in, to see her husband sitting cross-legged on the floor with some stripy fabric, a needle and cotton. Just what was he doing?

'Can you thread this for me? I've been trying for the last ten minutes and it's got a mind of its own,' he said, looking exasperated.

Taking in her confusion, he said he was making George a costume for tomorrow, it was Big Cat Day in reception and he'd managed to make a waistcoat from a pattern he saw on the internet but he was having trouble with this last bit, attaching the tail.

How did she not know it was a dress-up day? Lisa felt awful. No one had mentioned it to her, it was as if she was invisible. A different invisible to how she felt before, being taken for granted with the housework. Now she felt overlooked, out of the loop.

'You should've asked me to do it, the strike doesn't cover this,' she said, joining him on the carpet to help out.

'George wanted me to do it, Lees,' Adam said, getting up to go to the loo, unaware his words were stabbing his wife's heart.

11.14p.m.
Mandy lay in bed with a smile on her face.

This is ridiculous, she told herself, you only fancy him because he helped you out and that is pathetic. It shows how needy you are right now, her conscience said, as Mandy threw the duvet off her legs and pulled up the sheet. It was a warm night. And she had the hots for a stranger.

She relived the evening which she'd already played back many times since she'd got home. Her sister had babysat while she went back to recover the car.

Mandy had lifted the bonnet to check the oil and water, and all of that seemed OK. But the engine still refused to start. With the door wide open, she'd sat in the driver's seat and banged her head on the steering wheel, cursing Sandro for cancelling their RAC membership. He'd said there was no need, they had mates who could lend a hand if they ever needed it – but where were they now? His phone was switched off and the restaurant said he'd call her. He hadn't. Bloody Sandro, she said out loud, and then became aware there was a man on the pavement, looking at her.

'Do you need a hand?' he'd said, smiling, the exact same smile she'd seen in the photo earlier today. It was the man she cleaned for and she had a moment of fear – should she let on she knew who he was? Or would that make her look like a weirdo?

'Have you got any jump leads?' she'd asked, and he'd gone back through the front door of the house she knew so well to get his car keys.

Her heart had flipped when she saw the back of him, broad shoulders beneath a tightish grey T-shirt and a neat bottom beneath a pair of knee-length shorts. Her mind wandered to the tattoo she knew was hiding beneath his top and she blushed before telling herself to stop right there. This was not what she needed, a crush to complicate things.

He'd examined the engine then decided he needed some WD40, and that was when Mandy gave herself away. 'It's under the sink,' she said, which made him stop and stare at her as if she was some sort of mystic.

'I'm your cleaner, sorry, I should've said, I was just caught up here with this,' she said nervously, turning her attention to a frayed piece of cotton hanging down from her cut-off denim shorts.

'And there was me thinking you were Daisy Duke,' he replied, nodding at her legs before disappearing inside.

Was he flirting? Was he being kind? Was he just trying to change the subject? Oh God, it had been years since anyone had been like this with her. Most men she mixed with knew she was Sandro's 'property' and she was treated as such.

The jump leads did the trick. Mandy was relieved to be able to say thanks and concentrate on closing the bonnet. Then the man had started chatting with her, apologising for the mess he left her to clear up. She laughed and said it was nothing compared to some of the holes she went to and then pointed at his bald head.

'Shit, where's my hair gone?' he said, which made her laugh and then fumble her words.

'You've got oil on your head, that's what I meant,' she said. 'Anyway, must go, the kids, my sister's babysitting.'

He nodded and there was a pause. Something rippled between them, Mandy was sure of it. Or maybe he was embarrassed because she'd brought up her children and it was a sensitive subject. She said as much. 'Sorry, didn't mean to mention kids when you're – the kids in your pictures, you know.'

He looked confused, then it dawned on him: no, those weren't his, they were his nieces and nephews!

She wanted the ground to swallow her up. Trying to make it clear she wasn't after him because she was married, she said: 'My husband works evenings.'

He just nodded again. Why had she mentioned Sandro? Then why shouldn't she? I'm married, it's not something to hide, it's a fact. But why had she told him? Usually she was reluctant to reveal stuff about herself, it was no one else's business. His eyes, lovely crystal blue eyes, were locked on to hers as she blushed again. Then he broke the moment and headed back inside.

He hadn't looked back, Mandy remembered, her eyes closed as she tried to hold on to the image of his face. He's not interested in me, why would he be, I'm just a washed-up mum, his cleaner, he's probably with someone anyway and I'm married. Lying there, Mandy analysed her reaction to a bit of male attention. She had responded because she didn't get any, even though her female friends told her she was attractive.

A roar of engine in the street. Then the door banged and her dream splintered. Footsteps, Sandro appeared, his eyes narrow as he asked her how she'd got the car sorted. He'd been busy tonight, he'd sent one of the boys up to the address but by the time they got there, she'd gone and so had the car.

'Jump leads,' she said, fiddling with the strap of her nightie. 'Someone helped me.'

He was suspicious, but then he always was. That's why she came across so cagily. She had nothing to hide so why did she feel guilty? He could've quizzed her, she knew his mind was racing, but he left it dangling because he enjoyed seeing her squirm.

Without taking his eyes off her, he pulled at his tie, unbuttoned his shirt, unzipped his trousers, got onto the bed and climbed on top of her. She really didn't want to do this, it didn't feel right. She said she was tired.

'Come on, *amore*,' he said, pinning her down, pushing into her. 'Don't tease me any more.'

Then a sudden pain as his teeth sank into the flesh on her collarbone. He held on to the bite and then forced her face to the side with his hand, leaning his body weight into her cheek, his fingers smelling of foul cigarettes.

She braced herself. He was about to take her. She stared at a crack in the wall, focusing on it, willing her mind to have an out-of-body experience. If you're going to do this, just get on with it.

Without warning, Sandro took hold of Mandy's chin and twisted her face round to meet his. His eyes held hers; she was breathing quickly, terrified.

'Not tonight, I'm not in the mood,' he said. Then he rolled off her and spoke into the dark. 'Tomorrow.'

It was a warning, Mandy realised. A message to be careful. It was as if he was saying 'If I'm capable of this when you've done "nothing wrong", then imagine what I'll do if you have.'

Frozen to the sheets, she didn't dare move. One twitch and maybe he'd see it as provocation. So she lay there, her eyes clamped shut, her chest barely rising and falling, ordering herself not to even think.

But while she could control her body, her mind would not stop wandering to the stranger.

Day 14

9.39a.m., Wednesday, 28 May

A thud on the shop window made Lisa leap out of her skin.

A mixture of egg white, yolk and shell oozed down the glass and her reaction proved that habits died hard as she despaired at the mess, then the waste of food.

Mo hobbled down the stairs, her legs impeded by her punky bondage trousers and fuchsia stilettos.

'What the bloody hell is going on?' she shouted as she flapped the throng of shoppers towards the back of Vintage.

Lisa, reappearing from the office with the cleaning stuff, froze as she heard the clamour outside. There was a man, she couldn't see who it was because of the smeared window.

There was shouting then jeering, 'Where is she?' and 'I want a word'.

Lisa gulped. Mo instructed her to stay where she was, she'd deal with it, taking the Windolene and squeegee with her.

'It's my shop, you're my employee,' she hissed, marching towards the door.

She wasted no time at all, laying into the man, demanding an explanation first then an apology.

As the door shut, Lisa could see Mo's lips moving at speed but not hear a word she was saying. There was too much background noise from the shocked customers inside to make out anything.

It was a bizarre sight, seeing a flash of her tiny boss squaring up to somebody, who had clearly been stunned into silence because her mouth was going nineteen to the dozen.

Mo continued at full speed while a crowd four deep gathered round, more and more stopping to see what was causing such a bottleneck on the pavement. Toots from car horns indicated the road too was blocked by them and a jam built up in the street.

Lisa sensed it was about the strike. She felt dreadful, responsible for this whole situation. She'd have to resign from work, she felt awful for bringing Mo into this. She hadn't meant it to happen, Lisa thought, preparing her leaving speech in her head. Shit, she'd have to tell Adam that she'd lost her job over this. She'd been too ambitious, she was such a fool.

Suddenly the throng parted slightly, then

immediately clamped shut again, allowing a police officer to pass into the eye of the storm. It was Eric, the Special Constabulary bobby who'd walked the beat here for years, a regular in every shop and office in the town, popping in for a chat and a bit of banter whenever he was on duty. A cabbie by profession, the forty-something knew everyone and was blessed with exceptional diplomacy skills; he could judge a situation and the people involved then calm things down.

Dear God, what had Lisa done? She'd got carried away, this strike was bad news, she had to end it now. She took a deep breath then took a step towards the shop door to throw herself on Mo's mercy.

But, oh my goodness, what was going on? A man with dark hair, whose face was obscured by the slime, had taken the Windolene from Mo's hands, and was spraying it on the glass and now he was wiping it clean with the squeegee!

Just before a couple in the shop stepped in the way to get a better look, Lisa saw Mo stand over him, pointing out 'you've missed a bit', milking the drama for her own amusement.

Then, just like that, it was over. Mo walked back in, smiling, calm, checking with her customers if they had found what they were looking for as if nothing had happened. It was as if she'd waved a magic wand and everyone had had the memory of the egging erased from their minds.

A few sales then the shop was empty and Lisa finally got the chance to offer her resignation when Mo brought two steaming cups down to the till.

In return, Lisa got a faceful of coffee as Mo spat out her slurp with laughter.

'Are you serious?' she asked, once she'd got her breath back.

Lisa nodded, wiping the froth off her nose. She launched into her detailed apology and without waiting for a reaction began to walk towards the office to get her coat and handbag.

'Er, where do you think you're going, lady?' Mo said. 'You work here, you're my right-hand woman and there is no way I'm letting you go.'

Once more, Lisa was startled.

'In fact, Lees, I wanted to see if you'd take on a bit more responsibility here. I want you to be the shop manager. You've shown how hard-working you are, you've got an eye for all the details. I'm afraid you will have to do every other Saturday, we can share it, but you'll have an extra day off in the week to make up for it and you'll get more money. Plus, I was thinking about getting you some training. I'm a bit tired of all the boring paperwork and I'd like to focus more on sourcing stuff, which will mean I'm out of the office more. So what do you think?' Mo asked.

Thrilled, Lisa said she'd love to, she just had to speak to Adam. She gabbled on about her dream of a degree, which Mo agreed to consider sponsoring, and said how excited she was. And then she paused.

'Who was that bloke?' she said.

Mo tried to wriggle out of it; there was no need to dwell on it, it was just some silly misunderstanding.

'No, Mo, you need to tell me. Or I won't even think about accepting the job.'

'All right. I didn't catch his name but he said his wife had gone on strike and he was really pissed off about what it was doing to his marriage, he was blaming you for everything. It's Mandy's husband.'

12.59p.m.

Lunchtime, and Lisa walked to Cal's with apprehension. They hadn't seen each other properly for a few days; in the playground, yes, but only to exchange a wave. That was quite normal. They swapped texts and kept up to date with each other's news on Facebook, they were both busy.

But there was an unspoken tension between them now – Lisa was still troubled about Cal helping Adam and not telling her. She hadn't mentioned it to either of them because she was afraid of looking over-sensitive and accusatory in the eyes of two of the most important people in her life. And she'd noticed Cal hadn't 'liked' her Facebook page – not a hanging offence, obviously, and Lisa was probably being paranoid, but was it a snub?

223

She put her sunglasses on as she turned the corner into the road which led to Cal's new estate. She couldn't wait to tell her about her distance learning idea; she'd looked at courses last night online and 'An Introduction to Business Studies' seemed perfect. The prospectus was ordered and she'd already worked out she could afford to pay the fees with a combination of her wages and sponsorship from Mo – a small contribution would be enough. There was a load of baby stuff she could flog on eBay – she'd been meaning to do that for ages so it was a good kick up the bum to get on with it. And if that didn't cover it, there was always a loan. It would be a tough time with so much studying but she had her days off and evenings. Adam would come round, of course he would, he'd have to. And just think of the money in the long run. If she did start her own business, and it did well, well, then they could afford a decent holiday every October, somewhere warm, like Turkey, rather than a cottage in the cold.

And then there was the job offer. Cal had run the florist's and been absolutely brilliant at it. She could tap her for info and see if she had any advice.

Those were safe topics at least, Lisa thought, taking in the sunny day and admiring the trees in full leaf, swaying in the breeze. This road was Mandy's. She couldn't remember what number she was, but she knew it was on this side, up by the postbox, which was coming up.

That reminded her: she texted Mandy about earlier, tapping a cautious 'hi, how are you? Have you heard about Sandro? Hope you're OK, give me a shout if you need anything, xxx'.

A couple more minutes to go and she'd be there. When she walked, Lisa loved having a nose into the windows of other people's homes; it was like a snapshot of their lives.

Number 25, the small black china cat curled up next to the back of a silver A4 photo frame, thick lined curtains, she could see a floral design on the tie-backs, probably an elderly lady who used the sill as a shrine to her beloved grandchildren and special pet. Tasteful white shutters at number 27, open so she could see a blue glass chandelier hanging from the ceiling, probably a trendy couple who were on their way up in life. At 29, a topless Barbie in jodh-purs and a selection of mismatched Lego mini-figures lined up. George did the same, swapping the heads and accessories to create bizarre space cowboys and alien pirates. Definitely a family home with young kids.

Then, next door, by the postbox, number 31, she covered her mouth, whispering 'Oh my God' into her palm at the sight of Mandy's! There in the window, sellotaped to the glass, was a poster facing the street with the words MUM'S ON STRIKE. Bold black capitals like a newspaper billboard, contained within a red circle featuring a dustpan and brush, crossed through like a No Smoking sign. The window was filthy and she realised the homes before this one had had sparkling clean glass.

Absolutely brilliant! Mandy was clearly a bit bonkers, she thought, but goodness, she knew how to make an impression. I wonder if I should ask her to knock up a load, Lisa asked herself.

But she saw she wouldn't have to when the next house, then the next . . . seven in total, all had the same MUM'S ON STRIKE poster on display.

Lisa looked across the road – there were a few over there too, and more up the top which she could just make out if she squinted. She felt like she'd stepped onto a film set.

Coming soon, Lisa said as though doing the voiceover for a trailer at the cinema, *The Anti-Stepford Wives*!

If she'd had time she would've knocked on Mandy's door there and then but she was probably at work anyway.

She quickened her pace and arrived at Cal's, full of it from the posters.

Her best friend answered with a hollow 'wow, brilliant' as she led Lisa to the day room for a salad she'd knocked up. She's probably just tired, Lisa thought, as she gushed about Mandy, her new friend, who was absolutely lovely and so supportive and such a laugh.

Then she switched to her favourite subject, the lovely Dot. How was she, the beautiful little bubba?

'Asleep, thank goodness. Mind you, she needs it after last night,' Cal replied.

'Oh, I bet it's lovely having night-time cuddles though,' Lisa said, gobbling her bowl of chicken Caesar and mopping up the dressing with some French bread.

'So what's the patio like then?' Lisa asked, knowing Adam and Ginger Steve had just finished the job.

'Amazing! Come and see,' Cal said. Passing through the house, Lisa took pleasure in the shine of the tiles in the hall and the scent of the soft and spongy carpets; it was spotless. But the garden was still a work in progress.

'I don't suppose he brought our washing with him, did he?' Lisa said, laughing.

Cal stopped, took a breath and stared her straight in the eye.

'He did, actually, I offered. Look, I just wanted to help,' she said, wincing at her confession.

Lisa was stunned – she'd thought Rob had been exaggerating for dramatic effort but clearly Adam had been leaning on Cal. It felt even worse hearing it from Cal.

'God, when Rob said Adam had had some assistance off you, I had no idea you'd been that involved.'

'Oh. He told you, did he? Listen, I thought ultimately

it would help you, as well as Adam and the kids,' Cal said. 'I'm not interfering, honestly, look, I've sort of done a few bits you know, nothing major, just a few favours because Adam's needed some help and he's been good as gold to me too.'

This was getting worse – what on earth did she mean by that?

On a confessional roll, Cal continued: 'You know how rubbish Rob is at DIY. Remember that time he tried to put up the TV unit thing at our old house and he went through the electric cable and we had no telly for a fortnight because he wanted to "fix" it himself and we had to get a sparky in? So Adam's done a few jobs for me in his lunch hour, nothing major, just put a few pictures up. I've paid him in kind, just made him sandwiches and cooked a shepherd's pie, which he was going to freeze for a meal in the week.'

Lisa laughed bitterly. There were 101 jobs she'd asked Adam to do millions of times which he'd put off again and again.

'Great, that's just great,' she said, looking out at the freshly laid patio which was now blurred by the tears in her eyes.

Cal asked her to understand; her intention was to help, to make things easier, for George and Rosie, for Lisa.

Lisa swallowed her upset, she knew Cal had a heart

of gold. She was very domestic, very much the house-wife and this was her way of understanding and coping with Lisa's strike. But it still stung.

A gurgle from Dot echoed on the baby monitor, so Lisa volunteered to get her, both desperate to get away from the awkward atmosphere and savour her god-daughter-to-be.

Picking up the baby from her white cot in semi-darkness, Lisa inhaled her clean skin and laundered Babygro, kissed her deliciously warm cheeks and cherished the cuddle, taking in the sweetie-pink walls, the glowing bunny rabbit nightlight and a pile of fabric books scattered over a sheepskin rug.

She stepped back several years in time at that moment, remembering her two like this. Cal must be so happy – a second baby was so much easier, and blimey, with this one Cal is probably practically horizontal, more relaxed as the baby just falls into everyone else's routine.

Maybe she was on her third because she didn't want all this to end – to face up to the time when she decided she'd finished creating her family and moved on to the next stage. Carrying Dot down the stairs, Lisa felt calmer. There was something so grounding about the softness of a baby's feathery scalp.

'Oh, she's so beautiful,' she said, handing her over to Cal.

'We'll be all right, Cal,' Lisa added, offering a consoling smile as she picked up her bag and headed for the door. But would they? She wasn't sure any more.

5.14p.m.
'I'm home,' Lisa shouted, sniffing the air. Something smelt good. It had to be Cal's shepherd's pie!

'What we having, Ad?' she said, setting a trap to see if he owned up. He didn't.

'Just a little something I saw on *Masterchef*,' he said with a wiggle of his fingers, bending down to kiss his wife. Lisa left it – she'd thought about bringing it up but she needed him to be onside with her job offer.

'How's Mum? I popped in this morning before work and she seems to be coping really well,' he said, blissfully unaware that that was because Lisa had been going to and fro, tidying up for her, stocking up her cupboards and filling the fridge.

'Fine,' Lisa said, preparing the excuse that she'd had a quick swim after seeing Lesley if Adam picked up on her puckered fingers from wearing rubber gloves.

George and Rosie raced to hug their mum and started talking about their day at school, her son babbling his costume had won first prize while Rosie recited her spellings. Both were out of their uniform already because Adam had wanted to do the washing early; he was hoping to go for a pint with the boys later.

Whistling while he worked, he was in a brilliant mood, fortunately for Lisa. So she seized the moment and told him about her day: the egg, Mandy's husband, her resignation offer then Mo's surprise promotion for her. She was so chuffed – it'd require a bit of juggling but think of the money, it was a fantastic opportunity for her; the chance to learn valuable skills which would move her a step closer to her goal of running her own business one day. On the Saturdays she had to work, he could bring the kids in for lunch then they could afford to go out for pizza afterwards.

Adam's jaw dropped and an open bag of frozen peas fell from his hands, emptying petits pois across the floor in all directions, like ball bearings. George ran in and skidded onto his knees, delighted at the commotion, rolling his palms on the peas.

'GEORGE!' roared Adam. 'Go into the other room with your sister and find something to play with.'

Lisa knew what was coming. Or at least she thought she did.

But Adam composed himself and said Saturdays were family time, hadn't she always said that when he'd had to work to finish a job? The egg incident showed the strike had reached ludicrous proportions and she was putting herself in danger. And what's more, because he was so busy doing all of this – waving at the cooker and the washing machine – he was going on strike himself from 'his duties' so she could understand the pressure he was under.

'What do you mean "your duties"?' Lisa said, on

the back foot. 'You hardly do anything unless you're nagged.'

'I'm now you, yeah?' he replied, as he swept up the peas. 'So you've got to be me. I can't do everything round here. There's a handle on one of the kitchen cupboards that's loose, the downstairs loo isn't draining properly and the car insurance is up. You'll have to sort it.'

Damn, he'd got her over a barrel. 'That's so childish,' she said, realising the second she'd said it that it was a case of touché.

'Yes, it is. But you treat me like one,' Adam said from the floor. 'You have done ever since the kids came along. Anything I ever did wasn't perfect enough for you. When you've got a running commentary of "silly Adam" in your ear, it makes you think "balls to it". It's the same now, you walk around with a face like a smacked arse, disapproving of my attempt at doing all of this. So I can't wait and see what a mess you make of "my jobs".'

Well, if he was going to be like this, turning the tables on her, she thought, she'd show him.

'Fine, Adam. Not. A. Problem. I'll sort all of that out tomorrow, I've got a half-day, time owing, so I'll fix that lot in the time it takes you to huff and puff to get your tools together whenever I've asked *you* to do a job round the house,' she crowed, pointing to a missed pea under the table.

She told him she was off to get changed, then declared, 'I can't wait for Cal's shepherd's pie, it's my favourite' before licking her finger and painting a mark in the air.

8.57p.m.
Drying herself after her bath, Cal peered at her washed-out reflection in the bathroom mirror.

God, she was starting to look her age. It was hard to accept, having been the baby-faced one throughout life. The youngest of the sisters, the youngest in the year at school, the one people couldn't believe was thirty-five with two kids and one on the way.

No one had commented on her appearance now for months. Probably a good thing, she thought.

Her eyes were bloodshot, she had bags and her crow's feet were now proper wrinkles. She had deep lines coming out from her nostrils, bracketing her mouth, and her forehead had a slash mark where she frowned. Her complexion was sallow and her chin hung like a cat's belly.

Her hair was falling out because she was at that stage, post-pregnancy, and it looked thin and dank.

Nothing like that Mandy's, I bet, bloody perfect hilarious energetic amazing Mandy.

She'd tried to be magnanimous at Lisa's excitement for her new friend, but she felt sick at the thought of the two of them meeting up. The description

233

of Mandy as 'absolutely lovely and so supportive and such a laugh' rang round her head as she wiped off the mascara she'd put on for Lisa's visit.

Her rational side told her there was no need to worry, they were dear friends, they'd known each other for as long as they could remember and Mandy was no threat. She and Lisa had their own language, for goodness' sake, their own codes, which usually derived from some silly conversation they'd had years ago.

Lisa or Cal just had to say the word 'boys' in a feeble tone and they'd be gasping for air in hysterics because it came from their InterRailing trip around Europe together aged nineteen – Lisa had called out the word in a thundery campsite in Venice to next door's tent, which contained three blokes they'd met. She was terrified and wanted 'rescuing', but Cal was panicking like mad because she was in her specs and didn't want anyone to see her looking so 'square'.

If one of them was out and heard 'their song', 'Step By Step' by New Kids on the Block, they'd send a text saying '10,000 LOVE YOUS' because they'd spent hours on a fruitless begging letter to the band to meet them, with 10,000 'love yous' in multicoloured biros.

And they did this thing when they saw someone naff from school in the street, nudging one another with 'I'm so going to tell Miss Parker', which was the name of their strictest ever teacher.

To anyone else their exchanges would be

cringeworthy but to them they were an intimate record of their past, their history.

Whereas these memories might have tickled Cal in the past, now she felt sad. And jealous. In the steamy mirror she drew horns so they sat on the top of her reflected head. Mandy was so shiny and new. And I'm so dull and old.

Maybe I need Botox? she wondered, pulling the skin back at her temples. No, Lisa and she had both sworn never to have it because they wanted to grow old gracefully.

Maybe I should start jogging. No, our boobs are already saggy enough was their consensus on that.

Maybe we need a night out together. Just me and Lees. Yes, it's been so long – not since before Dotty was born. Six months plus, she realised. They needed the chance to reconnect, whether that meant they'd address the unspoken crack which had opened up in their relationship or not. Heart-to-hearts had always come easily to them but that was when they'd been sharing their experiences rather than discussing a difference between them. That time I snogged that bloke she fancied was the only time we fell out and we made it up when he tried it on with her the next night, Cal recalled.

Things were so much simpler then. This strike though has really changed things between us. I swear I went red when she complimented me on how tidy the house was, Cal thought, but there's no way I want to tell her I'm under the spell of the Housework Fairy. She'll think I'm letting the side down.

God, she's so lucky to have a husband who's around, frankly, Cal thought, knowing she'd be going to bed alone tonight because Rob was at a conference. Life was never all roses. Roses. Flowers.

Maybe she'd make Lisa a bouquet with a card suggesting going out tomorrow night? Lisa loved flowers and she always said Adam never bothered because he was sick of greenery by the time he got home.

Would be interesting to see if I've still got my floral fingers, Cal thought, it's been years since I had a go. I could go to the market tomorrow; yes, if I do it then, Rob won't know and he won't bring up the subject of me going back to work. He'd been dropping heavy hints recently, asking when, not if, she planned to look for a job. The thought made her shudder – he'd changed his tune of late. Sunday night was when he'd last brought it up: if you're so set on having a cleaner, why don't you go out and earn the money to pay for it? he'd said. It was as if he'd moved the goalposts.

Before Dotty, he was happy she was at home for the kids but now he'd emphasised that this was her very last baby and he wanted to know what she would do with the rest of her life. It frightened her.

She wanted to be at home forever; he earned enough anyway. It wasn't as though she didn't earn her keep, he had a beautifully home-cooked meal every night – well, most nights if he wasn't dining with a client. His clothes were always cleaned and ironed, she knew where everything was and he didn't ever have to do bed- or bathtime.

No, there was no way she'd think about going back to work until she was ready, that was one thing she stood firm on. She'd stayed home with the oldest two and Dotty deserved the same. When she was three and started pre-school, then she'd make enquiries. But not before.

Cal scooped up the last of her night cream and dotted it on her cheeks before smoothing it across her face.

At least she had an excuse to go and buy some more, she loved a good pampering; maybe she would get some of that posh retinol stuff when she was in Boots tomorrow. If she wasn't going to have Botox then she needed good-quality moisturisers if she was to hang on to her fast-disappearing looks.

WEEK THREE

Day 15

'Wow, you look amazing,' Mandy said to her newest client, when she opened the door and invited her in.

The woman, who'd looked haunted last week, was clearly back on form; she'd probably had a good night's sleep, that's what you needed with a young baby. Mandy remembered the intoxicating feeling of waking up after a long stretch of sleep when you were used to three, four hours at a time at the most.

'Baby doing well?' she asked Caroline, who was humming happily, arranging flowers in one of those plastic water pouches which florists used these days.

'Brilliant,' she said, 'she slept through last night for the first time!'

That explained it, Mandy thought, as she laughed and plugged in the steam cleaner to do the kitchen floor.

'It called for a celebration, so I went and bought a

241

load of smellies for myself,' she said, pointing at the mountain of expensive-looking potions on the island. 'Had one of those makeovers too, I feel about ten years younger!'

'Oh, good for you,' Mandy said, breathing in the fresh scent of foliage and flowers which were piled on the worktop. 'They're gorgeous too.'

'I'm making a bouquet for my best friend, we've had a bit of a falling-out recently, nothing major, so I just wanted to show her how much I think of her.'

'That's lovely,' Mandy said, genuinely touched by the sentiment. 'She's lucky to have you.'

'And me her, we've just sort of lost our way lately,' the woman said dreamily, snipping here and there, looking happily lost as she sorted through stems of flowers Mandy had seen at the florist's but never had the money to buy. She recognised some, orchids and palm leaves, but what was that exotic-looking orange and yellow budded one with huge green leaves?

'Heliconia,' Caroline said, reading her confusion, 'related to bananas, believe it or not! And these,' she added, pointing at some stalks with orange petals and a blue tongue, 'they're strelitzia, known as bird of paradise, for obvious reasons.'

'Beautiful,' Mandy said, mesmerised, her breath quite taken away. Christ, what she'd give for someone to think that highly of her. Suddenly tears pricked her eyes. Sandro hadn't bought her flowers for years, said they were a waste of money, they only went and died on you. The image of a vase of dead flowers came to her mind and at that moment she realised she was looking at what had become of her love for Sandro. Last night was confirmation of that.

Gulping hard, she felt a rising panic, so she made her excuses and went to the loo, where she threw up quietly. No heaving dramatics, just a short statement that she could no longer stomach Sandro. He deliberately frightened me, she thought, repulsed by the memory of his touch. He's an animal. A bully. I don't love him any more, I don't want him being around the kids. She'd felt it this morning but had gone into denial mode, busying herself around the kids at the table, pushing his bowls and cups and fags and cufflinks to the other end to clear a space for their bacon and eggs. Franco had asked why she wasn't having any, and Lola, the sweetie, even offered some of hers. But she had no appetite. I've had mine already, she lied, while you were getting dressed. God knows how but their beautiful innocence was so far untainted by Sandro; if they stayed together he'd end up corrupting them with his hateful behaviour. I need to leave him, for my sake and theirs, she thought.

They shouldn't grow up believing their parents' marriage was the way to do things. They needed to know it wasn't acceptable to shout and scream and argue and fight and hurt one another.

She still hadn't brought up the subject of him egging Mo's shop. She was too scared. It would end up in a row and God knows what he'd do to her. She cringed at his utter stupidity; targeting a woman who had nothing to do with the strike apart from employing Lisa. She wouldn't be surprised if Mo let her go now, just when she was saving for the kids' summer schools. He was fortunate that Mo hadn't wanted to take things further – but that was him all over, he was a law unto himself.

Bile dripped from her nose as she stood half bent over the toilet, waiting until she was absolutely sure there'd be no more. How ridiculous, throwing up in a house I'm supposed to be cleaning.

She checked her face, wiped away her panda eyes and went back to the kitchen for her bleach.

The room was empty, she could hear the sound of a mother cooing to her baby somewhere else in the house, and the bouquet was finished. It was glorious and so, so stunning. There was an envelope poking up from within on a green plastic stem – she gasped as she saw the name on it. Lisa.

My Lisa? I wonder if it is. Mind you, she knew several Lisas; no, that'd be too much of a coincidence. She tried to recall if Lisa had mentioned a falling-out with a friend, but no.

Embarrassed at nosing into someone else's business, she told herself to get on with her work, first detouring to the loo to clean that up before returning to finish the floor, dust the skirting boards before scrubbing the sink and marvelling at their modern bendy tap rinsing away the suds.

She was in the groove now, scanning what needed doing, moving from room to room of this lovely big house, with its huge windows and wide spaces; it was a pleasure to clean.

'I'm just off to deliver these, thanks ever so much, see you next week,' came Caroline's voice.

A door slammed and Mandy realised she'd forgotten to ask if it was OK if she could come an hour later next Thursday, she had a dentist's appointment, made six months ago, and you just had to take whatever they offered.

She went around the place, looking for things she might've missed – nope, it was perfect. Just the finishing touches now, which she thought of as her signature: arrange the cushions on the sofa just so and tuck all the chairs under the table, bar one, so it looked ready to receive a grateful woman who might need a sit-down and a cuppa when she got in.

She realised she was 'playing house' just as she had as a girl, moving the tiny pieces of furniture in her doll's house around until it felt right. She'd been mimicking Mum, who was the queen of clean; they didn't have much but they were always nice and tidy, as she put it, just like Granny Glitter before her. It's running through my genes, this need to make things ordered. So how have I put up with the chaos of Sandro for all these years? The revelation came then that she'd been trying to make Sandro the man she wanted him to be. That's why she'd gone on strike – that's why she'd wanted to test him. But it was time to walk away. There wasn't enough good in him for her to accept him as the person he was.

She scribbled a note explaining she'd be a bit late next week, then she packed up and left.

1.05p.m.
Oh the joy of a half-day in lieu! Lisa skipped out of Vintage and recited her to-do list. It was odd, she was actually looking forward to doing something around the house. This strike, now a fortnight old, had been an education: she'd achieved so much outside the home that she needed to go back and check her roots indoors were intact.

After a sandwich, she'd do the cupboard handle, after that the car insurance and finally the loo. She'd be done in an hour so she could watch some TV on catch-up before getting the kids. Bliss. It was another sunny spring day, Adam had suggested a BBQ tonight and he was going to get burgers, rolls, coleslaw and salad on his way back from work. She couldn't wait.

Opening the gate, she walked up their path and saw a most incredible bouquet in the porch. Wow! A huge burst of colour – orange, blue, yellow, green, red and purple – bunched with twine and a card peeping out. Who could it be from?

Adam! Was this a 'sorry' for being lukewarm about her job offer? Or was it the moment he surrendered? She hoped with all her heart it was, surprising herself with her strength of feeling. She wanted to get on with things, move forward, weary of the higgledy-piggledy state of the house. Adam was coping better but she still had a gnawing irritation in her stomach when she watched him make work for himself. Why hadn't he realised if he pegged the washing out properly, the ironing would be less of a job? Lisa clenched her jaw at the thought of him 'tidying' by simply moving clothes and toys and mugs from one room to another, forgetting to put the dishwasher on, floundering as he tried to do what she found so easy.

Please, let that bouquet be from him, I'm tired of all this.

But no. Her spirits crashed. It wasn't Adam, not his writing. What had she been thinking? He resented buying flowers when he spent all day 'with nature'. Bugger.

Hang on, she thought, it's from Cal! What on earth? The card suggested a night out tomorrow, just the two of them, like old times. Lordy, that'd be two nights out in a row, get me! Tomorrow with Cal then our anniversary on Saturday night.

Why not! Forgetting her disappointment, she was thrilled her best friend had gone to such an effort. She still had the florist's touch, that's for sure – was this a sign she was preparing herself to go back to work? But what about Dotty? So many questions, all of which would be answered tomorrow. How exciting! They hadn't been out for yonks, they'd both been so busy, it'd be like a reunion of sorts.

Letting herself in, she left a message on Cal's phone to accept, stuck the drill on charge so she could do the cupboard, then while she ate her lunch she finished off the long-distance-learning application she'd started last night then checked her Facebook page.

Almost coughing up her crisps, she saw fifty-one 'likes'. No. Way. Scanning the names, she recognised some, but not others, but by the looks of things they were all friends of friends. And there was Mandy, phew, she'd been worried because she hadn't heard from her after she texted yesterday; she was obviously fine, just busy.

Goodness me! Two weeks, fifty-one strikers: if this carries on, the whole town will be on strike! There were loads of comments too, all of which were supportive; soundbites from put-upon mums who had had their fill of drudgery.

Absolutely amazing! Just when she was feeling fed up with the strike, this was a shot in the arm, the confirmation she wasn't fighting a losing battle. Lisa reminded herself how she'd felt the day before the strike – it seemed such a long time ago; they all obviously felt the same. She realised she needed to encourage them – she knew how hard it was to give in to the 'it's easier and quicker if I do it' urge and panic at the mess.

Lisa updated the page with a photo she'd taken of one of Mandy's MUM'S ON STRIKE posters and asked if anyone wanted one. She could easily run some off. Her mind started racing – we could do badges, have a get-together and organise a rally. She laughed out loud at her ridiculous stream of consciousness. Stick with the posters, love, she told herself, you're not Arthur blimming Scargill.

Then she logged off and saw that the light on the drill battery pack had turned to green.

Feeling recharged herself, Lisa was good to go.

3.15p.m.
'Ad, there's shit emptying all over the downstairs loo floor and the kids need picking up any minute, where the bloody hell are you?' Lisa wailed down the phone, her left hand automatically touching the side of her head in anguish.

Oh, why the hell did I just do that? she asked herself, realising her hair would now be tainted with the murky and smelly effluent covering her rubber glove. That's the least of my worries, she thought as she raced back to the scene of her DIY disaster.

Towels, where are they? Up to the airing cupboard. Damn you, Adam, where the hell have you put them? Not in the chest of drawers in the spare room. The laundry basket? Obviously. Full of dirty ones, they'd do. Lisa ran downstairs, throwing them onto the pool of brown water spreading as the liquid spilled over the sides of the loo and seeped slowly across the tiles in all directions up to the skirting boards, little streams breaking free in straight lines as they followed the grouting.

Sheets. She needed sheets. Again, not where they were supposed to be but eventually located behind their bedroom door, where Adam must have dumped them then forgotten about them when he made a mountain out of the molehill of changing the beds. Grabbing them, she returned to the loo and chucked them on top of the stinking mess, as though she was covering a crime scene. It was now 3.18 and she had no choice but to get Rosie and George. Peeling off her Marigolds, she pulled a disgusted face, breathing through her mouth like she did in public toilets.

Her phone buzzed. What now? I'm going to be late, she cursed, I just hope the water stops. Where's the bloody stopcock? Do I need to turn that off?

A text from Cal: 'Adam getting kids, he's just left,

told me to text as he was rushing, hope all OK, let me know if you need anything. XX'.

At hers again? 'Probably picking up his bloody washing,' Lisa announced to the ceiling.

Back to the loo, where the Rivers of Babylon had ceased and the water level in the bowl was dropping ever so slightly. Thank God. This was her doing. Caustic soda, a plunger then repeated flushing clearly wasn't the way to deal with a U-bend blockage. Adam would love this. And he'd love the cock-up she'd made of the kitchen cupboard handle as well. She'd accidentally drilled too large a screw at speed at an angle so the tip pierced the wood all the way through to the other side and was not only visible but dangerous. A blob of Blu-Tack now rested on the sharp point, which inevitably George would spot and, much as he fought the urge not to touch, he'd probably nick his finger.

As for the car insurance, well, their premium had gone up by 30 per cent for no reason. Their circumstances hadn't changed, they had clean licences and no claims. After giving up on all the confusing websites, she was repeatedly told over the phone how the collapse of the financial markets, an increase in crash-for-cash scams and car insurance being sold too cheaply in the past were to blame.

The door banged and in trooped her family. Bags, shoes and coats were thrown off and a high-speed shouty chitter-chatter filled the house as Lisa braced herself for a very smug husband indeed.

'Before you say anything, I'll fix all of it, Adam, all of it,' Lisa volunteered, kissing the kids, who screeched at her stinky odour. 'I'll get a plumber and a handyman in, I'll ring now.'

But Adam wanted his piece of flesh. Oh no she wasn't going to buy in help, he said, not when she'd pooh-poohed a cleaner. He wanted to rub her nose in it big time.

But this is different, Lisa argued as Rosie and George rifled through the snack drawer for sustenance. Adam refused to compromise. He insisted his wife would have to deal with it herself and he wasn't going to help because he had to go out to get the barbecue stuff.

One thing she had to know before he slipped out: 'What were you doing at Cal's?'

'A slab on the patio was loose,' he said. 'Anyway, I prefer it there, at least she makes me a cup of tea.'

Slam. Grrrr, men. Lisa shouted at the kids not to touch anything.

Then she stormed off into the garden, stuck a spade underneath the lip of the drain lid and hoiked it open to see if there was a blockage down there. Aha, there beneath her was the cause: a load of toilet roll and worse caught on an unidentifiable piece of red plastic. She found George's fishing net, bought on a happy day at the seaside last summer, and freed a toy car which she promptly stuck in the bin and then took the garden hose, turned the tap full blast and swished away the obstruction until she was sure the pipe was clear.

Back inside, unscrewing the cupboard door from its hinges so she could replace it at the weekend, she couldn't wait to tell Adam he had to bleach the floor.

5.45p.m.
Cal had heard Madonna singing 'Holiday' three times now.

At first, she had tapped her foot along, remembering her and Lisa singing into their hairbrushes one afternoon after school, their faces painted with 'borrowed' Rimmel products sneaked from one of Cal's sisters' make-up bags. They'd spent ages riffling through copies of *Smash Hits!* to find a photo of their favourite pop star so they got their eyelinered beauty spots on the right side.

But now she was getting annoyed with Madge on loop. She'd been on hold to the travel company for nearly ten minutes and a voice kept telling her she was next in the queue.

A scream came from upstairs then a riot of feet. What were Ted and Molly up to? Dotty was getting fed up too, squirming on her knee, yelping for milk.

She'd thought she'd be safe, calling now, with the kids fed and Dotty bathed. Famous last words.

You'll be next, she told herself, hang on in there. She plonked Dot on her boob and waited.

Why had she told the cleaner about her falling-out with Lisa? She didn't know if the Housework Fairy was Lisa's Mandy but she couldn't think of any other women by that name round here. Even if she wasn't, what if this Mandy was a gossip? Cal searched her memory to see if Mandy had been indiscreet with other people's business – undoubtedly she had access to people's secrets through her cleaning job. But no, she'd never dropped in any juicy titbits in her company so perhaps she was trustworthy. What did it matter anyway?

If she was Lisa's Mandy, she could see why Lisa was so taken with her. Mandy was gorgeous and sparkly and, yes, nice. She was professional yet warm without being overbearing.

Whether she was or whether she wasn't, Cal decided she'd fess up to Lisa tomorrow about having a cleaner – this had just highlighted an issue between them. Lisa won't go mad because she's not like that, but I feel awkward about it, especially after that business with Adam. At least we're going out, at least we'll have the chance to talk.

'Thank you for waiting, this is Emma, how can I help you?'

Cal explained they were going away in nine weeks and she was probably being silly sorting this out now because it could be fixed when they arrived but she wanted it to be perfect from the minute they got there. She wanted peace of mind and knowing her husband he wouldn't have thought of it so would she be able to book a cot and a high chair for the villa?

The call centre worker gave a tinkly laugh and reassured her she understood how precious holidays were and that she was right to think ahead. She asked for their booking reference so she could check.

'Oh, sorry, my husband's got all the paperwork, I only know we're going with you, don't tell me I've got to ring back!' Cal said.

No, it wasn't a problem. All she had to do was give the family name, their address and destination and Emma could access their details that way.

'That's a relief!' Cal said, their details tripping off her tongue.

There was a pause as the woman waited for the computer to work.

'It's been dodgy all day, nothing to worry about,' she reassured Cal before saying she'd been to their resort at Easter and it was fantastic, perfect for the kids, she had two little ones and honest to God, she had no complaints whatsoever, the food was incredible and the accommodation was brand new. 'Hmmm,' she added, 'I can't seem to find you on here, let me recheck your details.'

Cal wasn't fazed, she'd probably given out the wrong postcode in her excitement!

Another minute passed and again nothing came up. She took Cal's number and said she'd ring her back in five so she could speak to her line manager first, it was probably her fault, it'd been a long day.

No worries. Cal put the receiver down and sat back, stroking her daughter's soft scalp. Ted raced in, laughing, squeezed into Molly's Hello Kitty pyjamas, the sleeves halfway up his forearms and the legs around his calves. His sister was in hot pursuit, giggling, demanding he take them off right now.

'You two are funny!' Cal said, watching them with delight as Molly grabbed Ted's waistband, pulling him to the floor.

The phone rang. She shushed them with a flap of her hands, telling them it was probably about the holiday so they had to be quiet as it was important.

'Hello?' Cal said, smiling, ready to thank the woman for going to so much effort and awaiting the feel-good factor of knowing she could cross something off her list.

'I'm awfully sorry but I'm afraid we have no record of a booking under your husband's name, we've looked everywhere, but nothing's come up,' Emma said. 'Our searches are very thorough – they have to be with the number of clients we have. Of course, it could just be a mistake so if you'd like to get your husband to ring back later, we're open until 9p.m. . . .'

How weird, Cal thought, as she ended the call, holding her fingers over her mouth to think.

It'd be nothing to worry about, she was sure of that, Rob had probably given her the wrong company or she'd misheard him. She was still a bit baby-brained, after all. Rob would sort it when he got in.

257

Day 16

9.16a.m., Friday, 30 May

Mandy moved quickly and quietly around the house. She didn't want to wake Sandro and risk a confrontation.

She gathered up essential bits and pieces the children would need – pyjamas, Lola's comfort blanket and Franco's battered teddy, their toothbrushes, pants, shorts, T-shirts. There'd be no swimming later, it just wasn't important today. Her things, in the bedroom, would have to wait.

Stuffing them into the bag, she shoved it in the cupboard under the stairs and wondered where she was going to stay that night. Mum and Dad are in Spain and I don't want to be there alone with the kids, just in case. How about Shelley, her sister? Nope, she'd said she had friends staying tonight and there'd be no room. Who else was there? She scanned through a list of people she could call on but all of them were friends of both hers and Sandro's and she didn't want to put them in the position of thinking they had to choose sides.

Lisa's name sprang to mind. But she hardly knew her. Mandy was not one of those women who would tell her life story on the first meeting, she wasn't one of those leeches who wanted to be best friends the second you'd met. It was far too soon to be involving Lisa in her dramas. And yet, they had clicked, Lisa had a spare room, there was a man on the premises should Sandro get tasty, and it was only for one night. We can go to Shelley's tomorrow. And I'm completely desperate. If I don't do this now, I never will.

So she sent one of those huge texts, apologising profusely for asking, it would be fine if you said no, it's only for tonight, I need someone who doesn't know Sandro. She added a PS of 'I'll bring wine' to try to make it seem a bit more light-hearted and then she pressed 'send', crossing her fingers for a 'yeah, sure, no probs'. A response that mirrored her own tone, an acknowledgement that she wasn't getting heavy, trying to be Best Friends Forever. Just a favour, that was all.

Then she got on with the task she'd been dreading. Writing a letter to Sandro explaining it was over: she didn't want a messy separation, just think of the kids, you can see them whenever you like, it's not been working for a while, let's have a break. Making it seem temporary might appease his temper, she thought, knowing deep down however it would be in vain.

She didn't mention the other night when Sandro bit her, that would only make him angry. She hated doing it but she had to make it seem that it was her fault, that she'd realised she wanted different things in life and she was going through a difficult time.

Then came the bit she knew would hit him hardest. She told him he had until Sunday lunchtime to leave. She was going away for two nights to give him time to sort something out.

This would be an affront to Sandro – he would care more about losing his stake in the house than his kids. He behaved as if it was his castle and they were his subjects. But it wasn't his. It belonged to her parents, it'd been Granny Glitter's place and there was no way she was going to let him stay in the house. The kids were settled here and that was that.

A cough came from upstairs. Sandro was preparing to get up.

'*Amore*,' he shouted. 'Are you there?'

She stiffened, praying he'd think she was at work. The only sound was the ticking of the clock as the seconds passed. Mandy braced herself for the rustle of the duvet and the creak of a floorboard. Then she relaxed as it became clear he hadn't got out of bed. She realised it was his way of finding out if he had to get up – if she was in, he'd do it so he didn't look so lazy. The coast was obviously clear and he was dozing.

In the future, she told herself, remember this moment: if you ever doubt yourself for ending this, remember you couldn't bear the thought of seeing him. You were terrified of him.

A 'boing' came from her phone. Shit. If he heard that, he'd come down to investigate – he knew she was never without her phone, it could be a client or school. Another cough from upstairs. She hardly dared breathe.

Footsteps. Where was he going? Her heart thumped as she waited to find out. A groan and the sound of liquid hitting liquid – he was having a wee. Probably admiring his muscles as she'd once caught him doing, flexing as he emptied his bladder. His feet again, then silence. He'd gone back to bed, thank God.

Mandy swiped her phone. A message from Lisa. Come on, come on, come on, please let it be a 'yes'. Hallelujah, it read 'course, no worries, come over after pick-up'. Her soul soared – she had an escape.

It was like hearing a starter's gun. Who'd have thought the strike would lead to this? So Mandy signed the letter, left it on the table, tiptoed to the cupboard for their bag and went into the hall.

She saw a woman's face etched with anxiety looking back at her from the mirror.

'You're nearly there, Mand,' she whispered. 'Go, go, go.'

Slowly, she pulled the latch and opened the door, the noise of birdsong and traffic suddenly deafening her. She stepped outside, blinking in the sunlight, then grimaced as she eased the door shut, willing it to close without a sound.

Almost there, girl. The faintest click. She'd done it. She'd left the bastard.

11.04a.m.

Staring out of the window, Cal toyed with the idea of cancelling tonight. She couldn't bear the thought of telling Lisa the truth.

She could barely believe it herself. Her world had been turned upside down when Rob came home last night. She was still coming to terms with his confession, trying to work out how she should react beyond the anger. She hadn't wanted to share this with anyone as yet – that's why she hadn't turned to Lisa. In her younger days, the first thing they always did in a crisis was to contact each other. But that was before they became 'grown-ups', when tears become more private, when you try to work out how you're feeling before seeking a shoulder.

The view was the same as yesterday, the same as it would be tomorrow: a lovely street of modern houses, trees dotted in the style of a boulevard and a breeze tickling the leaves. How could it be so constant when her world had come crashing down? Why wasn't there a crack in the road to acknowledge her hurt? Why was the sun shining when inside she was grey and cold?

Last night the children had been in bed when Rob got in, looking haggard and harassed.

'What's up, love?' she'd asked, giving him a hug, hoping he'd notice how good she was looking. OK, it had been hours since her makeover but her new foundation was amazing, it'd lasted all day.

Instead, he'd grunted at her and gone to the drinks cabinet for a very large G&T.

He'd eaten his dinner in silence while she chit-chatted about her day. Dotty had just about been able to sit up in the high chair for the first time, Ted had been made Star of the Week for his reading and Molly had her first wobbly tooth.

None of that worked, so she mentioned the holiday, trying to get him to see all his hard work was worth it for two weeks off in the sun.

That was when he'd thumped the table and told her to stop going on about bloody Greece.

'I don't go on about it! Well, not that much! I'm just excited, that's all,' she'd said softly, hoping he'd calm down when he saw it was just enthusiasm.

It failed quite spectacularly.

He'd turned his head, there was sweat on his temples, and he stared her straight in the eye. Then he dropped the bombshell.

There was no holiday. He'd tried to book it but his credit card had maxed out. Just like all of his other ones. His last few bonuses hadn't arrived because he hadn't hit his ever-increasing targets. He didn't say anything because he was sure he'd cover his losses the next month. But the bills kept stacking up, then the move, the baby and he didn't blame her but Cal kept spending as though money grew on trees. Their account was £10,000 overdrawn and he felt he couldn't ask for help because she'd been struggling with a new baby.

Then his shoulders rocked as he started to sob, apologising over and over, telling her he was scared and unable to see a way out of it.

Cal's mind raced for signs of their predicament – that was why her card had been refused. That was why he'd gone mad about the cleaner. That was why he'd had a piece of bloody toast at the café. He'd been so distant of late. Why hadn't she seen him suffering?

She'd gone to console him. But then the fury came.

She was angry, my God, she was angry. He'd taken all of that on himself, without asking for help, thinking it was down to him. And the lies, the fact that he'd kept something from her that endangered the roof over their kids' heads.

Then came the fear that they could lose everything. Their lovely lifestyle which they'd worked so hard to achieve.

After that, the realisation she was going to have to step out of her cosy comfort zone, support him and take some responsibility for this mess. They'd have to sell up. This place and her car, they'd have to cancel their Sky TV package, sell the iPads, stop their gym membership and meals out, shop at Lidl, get rid of Mandy, cut back wherever possible.

And then he'd said it. The thing she'd been dreading all along.

'That's all incidental,' he'd said, shaking his head. 'We owe thousands, I need to pay back these debts straight away. I haven't met the payments for months.'

The memory of her husband's words made her shudder as she debated whether she would go out tonight.

'There's only one thing we can do, Cal, and you have to face up to it.'

5.01p.m.
'You bloody what?' Adam hissed in a shouty whisper. 'First you're on strike and now you're setting up a women's refuge! When is this going to stop, Lees? When?'

Perhaps the second he got in, caked in mud, hadn't been the best time to break it to him.

265

But Mandy was already here so she'd had to tell him as soon as he'd come home, it wasn't her fault his phone was out of battery. Lisa had offered her the spare room, her kids could go in Rosie's bunk and George would share with his sister – thank God they'd bought him a pull-out bed.

'I know, I'm sorry, Ad, it's just for the night, she had nowhere else to go,' Lisa said, mouthing 'she's left her husband.'

'Oh, that's OK then,' he said, giving her a fake happy face.

'Daddy, we're having a sleepover!' Rosie said, running into the hall, out of breath, hotly pursued by her brother, Lola and Franco, who'd gone from shy strangers to head-over-heels best friends in three seconds flat when they'd discovered they were staying over. In that time, they vetoed the sleeping plan and decided the boys would share one room and the girls the other. They galloped off to play spies, just as Mandy hesitantly came down the stairs.

She gave Adam a grateful smile, thanked him profusely and promised they wouldn't get in the way.

Lisa waved her words away. 'It's no problem at all. The kids are loving it. Really sorry about this but I've got to go out tonight, won't be late though so we can catch up when I get in. Have you heard from Sandro?'

Mandy shook her head then pulled her phone out of her pocket – it was switched off. She clearly didn't want to discuss it while the kids were up; she was yet to broach the subject of chucking Daddy out. She moved on swiftly, offering to make the tea, she'd go out and get some pizzas, she'd brought some wine though, and she'd put the kids to bed 'to earn her keep' because her strike was over.

'Wicked,' Adam said, giving Lisa a smug look as he disappeared for a shower.

'Typical,' his wife said, rolling her eyes – how many times had his friends and family descended on them and she'd been expected to cater and serve just like that without his help? But she let it go because this was an emergency and everyone had to muck in. The strike had taught her to 'go with the flow', something she'd been afraid of doing a little more than a fortnight ago: organisation and control had been good; spontaneity, bad.

'Hey, have you seen my flowers?' Lisa asked, changing the subject because she didn't want Mandy to feel awkward, proudly pointing at them in the hallway. 'From my best friend, aren't they beautiful?'

Lisa saw a flicker of something cross Mandy's face.

'What is it? Are you OK?' she asked. Oh God, it was bound to remind her of happier times, why had she opened her big mouth? 'Sorry about Sandro and everything.'

'No, it's not that, it's just I've seen those flowers, I

clean for that lady,' Mandy said, looking unsure if she'd said the right thing.

Lisa cocked her head as if she was checking her hearing.

'Right, oh, OK, wow, small world,' she said. It felt odd finding out something she didn't know about Cal. How did I not know that, she wondered, why hasn't she told me? A cleaner? There was a quick analysis in her brain: Cal had always done everything round the house and said she'd loved it, why would she take on a domestic? It wasn't as though she was struggling – she'd got everything she'd ever wanted. It was all very confusing.

'I can tell the kitchen has seen better days,' Mandy said, bringing Lisa back to the here and now as her guest took in the festering collection of breakfast things still on the kitchen table. 'At least you don't have to say excuse the mess to me,' she said, wryly, unscrewing a bottle of white.

Glowing from his shower, Adam wandered in smiling, asking if this was the right place for the soup kitchen. Phew, at least he'd come good about this, Lisa thought, shelving her thoughts: they could wait till later. In their place, she had one of those moments when, despite everything, she knew exactly why she'd married him.

'Pour me one, Mandy,' he said, sinking into a seat, making a show of having a night off from wearing the muscleman pinny which Ginger Steve had bought him as a piss-take.

'No eggs for tea tonight then, I assume?' he said and the two women laughed their heads off. Adam does get it right sometimes, Lisa thought. She'd never have dared make a joke like that but from him it just seemed to work.

Then he decided he was going to order in pizzas. Lisa was having a night out so he wanted to have a treat too and Mandy was their guest so that was that.

'Hang on, Adam,' Mandy said rifling through her purse when he'd put the handset down.

'Don't be silly, it's on us,' he said. 'Besides, I've got vouchers. I love a deal. I'm not one to brag but since I started doing the shopping, our bill has gone down and so we can afford it. Just call me the coupon king.'

He was enjoying this, Lisa knew, and poked her tongue out at him. But she let him have his moment in the sun. She was so grateful he hadn't kicked off tonight. In fact, she was dead proud of him; for seeing the bigger picture, for being so laid-back when it mattered.

She went to sit on his lap and gave him a kiss. 'Great idea, Ad,' she said, 'who needs Pizza Saturdays, eh? Besides, you don't want all that extra washing-up, do you?'

He laughed and pulled his top half away from his wife so he could look into her eyes.

'Cheeky, Mrs Stratton,' he said, gently flirting with her, 'very cheeky.'

Lisa flushed, feeling flattered by his attention, which had come out of the blue. Then aware it might make Mandy feel funny, she jumped up and announced she was going to get ready. She felt nervous about tonight and wanted to get herself together.

Adam followed, saying he would go and make the beds.

'Blimey, you're keen,' Lisa said as they leapt up the steps two by two like children. He grabbed her arm and pushed past her. He got to the top and turned round and with a glint in his eye he said, 'Yeah, well, I'll be coming back in with you tonight, it's been too long.'

Lisa's tummy flipped. She'd missed him too, the feel of him and his body heat he generated beside her.

Then his face turned conspiratorial as he whispered to Lisa: 'Have you seen her love bite?'

'No! Never! Really?' she said.

Adam nodded then raised his eyebrows, before adding: 'I wonder if there's someone else?'

7.12p.m.
Lisa took a swig from her glass of wine, trying to calm her nerves.

Sitting alone in a packed airless bar didn't help.

270

She fidgeted with her loose hair, adjusted her black tunic top, twisted her earrings, picked at non-existent fluff in her leggings and played with her face as she watched the door, ping-ponging between willing Cal to come and fearing her friend's arrival. She felt exposed. She might as well have ordered a can of worms with that bottle; something was up with her and Cal but she didn't know what. Oh this is silly, she's your biggest buddy, I bet it'll be just like it always is when we go out. Too much wine, lots of honking and millions of 'Love You Loads' texts when we're lying dizzy in bed.

Then there she was.

Lisa saw Cal before Cal saw Lisa. She looked awful. Her hair and make-up were 'done' and she was wearing a lovely red and black striped wrap dress and heels, but there was no spark. No wonder – she'd been crying; no one else would know but Lisa could see by the red patch on her chest that always came up when she'd been in tears. Lisa stood up, first to wave at her friend then to shuffle forward and shuffle back, not wanting to risk losing their table but desperate to hug her and make everything better. Whatever this was about.

She's the dearest person to me outside of my family, Lisa thought, as she took hold of Cal, breathed in the smell of her oh-so-familiar shampoo, and stroked her back as Cal gave in and sobbed into her collarbone.

They were quiet for a time as Cal got it out of her system, sitting with her back to the room to protect her privacy, wiping mascara from beneath her eyes with her ring fingers.

'Oh darling, what is it?' Lisa then asked, leaning forward, full of concern. 'Whatever it is we can fix it.'

Thick and fast, words tumbled out of Cal's mouth: huge debts, secrets, lies, betrayal. There she was thinking they were the lucky ones with a happy home and it was all built on sand. Her voice fractured as she delivered the bit which obviously hurt the most.

Rob had told her she had to go back to work. Straight away.

'I know it has to be done but that doesn't mean I'm not devastated,' she said. 'I'm going to have to hand Dotty over to a stranger, it makes me feel sick, the thought of doing that. She won't have what I gave Ted and Molly. I feel so guilty.'

And a part of her hated Rob for doing this to her. If he'd admitted their financial situation earlier perhaps they could've sorted it out and she wouldn't have had to spend today on her CV. 'He's robbed me of my baby, that's how it feels, Lees. I don't know if I can forgive him for that.'

In her next breath, she said she knew she was being self-centred; Dotty would be fine, that's life, her head had to rule her heart on this, being practical was the only way they could get through this if they were to save their home. But even so.

Lisa felt her pain acutely, she knew how much her stay-at-home dream meant to her friend.

'It's awful, Cal, I'm so sorry, I just don't know what to say, I wish I had the money to help,' she said. Then it dawned on Lisa that the strain on their relationship was nothing to do with this because Cal had only found out about their money worries last night. Maybe she was being paranoid. She wouldn't ask 'is there anything else?' – the debts were more than enough and if she did probe further, she would only be trying to appease her own concerns.

Instead she said: 'I know it doesn't make it all right but at least you found this out after having Dotty, otherwise you might never have had her, and those precious first few months, no one can take that away from you.'

Cal stopped. Took a breath. She seemed to be weighing up something.

'Look, I don't mean this the wrong way, Lees, but how would you know?' she said sadly, searching Lisa's face for understanding.

'You haven't been there for me since Dotty arrived. I don't mean to have a go but you popped in every now and again to see her and yet it never felt like you were coming to see me.'

Lisa was bewildered. She felt instantly defensive but

when Cal sighed deeply and dropped her shoulders she knew her friend had thought deeply about this.

'I'm saying this because I care about us, because you're my best friend, because I want to address it and not let things deteriorate,' she said. 'I don't think you've asked in months how I'm doing. I feel inconsequential. I've been really down in the dumps and I was just starting to feel like me again when I found out about Rob's debts.'

Cal explained how tired she had been. Dotty wasn't like the other two. She was a handful. Cal had been back and forth to the doctor's with the baby because of her reflux, then she reacted to the jabs, and Rob was never around. All she wanted was sleep. She just felt so alone.

'So while you were going forwards, with your job and your strike, I was going backwards and then you met Mandy. It feels like I'm losing you.'

Lisa put her head in her hands. She felt nauseous, as if she'd been winded. She was mortified and filled with disgust.

'Oh, Cal, no one would ever replace you, this is all my fault. I've been such a rubbish friend. You're right, I haven't been there for you,' she said, shaking her head in shame.

'I'm so, so sorry. I thought you were doing so well, I assumed you were loved-up with Dotty, you always seemed so together and serene. But I guess that's what I wanted to see, and then I felt snubbed by you over the strike.'

Cal gave a small laugh. 'And the worst thing is, I've been hiding something from you. I've got a cleaner and—'

Now it was Lisa's turn to smile. 'I know. Mandy saw your flowers and assumed I knew. Not that it matters, how could it? This strike is about my circumstances, it's a personal thing, I'd never judge anyone, you, if they had a cleaner.'

Cal looked relieved to have it out in the open. 'I wondered if it was her. And she's lovely and I'm just jealous, not of her, but of you finding someone else and wanting to spend time with her. And I got her in because I wasn't coping. I wanted everything to be perfect. And now look.'

The friends hugged. The air was clear. And it was full of love; the bond between them might have been battered about a bit but it was as strong as ever.

Looking at Cal, Lisa took in her lifelong soulmate: in this moment, she saw a sepia cine film reel of their friendship. She saw Cal in pigtails, chasing her around the playground, crashing over and scraping her knee, and Lisa kissing away her tears. Then she saw herself as a teenager, being consoled in Cal's bedroom when Michael Brown had dumped her and told everyone Lisa was a 'weird snogger'. And as Cal's bridesmaid and then Cal as hers, fluttering confetti, and newborn babies passed to one another, so proud of each other's achievements.

They'd made up because of all those memories.

'We'll be all right, Cal,' Lisa said, knowing this time it was fact.

Lisa poured out a promise to listen to her, to make time for her, bringing in Mandy's situation, reassuring Cal she wasn't a threat. Then Cal admitted Adam had tried his hardest not to accept any help from her but she'd insisted, believing it really was for Lisa's benefit.

Lisa went to top up Cal's glass but stopped when she remembered she was breastfeeding – there'd be no raucousness and late-night texts. But that was fine. Those days would return.

8.15p.m.
Oh my God, it's him, Mandy realised, when she came out of the loo and saw the back of his head in the kitchen doorway.

Fuck. Fuck. FUCK. What the hell is he doing here?

She considered darting back into the toilet to check she was looking OK – she didn't want him to see her like this. Scruffy hair in a ponytail, jogging bottoms and a hoodie. And she was a bit pissed, which meant she might say something she'd regret.

But it was too late, Adam had heard the flush and he was calling her.

'Come and meet Ginger Steve,' he said, 'he's a

legend. Well, he thinks so. Just dropping off some paperwork. He's my business partner.'

Ginger Steve! So that was his name! He swivelled round, caught sight of her and did a double-take move. 'It's you! Are you following me?' he said, his mouth curling up at the edges in a show of genuine delight, as he ran his hand over his chest. His lovely chest.

Mandy beamed. Far too obviously. Shit, way too keen there. How embarrassing. She ignored his question, she avoided looking at him because it made her feel funny. And excited.

'Oh, I'm his cleaner, he helped with my car the other night,' she said, then pretended all of a sudden she might just have heard the kids and made an excuse to leave.

She heard Adam explaining she was one of Lisa's mums on strike and then it turned to mumbling as she went upstairs, where she finally allowed a massive smirk to creep across her face. So, it's true then, she told herself, you fancy him. A bit, she admitted. Well, a lot, actually but I don't know him, he's probably got a girlfriend and what are you thinking, you nutter, he'd never fancy you, look at you. And all your baggage, yeah, a bloke is really going to fall for a mum-of-two who's estranged from her psycho husband. Especially in these saggy-bummed trousers.

That was enough to convince her she didn't need to be self-conscious in front of him; there was no point. It'd look so sad if you acted all shy around him, you silly deluded old cow, she told herself.

While she was up here, she might as well check her phone. She'd avoided it all day, wanting to get her head straight, focus on Franco and Lola, give them all of her attention. She'd spent too long wasting her energy on Sandro. So she sat down on the top step, waiting for the phone to wake up.

A buzz. Then another. Then three, four, five, six, seven and on and on as messages and the voicemail symbol flashed like some awful Morse code SOS.

'Where are you?' at 11.07a.m., obviously when he'd climbed out of his pit.

'Very funny, I take it this is a joke' at 12.13p.m. His ego was in denial.

'You bitch' at 1.13p.m. Angry now.

'*Amore*, come home, I love you' at 1.57p.m. It was his Plan B, thinking she'd fall for it.

'Who is he?' at 2.23p.m. Ah, she'd been waiting for the accusations to start.

'Will you just pick up, keep trying to ring you, stop playing this stupid game' at 3.47p.m. He'd started to believe it.

'There's no way I'm leaving this house, I'm not going anywhere' at 5.14p.m. He was going to be awkward, of course, she should've realised.

The voicemails went along the same lines. But not one mention of the kids or 'we can work this out'. Both were conspicuous by their absence – that was all she needed to know to convince her she'd done the right thing.

But how was she going to get him out of the house? That was the issue here and now.

She needed to sleep on it, to have a clear head. But that was for tomorrow. Tonight she was going to revel in her new freedom and raise a glass to flying solo.

So she went back down to the kitchen for a refill.

9.39p.m.
Lisa fumbled around with the key, trying to focus on not looking too drunk. She hadn't meant to have three-quarters of a bottle of wine but they'd ended up having such a laugh that she'd swigged it down like Ribena.

What a fab night, in the end. The two friends had left the bar when Cal was called back for a feed. Hugs and kisses and promises to always be there for each other, to listen and to make sure they made a date every week or so to have a night out together. Friendship's like a marriage, you have to work at it, that's what I've learned tonight, Lisa thought as she fell into the hall.

Hearing voices, music and laughter, she performed an inner whoop – she didn't want to sober up yet.

So she weaved her way in to find Adam, Mandy and Ginger Steve at the kitchen table, which was covered in empties. They cheered at the sight of her, which she met with a fist pump as though she was Rocky.

'Hurrah!' she said as Adam immediately introduced her to the argument he was having with his best mate as they competed on Spotify to find The Best Album Ever. Adam was slurring praise for *Pet Sounds* by the Beach Boys while Ginger Steve was having none of it. *Now That's What I Call Music 10* was his choice – how could you beat a compilation featuring 'Pump Up the Volume', Kiss, The Housemartins, 'La Bamba', Hue and Cry, Bananarama and 'Sweet Little Mystery'?

Grinning madly, Mandy stood up, a little wobbly on her feet, and suggested they should check on the kids. Lisa went first up the stairs, delivering a drunken 'shhhhh' so they wouldn't wake the children.

'Having a good time, Mandy?' Lisa asked. 'I did, I love Cal, tell you what – we should all go out the three of us, you'd love her.'

'Yeah, defo,' Mandy said in pursuit on cartoon tiptoes. They went to Rosie's room first. Poking their heads round, they saw the two girls snuggled up sharing the top bunk. Lola was spooning Rosie, both were rosy-cheeked, their long hair fanning the pillows, and their soft breathing was in tandem.

Mandy and Lisa looked at one another and shared one of those 'oh, aren't they beautiful' moments then went to see the boys.

Franco was in the bed, turned to the wall, the duvet pulled right up over his head so you could only just make out the top of his shaven head. George, who was snoring gently, was meant to be on the pull-out. Instead he was half on his mattress, half on Franco's, spreadeagled flat on his back. The covers were twisted up around his knees in a jumble of soft toys and books; he'd obviously been doing a show and tell to his substitute big brother, desperate to win his approval.

'Oh, bless,' Mandy said, as they padded away to get back to the party. 'Thanks so much, Lisa, you just don't know how much I appreciate this.'

'Hey, don't mention it,' Lisa replied, stopping so they were out of earshot of the kitchen. 'How are you? Have you heard from Sandro?'

Mandy filled her in, ending with the challenge of evicting Sandro. 'You don't happen to know Davina McCall, do you? Or any *Big Brother* bouncers?' she said, making a joke out of her terrible situation.

Lisa suggested getting Adam and Ginger Steve to have a word but no, that would only convince Sandro she had been up to no good and that'd send him wild.

'So there's no one else then,' Lisa tentatively said,

before apologising, excusing herself for such a stupid question. She'd drunk too much and she was being gobby and it was none of her business.

'I s'pose you've seen this,' Mandy said, arching her neck to show a bruised patch of skin near her breastbone.

Shit, that looks sore, Lisa thought; so that's what Adam had been talking about.

'It looks like a love bite, if only it was,' Mandy said, quietly, her eyes suddenly losing their sparkle. Then, staring into the distance, as if she was in a trance, she said: 'Sandro did that. He bit me. That was kind of when I realised it was over.'

From nowhere, Lisa felt a protective urge take hold of her. She grabbed Mandy and hugged her, rocking her gently from side to side, unable to imagine the fear of living with a man like that.

'It's OK,' Mandy said, pulling away, staring into her eyes as her hands gripped Lisa's forearms.

'Well, it's not, it's horrible, but if it wasn't for that then I'd still be there with that animal. He's lost control before, gone for me in the past in fact,' she stammered, 'that's how I lost my first baby. He pushed me down the stairs, and we were just married so I couldn't walk away.'

My God, she has so much strength, Lisa thought as she shook her head and tried to picture what kind of a person would harm someone they supposedly loved.

'I could kill him,' she said, bubbling with fury.

'Ha! You've done enough already. Not just putting us up but the strike. If it wasn't for you, I'd still be in that miserable marriage. I really mean that.'

As Lisa pulled her in again for a cuddle, she vowed to come up with a plan to pull together every single strand of this journey and tie that bastard in knots.

'I have no idea how we're going to get him back but we will, I promise you,' she said.

Mandy nodded and pulled herself together.

'Let's have a nightcap,' she said, leading the way into the kitchen. 'Two heads are better than one.'

Day 17

8.23a.m., Saturday, 31 May

What an angel Adam is, Lisa thought, as she woke up
to the waft of something cooking. She could murder
a bacon sandwich after last night's shenanigans.

Hang on though, the fire alarm would be going off
if that was him, he has yet to work out that the grill
needs to be cleaned after every use, and that stomach
rumble just then wasn't mine.

She rolled over to find Adam waking up. Yes, that's
right, he's back in with me now, what with Mandy
staying over. Mandy! And look at the time, our first
lie-in in donkey's.

Relieved she'd taken a cup of tea and two paracetamol
to bed to stave off a hangover, Lisa relaxed into a
sleepy smile, stretched and burrowed into Adam's
neck. 'Happy anniversary,' he said, kissing her as he
curled his arm around her.

Bugger, she'd completely forgotten to get him a

card. It'd been on her mind all week but all of this drama had got in the way.

Thankfully, Rosie bounded into the bedroom, landing on her dad's tummy with a 'woohoo'.

'Breakfast's ready!' she said, before running off back downstairs where the other three were clattering about.

It was a blissful feeling being spoiled, Lisa thought. Blokes just don't get that, they're so used to it.

'What a treat, a cooked breakfast,' Adam said, shocking Lisa to the core. Blimey, maybe he's coming round.

Then he added: 'Eight years, eh? Best eight years of my life, apart from the last two weeks.'

'You've got a nerve!' Lisa laughed, hoping he wouldn't realise she hadn't produced the usual card and present from her side of the bed, as she did every year. 'Where we going tonight then?'

'It's a surprise, nothing fancy, just somewhere meaningful,' Adam said, getting out of bed and sticking on pants and a T-shirt. 'Let's go,' he said, 'I'm starving.'

Wow! Mandy had not only made a fry-up but she'd tidied up every last spillage and empty glass from their impromptu party. Lisa had a flashback to Adam and Ginger Steve doing the 'Ooops Upside Your Head' routine on the sticky floor. After that they'd attempted breakdancing and devised a 'brilliant idea' to start up a middle-aged male dance troupe called The Landscaping Lads. The silly sods!

Lisa came to her senses at the sight of Adam producing two packages and a couple of cards from one of the cupboards. Oh no, I feel awful now, he's gone to such an effort, she thought. His card was her favourite photo from their wedding day, the pair of them nose-to-nose laughing with joy, while the other was from the kids, a home-made one drawn by Rosie, of Mummy and Daddy holding hands. She stole a kiss each from the children, who went to great pains to point out which bits they'd done, and then unwrapped her parcels. She laughed at the first, a Che Guevara tea towel and a pair of rubber gloves with Lady Muck printed across the sleeves, a hint, Adam said, that it was about time she ended the strike. The second took her breath away. A gorgeous heart-shaped pendant and chain, which he immediately put around her neck.

'It's Cornish bronze. Bronze is the traditional eighth wedding anniversary gift and Cornwall is where I proposed, remember?'

'Honestly, Adam, I'm so touched, it's beautiful,' she said, full of love for the man who'd got down on one knee all those years ago on the sand of St Ives. 'I feel terrible, I haven't got you anything. I was just going to pay for the meal tonight,' she made up on the spot.'

Funny how he'd got it pitch perfect this year, she

thought, she couldn't recall a year when he'd gone to so much effort. Was it the strike? Had it given him an insight into her life? Made him feel how nice it was to be appreciated. Whatever it was, she felt enormously lucky, considering what Mandy was going through.

With seven at the table, it was a bit of a squeeze and there were hands everywhere, reaching for bacon, eggs, sausages and tomatoes. Lisa surveyed the scene with total happiness: who'd have thought we'd be here, all of us, a little more than a fortnight ago? she thought. Franco, who was such a cutie, was helping George butter some toast while Lola and Rosie insisted on sitting on the same chair, a real sign of their new friendship.

'We're off to my sister's tonight,' Mandy said, sending the kids off on a chorus of boos.

'You don't have to go,' Lisa answered. 'Really. Stay as long as you need to.'

'Yeah, I second that if this is what it's going to be like every morning,' Adam said, his eyes closed, biting into two slices of bread oozing egg yolk and bacon.

But Mandy wouldn't have it. She'd said one night, and one night it would be and besides it was their anniversary and she didn't want to impose.

Talk about timing, Lisa thought. The poor thing. It must feel like we're rubbing her nose in it.

When the children had finished and gone off to make the most of their last hours together and Adam cleared away the plates, Mandy began to agonise about how she was going to get rid of Sandro.

'We'll work something out,' Lisa said, more confidently than she felt. She'd had a think and come up with a big fat zero. But she wouldn't let Mandy down. Something would come to her.

'Whatever it is we do, Sandro won't have a hope in hell.'

7.28p.m.

'Cibo?' Lisa said as Adam pointed at their destination. 'But that's where Sandro works. He's the one who threw the egg, what if he's there?'

Adam tutted. 'He won't recognise you,' he said, 'you're far too dolled up.'

'Charming,' Lisa said, as Adam opened the door for her and pushed her in.

A quick scan and phew, Sandro was nowhere to be seen in the candlelit restaurant, full of murmuring diners. Their table for two was in 'their spot', in the bay window on the left where they'd gone on their first 'proper' date ten years ago having met through friends of friends in the pub, realising they'd known each other from school and wasn't it weird they'd lost touch.

'Remember when I knocked my glass of wine over and dropped spag bol down my front?' Adam said as they sat down.

'How could I forget? I should've run there and then,' Lisa teased, reaching for his hand across the red and white checked tablecloth. 'You were so keen, Ad, and I was trying to play it cool, but God, I fancied you, always did. Whenever I passed you in the corridor at college, my tummy somersaulted. Even when you went through that Sun-In phase.'

Adam always tried to rewrite history, claiming he'd had the hots for her too but if that was the case why didn't he ask her out? It made Lisa laugh because it still annoyed her, even though she'd married him! But then she was glad she'd had a life before meeting Adam properly – had a couple of boyfriends who'd been no-hopers, enjoyed girly holidays with Cal before she'd settled down, worked hard to become a PA and saved up for the deposit on her old flat, which they'd sold, along with Adam's apartment, for their first home after a year together. They'd moved to their present house when Rosie was a year old, needing a bigger garden and more space for when George arrived.

'You happy then, love?' she asked, hoping she could steer the conversation round to the strike. The only time they'd discussed it was during arguments, and that was no good.

Adam nodded. He loved her, he was so proud of their kids, his business was doing just about OK and they could pay their bills.

'But what about recently?' she probed, clenching her bum cheeks because she couldn't tell how he was going to react.

'Not tonight, Lees, let's just enjoy this, us. And marvel at how good-looking I am. A bottle of that, please,' he said as the waiter arrived to take their drinks order.

Then he got up to go to the loo and told her not to neck it all, he knew what she was like.

Lisa sighed, fair enough. Fiddling with her glass she thought about how she felt. It couldn't have gone better, if you ignored the mess. She had stepped outside her comfort zone, pushed herself at work, had the possibility of studying for a degree at her fingertips and she'd made a new friend. The kids were unscathed and Adam was no longer indulging in man sulks like he had at the start. He was just getting on with it. But surely he had to crack soon? He had lost so much of his own time and she had gained. It wasn't fair, she knew; she wanted to shift the weight back to the middle, he was looking so tired. But still he kept on. He must be enjoying the martyrdom, just like I did, there's no other explanation for him holding out. Maybe he was finding it hard to admit it and he just wasn't there yet.

Adam was on his way back. He looks so handsome tonight, Lisa thought as she watched him walk back to their table. He is lovely, he really is; she felt a hot flush creep up her body. That sensation wasn't a surprise – she noted his charisma every time she saw him, particularly when he'd just stepped out of the shower, lifted both kids with one arm, cuddled her or laughed at one of his own awful jokes.

But it was unusual to have the chance to bask in his sunshine; mostly it was a fleeting appreciation because there was always an interruption.

With the kids on a sleepover at Cal's, who'd stepped in when Lisa had told her about Lesley's arm, tonight she could take it in. His stubbly blond jawline, which was strong and angular; his sandy hair, like David Beckham's she always liked to think. A smattering of freckles on his straight nose, weathered crow's feet which were always sexy on men, very unfair to us women, she thought. White teeth, full boyish lips with a perfect cupid's bow and breathtaking blue eyes, all wrapped up in olive skin.

He sat down, picked up the menu and without looking at her said: 'What are you going to have then? By the way, Mrs Stratton, make sure you leave a bit of room for afters.'

She gasped. He did this to her every now and again, talking sort-of-dirty in a way that appealed to her basic 'You Tarzan, me Jane' instinct, which were buried deep underground most of the time because of life and stuff. On a day-to-day level, she forgot they were married, a unit independent of the world. The kids came first, naturally. Both of them accepted that, wanted it. Yet Lisa and Adam had been there before them and when they remembered that it had started off just the two of them and they'd fallen head over heels, lost their appetites because they were so in love – well, it was intoxicating.

Adam wouldn't go over the top with it, which was why Lisa loved it. He knew perfectly well how to flirt with his own wife. A few things here and there, at inappropriate times, would make Lisa's heart – and downstairs bits – flutter.

Who'd have thought she'd feel this way on their eighth wedding anniversary? They'd survived the seven-year itch, something a few of her friends had experienced: feeling dissatisfied with their marital lot, starting to eye up blokes, making snide remarks about their other half, feeling trapped and without hope.

But Lisa never felt like that about Adam. They were rock solid.

'I think I'm going to have the garlic prawns to start, then the tagliatelle. What about you, Ad?' she said, curling her naked foot around his calf underneath the table.

'Oh, I dunno. Anything, it's so nice to be cooked for,' he said, mocking her with one of the lines she always came out with when they ate out.

Then he tempered it with flattery.

'You look amazing tonight, by the way. Not that

you don't always look amazing. But tonight you've done something to your hair, haven't you? Have you? Please tell me you have or I'll look a right dick.'

Oh he was good, very good. Lisa had taken extra time to condition and straighten her hair when she was getting ready.

'And I like your top. That midnight blue colour really suits you, makes your hair look even more chestnutty.'

Lisa peered at her husband in an exaggerated fashion. 'You look like Adam, but you don't sound like him. Are you in there or has an alien life force taken over your body?'

Come to think of it, there was something odd about him, she thought. He had some kind of wax in his hair, his stubble was very neat as opposed to his usual scraggy style, and – sniff – yes, he was actually wearing something smelly. In a nice way smelly, not his usual eau de backside perfume. He didn't look rugged, she realised, more Shane Warne.

'Adam, I've just realised you've tarted yourself up! For me! Excuse me while I pass out. You look so funny!'

Oh dear. Funny was obviously not the word Adam had in mind. He looked slightly hurt, she thought. Quick, backpedal.

'But gorgeous, as ever. I'm so flattered, really I am, wow, you look lovely.'

He smiled. 'It's just nice to make an effort every now and again, isn't it.'

She'd got away with it. But the truth was she wasn't actually sure if she wanted a husband who spent hours in front of the mirror. Not to worry, she thought. He'll be pissed in a bit and he'll be back to his normal manly self.

Just like he was at their wedding reception! He'd started off all suited and booted, his face spit-licked clean by Lesley, and by the end he had his bow tie undone, shirt untucked and was barefoot on the dance floor. It was such an incredible day, that warm spring afternoon at St Augustine's church. Her beautiful champagne-coloured, puddle-trained dress, which she still had in the loft; his squad of best men, who gave them a cycling pump guard of honour when they walked out into the sunshine as man and wife. Their reception at the posh Manor House hotel had been the best party ever – all their friends and family together, tables decorated with red roses, brilliant speeches, the disco; and saving hard for their dream do, which they'd insisted on paying for because their parents weren't well off, had been worth every night stayed in, every meal out they'd turned down. Then their honeymoon in Tenerife when they soaked up the sun and each other for ten unforgettable days.

Theirs was a proper love story.

She just wished she hadn't caught him tilting his dessert spoon so he could check his hair.

10.14p.m.
When they'd finished their Irish coffees, Lisa suggested the bill. Adam nodded in agreement and called the waiter while she went to the loo.

She sniggered when she got back and it was his turn to go to the toilet, we're worse than the kids!

Bending down to the floor to dip into her handbag, she had a lengthy rummage – why was her purse always so hard to find?

Looking up, she saw a dark-haired figure before her. Sandro. He glared at her then threw the bill down, an action cleverly hidden from the manager as he had his back to the restaurant floor.

Lisa gulped. Shit. 'I didn't know you were working here tonight.'

He smirked and pointed at his whites; he was cheffing. 'One of the boys told me you were in,' he snarled.

Then he leaned forward, placing his hands on the table, his face inches from hers. 'You can tell Mandy from me I'm not leaving that house. This is all your fault, that stupid strike, you—'

'Problem, mate?' said Adam, smacking his hand on Sandro's shoulder. 'Because I can have a word with the boss if you're causing trouble.'

Sandro's body recoiled from the table. 'He was

just going,' Lisa said, standing up, realising how important it was to confront him. 'I've paid in cash, let's go.'

She grabbed her bag as Adam puffed his chest at Sandro, who sloped off back to the kitchen.

'What a nasty piece of work,' he said.

'Don't worry, love. Slowly, slowly, catchy Sandro,' she said as they stepped out onto the street. It was a lovely close night. Adam, who was obsessed with the weather thanks to his trade, told her the forecast. The last day of the fabulous stretch of weather they'd been having. Tomorrow there would be rain and possibly a storm. Lisa could smell it in the air and – listen – thunder, there was a rumble in the distance.

We still have tonight, Lisa thought as Adam took her hand.

'Feeling shultry?' he asked, in his best Sean Connery voice, raising his right eyebrow for effect.

She laughed and started poking fun at his new-found vanity. There was electricity between them as Adam pretended he was her, tiptoeing awkwardly, yelping at dog poo, giving it the Little Miss act.

Lisa knew just what to do to get back at him: she'd seduce him – that'd bring out the man in him.

Waiting for the traffic lights to change, she whispered in his ear: 'I've got that underwear on, the one you like.'

Bang. Instantly, his face turned to her, his eyes

heavy with lust. She had him hook, line and knickers.

He pulled her towards him, started kissing her neck, one hand on her bottom, searching for the outline of her pants to feel the evidence. He pushed himself against her, making it quite clear he was up for it. They had a full-on snog on the pavement until a car that had stopped at the red light beeped them out of the moment.

He dragged her across the road, clutching her hand tight, saying nothing, walking at speed, until they were on the doorstep. Fiddling for keys, not bothering with the light, kissing in the hall, pulling at each other's clothes, exposing flesh, sighing, stumbling towards the nearest room, the lounge, collapsing on the sofa, his weight on hers, Adam holding her wrists down, his breath fast and shallow, then letting Lisa climb on top, gazing up at her, his lips flushed, his shirt off, willing her to say she was ready, her mouth travelling all the way down.

Suddenly, everything turned to marshmallow. The image that came straight to Lisa's mind was a Flump, George's favourite sweetie, one of those bendy pink tubes, which reminded her of that joke 'what's wrinkly and hangs out your trousers?'

'Oh God, is it because I wasn't really wearing those pants? Your favourites?' Lisa asked, suddenly feeling her skin smarting from Adam's bristles. 'I wasn't lying, I mean I was because I had my M&S black ones on, but I was just trying to get you in the mood. I'm sorry.'

Adam shut his eyes, sighed and screwed up his face, saying: 'Fuck, fuck, fuck. Fuck you, Mr Floppy.'

'What? It's fine, it happens, I've read about it in magazines, it's normal during times of stress, I don't care that we didn't do it, that was amazing as it was,' Lisa said, honestly.

Adam wasn't listening to her. He made a fist and slammed it down on the sofa.

'Seriously, Ad, it's fine. I think you're over-reacting. Maybe it was the wine?' she asked, lying back down with him, so he didn't have to meet her eyes if he felt embarrassed.

As she snuggled up to him, burying her face in his neck, she felt something wet on the top of her fore-head. Looking up, she saw that Adam had two tracks of tears running down his cheeks. No sobs; he was silent, staring up at the ceiling, running his right hand through his hair, which was still holding its shape quite nicely, thanks very much.

'Maybe you should've used some of that wax on it?' Lisa said, kissing the drops, thinking a joke might lighten the atmosphere, might make him realise she loved him and that was all there to it.

She felt him flinch.

'Look, Lees,' he said, 'I'm not blaming you or anything but I think this whole strike thing is getting to me.'

She nodded supportively. She'd felt like that for years, up until seventeen days ago. It was so tiring being on call 24/7, only allowing yourself to fall asleep when you'd made completely sure you had everything sorted for the next day, running at 100mph to stop yourself falling behind, always thinking 'what needs doing next then?', the constant demands of others – all of it was exhausting and the last thing you wanted after all that was sex.

'I dunno,' he continued, 'I'm just . . .'

'Knackered, worn out, deflated, desperate for a day off?' Lisa suggested, expecting a hug in appreciation of her understanding.

'Actually, Lees, it's not that at all, even though I am tired. But it's "it's not me, it's you" if you get me,' he said, blowing his nose on a sock he'd retrieved from the floor.

'Me? What have I done? I don't understand,' Lisa said, sitting up and pulling her top back over her head as if she needed armour.

'The strike, it's left me feeling less like a man, less male, you know, I don't seem to be Adam any more and it's really confusing, and look, I'm even talking about my feelings and that's not me, is it? I just feel smaller and weaker and strange and weird and you, well, you've become more like me and you seem larger and stronger and you're flourishing.'

His voice trailed off. Lisa was stuck for words. It

was all true. But whereas before in the restaurant she'd wanted to talk, she couldn't be bothered now. The drama of the last few days was finally catching up with her, the stuffing had been truly knocked out of her. All she wanted was sleep.

A loud yawn came from nowhere so she gave him a cuddle in the hope he didn't think she was bored. Then she got up and walked towards the hallway.

'Lees,' he called as she went out of the room, 'what are you doing? Can't we talk about it?'

'Going to bed. I'm tired, love. We'll chat tomorrow. Come on, the kids will be back at 9a.m.'

And as she climbed the stairs, she felt relieved she'd got out of a heart-to-heart. It was odd, very odd. Usually I love a deep and meaningful, she thought as she scratched her bum on the way up.

Day 18

11.49a.m., Sunday, 1 June

The so-called Glorious First of June and it was pelting it down. Lisa ran from the car up the path, thinking that at least her hair was already wet from the swim. Not even midday and she'd thrashed out thirty lengths, peeled the spuds and carrots at Lesley's, slammed in some lamb, made a bread-and-butter pudding and tidied the place.

'Didn't you get my text about the broccoli?' Adam asked in a panicked voice as Lisa pushed open the front door.

Her eyes widened at the ridiculous sight of her beefy husband's face which was etched with anxiety, face-painted soldier's camouflage and pink eyeshadow.

'Have you been waiting for me, right here, in the hall?' she laughed, then stopped, noticing his wounded look, as if she'd snubbed him.

The kids dashed up to her, pulling at her clothes, wanting her to come and see the plastic milk carton and egg box igloo Daddy had made them out of the recycling stuff. Blimey, Rosie had a lovely fishtail plait – Adam had obviously done it: amazing. I've never mastered the technique, Lisa thought.

'Wow! Adam, I'm impressed!' she said. He'd clearly been busy playing and crafting – and cooking, by the smell of the roast coming from the kitchen.

She dumped her swimming bag on the floor and went to walk off with the kids.

'Lees, don't just leave it there, aren't you going to put it away?' Adam said.

'I bet Rebecca Adlington isn't spoken to like that,' she joked.

'And where's the broccoli? The dinner will be ready in ten minutes, I did tell you this morning we were eating at twelve,' Adam said, pointing at his watch.

'Right, it'll have to be tinned sweetcorn and frozen beans then if you don't take your children's diet seriously,' he said, walking off in a huff towards the freezer.

He was beginning to be a bit of a nag, Lisa thought.

With her bottom poking out of the igloo, Rosie gabbled away breathlessly how Daddy hadn't gone mad when she spilled some glue and then George produced a cardboard sword Adam had made for him. Rosie yelled: 'Daaaaad, can I have a drink?'

Lisa felt her stomach flip.

She felt like an observer, redundant. Useless. This wasn't what she'd been fighting for.

This was by far her worst moment of the strike so far.

Damn, it had taken the wind right out of her sails. Focus, she told herself, focus on the strike. It's not harming them, it's doing them good. Really, she should be happy, over the flipping moon at the way the kids had adapted. At how they weren't suffering. How she was teaching them a life lesson, that they'd grow up accepting that housework was not automatically women's work.

Losing her kids ever so slightly to Adam was a consequence. And she had to deal with it.

Over beautiful roast beef, her husband delivered another blow to her quickly diminishing sense of her superiority in the house. As if she was in the passenger seat of a car, her feet pushed at imaginary brakes as he announced the advent of pocket money to the kids.

They whooped and yelped in excitement as Lisa tumbled down from the summit of the moral high ground which she'd occupied for their entire lives. He was a hero in their eyes now.

And, begrudgingly, he was in Lisa's eyes too

because his pocket money pact depended on one condition: the kids could choose anything they liked to spend their money on as long as they did two allotted chores every day. George opted to tidy his room and lay the table at teatime while Rosie volunteered to feed the cat and get their school uniform ready before bed.

Why didn't I think of that? she asked herself. It was a stroke of genius.

For £2 a week, Adam had not only roped the kids into helping him but had introduced the concept of responsibility – and equality.

Lisa comforted herself by telling herself that he wouldn't have done this if she hadn't gone on strike because he would have had no insight into the domestic front. And she knew she wouldn't have had the patience to watch the kids doing their jobs either too slowly or haphazardly. She had been a bit of a control freak before this, she admitted, too quick to jump in and correct their attempts at whatever they were doing. Into her mind sprang the memory of making cakes with George one afternoon before they went to pick up Rosie. He was giggling as he whizzed the mixture in the bowl and he proudly spooned it into the cases like a big boy. Then – she winced at the recollection – she saw his panic when he splodged the worktop and his trousers. 'Sorry, Mummy, sorry, sorry,' he'd said when she'd sighed

'Oh, George.' Only three at the time and he was already programmed to apologise ahead of his mother's disapproval when all he'd done was have some fun. She'd insisted on finishing off the cakes while he sat quiet on the floor.

She promised herself that when the strike was over she'd relax and let the kids do things for themselves without getting in a flap. Her upbringing had so much to answer for, she thought, she'd been trying to be as perfect as possible because her childhood had been so chaotic.

She came to at the table when George knocked over his cup.

He automatically looked at her, fearing her reaction. Instead of scolding him, she smiled and said, 'Don't worry, it's only water, love.'

Adam pulled a face of fake shock. 'Breaking news – Mummy hasn't gone bananas! Maybe this strike is teaching you a few things, Lees. And you did notice it's water, didn't you? The kids don't have juice any more with their meals, I read somewhere it got kids to eat better, cos if it was juice they'd knock it back then feel fuller than they really were. So there! Daddy 1, Mummy nil.'

He got up and with one hand mopped up the puddle of water which was trickling its way down the leg of the table, and with the other stacked their plates and carried them to the dishwasher.

'Adam, you're doing really well at, well, every-thing,' Lisa said, as though seeing it for the first time. 'He is, isn't he, kids?'

Rosie announced that some of her friends at school were jealous of her having a 'housedaddy' because they hardly saw their dads.

Lisa smiled encouragingly but found herself wondering, what the hell have I done?

'Oh and there's another thing,' Adam said as he loaded the dishwasher. 'I've spoken to the kids and we've decided that it's best all round if they have school dinners. They'll be free soon anyway so it'll be good to get them used to it.'

In an instant, Rosie and George hissed 'yessssssss!' to each other; they had been asking for months to have school meals so they could sit with their best friends who had them. Even though Lisa knew she was making work for herself, she'd been a firm believer in packed lunches – she could decide what went in, she knew how much they'd eaten and it saved them money.

Reluctantly she could see that Adam was right. The menu was healthy, there was always fruit and veg available, and now she was working they could afford it. And she had to admit her lunchbox obsession was another way of controlling things for her own peace of mind when really parenthood was about preparing them for independence. But the way he'd gone about it was awful – why hadn't he at least told her beforehand he was going to do it? And she suspected he was doing it to save himself a job rather than thinking of the kids' benefit.

Well, he's not the only one who can pull rabbits out of a hat, she thought. If he's going to be the one making announcements left, right and centre, I'll give him one of my own.

'Kids! KIDS! Calm down! That's not all!' she said. 'You'll never guess what – Mummy has been offered a better job by Aunty Mo and it means you get Daddy to yourselves every other Saturday! How's about that?'

Had she mentioned this prior to the school dinners and pocket money news, she might've expected a vague cheer at the prospect of pizza out rather than in. Or even sad faces at missing more Mummy time. But because they were whipped up already, they went berserk with excitement.

She expected Adam to bite. Instead, with his back to her as he put away the salt and pepper, his shoulders and head dropped and he placed both hands on the worktop to support himself.

He looked defeated and though she'd expected to feel victorious, instead she felt a complete cow.

Lisa felt something – she wasn't sure what – pop. She didn't know it yet but this was the beginning of the end of her strike.

1.57p.m.

'Mum, it's me,' Lisa called as she let herself in and searched the house for her parents.

The *Observer* was scattered round the front room and their washed-up dinner plates were draining by the sink so they were about – but where?

The back door was open so she peered out into the gloom. She heard laughter coming from the shed. She stopped and took it in: her mum and dad who she thought were mismatched and leading separate lives were sharing a joke and through the shed window she could see them moving together. Oh God, they weren't, were they?

A wave of relief came when she realised they were dancing, there was some kind of classical music on Dad's ancient radio which he kept in there and they were having a slowie!

Dad was keeping time by nodding his tufty-haired balding head while Mum veered between apologies and giggles because she kept missing steps. It was a sight Lisa had never expected to see. Never.

Then Dad saw her, told Mum and they bustled outside in their slippers, delighted to see her and explaining they'd taken up ballroom dancing and they were practising. But why in the shed? It was tiny. Well, they were both in there potting some plants and then the mood took them, Angie said, elbowing Wolfie in the side, which was his signal to explain how awful she was. 'Your mother is dreadful,' he said, smiling.

'But you two . . .' Lisa spluttered.

'Yeeees,' said Dad.

'But you never do anything together,' she said.

Her parents swapped smiles and Mum looked a bit coy as she went into an explanation about keeping a marriage going and it was the time of their lives when couples came back together after years of raising children and working and they'd always wanted to learn to dance and they'd done things before like bowls last year, and the year before they played bridge but that was too boring and . . .

Lisa was stunned: this was all news to her. Suddenly she saw why – she'd been so engrossed in her own life, her children, her marriage, herself, that she hadn't noticed her parents had knitted themselves back together and were still very much in love. She'd grown up but her perception of them hadn't grown with her – in her mind they were still Angie and Wolfie, him working nights and her going to meetings.

Standing there, she knew she'd been misjudging them all these years. She'd never seen Dad as anything but a walkover when in fact he was gentle and laid-back, and Mum, she was so much more than the loony leftie Lisa had thought she was: she was colourful and vibrant and, to Dad, enchanting.

Her face must've told them what was going through her mind and a look passed between her parents as if to say 'the penny has finally dropped'. She waited for a lecture, but then gave herself a ticking off, that's exactly how you shouldn't be thinking.

Instead, they came over to kiss her and as it started to rain again, Mum said she'd put the kettle on, she had some lovely Fairtrade coffee in the cupboard; she told Dad she'd bring his out.

'But I thought you were on strike, Mum?'

'Oh, that, well, in public I am,' she winked, 'but your father, well, he's got a bad back at the moment and it's not fair to make him do things and I like looking after him.'

Lisa instantly understood that the glue keeping them together was love and acceptance and knowing when the other person really needed you. That was the difference between her parents and Adam's – Lesley was still keeping up appearances and Roy hadn't made any exceptions, not for her broken arm nor for any other moment in their lives together. That was the stiff upper lip in them; formalities and manners and roles were how they made sense of life.

'Mum, I think I've got an apology to make,' Lisa said to her mother's back while she stood at the sink to fill the kettle. Lisa felt cowardly, beginning remorse without eye contact, but it committed her to finish it, just as if she'd jumped off a diving board.

Angie plonked the jug onto its base, flicked the 'on' switch, and turned around with kind eyes.

'I've been a bit off with you, a bit judgmental and I'm sorry, I really am.'

Her mother sighed then sat down at the table to join Lisa.

'I think you cope very well with a mum like me,' she said, graciously.

'I've never been very good at motherhood, not like you, and there's no need to protest, love,' she said, silencing Lisa's 'buts'. 'I struggled in the early years when Dad was working nights; looking back I probably had post-natal depression but back then we didn't talk about it. And the only way I could deal with it was to busy myself, hence the meetings and things. I told everyone we only wanted one child because the world was over-populated already but the truth was, I was too afraid.'

Angie's voice cracked, she fanned her face with her fingers and claimed it was the menopause. But Lisa felt desperately sorry for her – there's nothing worse than carrying that feeling of not being a good enough mum. 'Oh, Mum,' she said, taking her hand across the ragged red and green Oxfam raffia table mats she'd given her on a Mother's Day years ago. Then it struck her: perhaps Mum hadn't chucked them not because she was an eco-warrior but because she treasured them.

Wiping a silent tear from her cheek, Angie continued: 'Did I ever tell you I applied for university but my father wouldn't let me go? He thought it was a waste – "women don't need to be educated, it's more important to get married", he'd say. That's why I turned out the way I did. Maybe I was trying to set a good example to you too, to go for what you believe in. But it never quite works out how you think it should.'

It all fell into place, Lisa thought. How could she have been so stupid as not to think there was a reason why her mum was the way she was.

'Oh, God, and you've carried all of this and never told me,' Lisa said, beside herself with upset.

'Don't you worry,' Angie said, shaking herself out of the memory, resuming her role as elder, 'families are funny things. Now,' she said, adjusting her batik scarf, 'what's going on with you?'

It was clear she didn't want to dwell on herself, so Lisa explained the problem. Mandy was trying to kick her bully of a husband out of the house which belonged to Mandy's parents. He was refusing to go. Lisa was determined to help but she just wasn't sure how.

Angie listened attentively, poured the coffee then took a breath.

'Do you remember when you were small, we had lots of aunties come to stay every now and again? Some for a night, others for a few days?'

Lisa nodded slowly, yes, she vaguely recalled visitors turning up in the middle of the night with kids and suitcases and then as soon as she'd got used to seeing their faces at the table, they disappeared.

'I thought they were your friends, Mum.'

'Well, they were sometimes, but most of them I didn't know at all. They were battered wives, Lisa. All those meetings I went to were to do with an underground support network I set up for women who wanted to leave violent husbands. There was no refuge for victims of domestic abuse, so we campaigned for one, which you know we achieved, but in the meantime a handful of women, me included, put up desperate souls who had to get out of abusive relationships.'

It all made sense now, the whispers on the landing at midnight, the spare bundles of bedding Mum kept behind the sofa rather than in the loft: she was always on standby for extra bodies staying over. Her mum was a complete hero! Lisa was enthralled. But still puzzled – how was this going to help Mandy?

Her mum took a slurp from her mug – which featured the slogan FEMINIST AND PROUD – and continued.

'And do you remember we once spent a week with a load of mums and their kids staying with Auntie Janice at her house? It was in the summer holidays and you had a ball with her two, Sally and Michael?'

Yes, I do, thought Lisa: we all bedded down

wherever we could, doubling up with others and there were those funny camp beds too. But what was Mum on about? She's off on a tangent, Lisa thought as she nodded frantically, hoping she was going to get to the point.

'It was like a commune, wasn't it?' her mum said dreamily, staring out the window. 'We all mucked in, taking turns to cook, cleaning, telling stories and playing games. But we never left the house, did we?'

Oh, yeah. Lisa's brain clicked. A smile spread across her face as she clocked what her mum was telling her to do.

Angie clicked her fingers as the understanding dawned on her daughter.

'It did the trick, love, he never came back,' she said as a crack of thunder bellowed overhead.

'You can't beat a peaceful protest, love.'

4.05p.m.
Mandy saw Cal and Lisa dashing up the path as the coats they held over their heads to protect them from the downpour flapped in the wind. They looked like two crazy caped superheroes on a mission to rescue her.

Which, in effect, they were; that was why they were calling round. Lisa had made it clear in her text an hour ago.

She'd simply typed 'We're coming to get you' with

an ETA of 4p.m. or as soon as they'd finished the homework hour.

The soaking-wet women shrieked their way in, eyes wide from the thrill of escaping sheets of rain and flickering bolts of lightning. Mandy banged the door shut on the elements and excused the boxes littering the hall.

'I got them for Sandro from the supermarket. As you can see, they're empty, he hasn't packed a thing. He's refusing to go,' she said, showing them into the kitchen because Franco and Lola were watching a DVD in the lounge. Lisa and Cal looked around for their victim but he was at his brother's. At least the coast was clear for now.

'So what's all this about then?' Mandy asked eagerly as she opened a packet of muffins and offered them round. 'Tea?'

Lisa and Cal nodded as they got their breath back.

'Right,' Lisa said, wiping a raindrop from her forehead, 'how do you feel about us moving in tomorrow with the kids and staying until Sandro gets sick of us?'

'What?' Mandy said, choking on a crumb. 'Living here? With the kids? That'd make four adults and seven children. Where are they all going to sleep? This is completely bonkers!'

Lisa whacked her on the back then spelled out the details.

If Sandro wouldn't leave then they'd have to be clever. If they worked together to make life so unpleasant and noisy and irritating that he couldn't take it any more, he'd go of his own volition. If he got angry, there was no way he'd hit out, because he was a coward – he couldn't take on three women. Lisa and Cal had worked it out – Cal would arrive in the morning with Dotty so Mandy wasn't on her own with Sandro, then after work Lisa would do the pick-up and they'd all stay over. There would always be two mums there at any one time so he couldn't intimidate one of them or get the locks changed. 'Give it a few days and he'll walk, no doubt about it,' she concluded as Cal echoed her support with 'I'd bet my life on it'.

It was brilliant! There would be no force involved, that was the important bit, Mandy knew, because if push came to shove, Sandro couldn't claim he was the wronged party.

Cal said they wouldn't tell the kids what was going on, they didn't need to know, they'd just accept it as an adventure. She'd had to persuade Rob because he was worried about the kids, which was a fair point, but they all had mobiles, there'd be ten against one, and no one would be left alone with him. And if it was OK, he could come over for tea if he wasn't happy.

God, yes, yes, of course, Mandy agreed.

Lisa on the other hand had had to bar Adam from

joining in too – he wanted to punch Sandro's lights out and he was talking about being on bouncer duty if they needed him. 'I can understand the men's concern,' she told Cal and Mandy, ' but I think we've got the measure of Sandro. No offence to the menfolk but three women and seven kids will beat him hands down.'

So what did Mandy reckon? Cal and Lisa awaited her verdict.

'I think it's genius,' she replied. 'Completely and utterly.'

And yet she was a little taken aback. 'I'm so grateful, really, and I'm touched . . .'

'But?' Lisa asked, looking anxious.

'But why are you doing this? I've only just met you and Cal, I'm just a cleaner.'

Lisa went to open her mouth but Cal got in first.

'A friend of Lisa's is a friend of mine,' she said softly. 'But this isn't just to do with you – well, it is because what you've been through is awful, and I like you very much. But what I mean is this: Lisa and me, we've had a bit of a funny old time of it, and we've worked it out and I've got issues of my own and while I want to help, I also think I need to do this for our relationship. I need to show her I'm here for her, but also for me, to stretch myself. It's a long story but I've got to go back to work and it's going to shake everything up, so I may as well get used to it with this.'

Mandy was bowled over. 'Even if it doesn't work,

I'll never forget this. If there's anything I can ever do for you.'

Lisa butted in – hold your horses, she said, it might go belly-up but if she really wanted to repay them she could do the cooking! 'I'm still on strike, remember?'

Mandy giggled and put her right hand out for the women to shake.

'Deal,' she said, with an emphatic pump of her arm.

And then she called to the kids to tell them they were going to have their friends staying for a sleepover but they weren't to tell Daddy because it was going to be a lovely surprise.

Day 19

8.45a.m., Monday, 2 June

Battling nerves, Lisa marched to work, keen to have a word with Mo before Vintage officially opened.

Butterflies didn't cover it. Enormous ocean-going stingrays were more apt, gliding around the depths of her tummy, looping the loop every time she thought of the challenge she was facing.

She was going to accept the role of shop manager, which sounded grand, but she knew she was starting on a vertical learning curve. Working Saturdays would be hard, she finally admitted to herself, knowing the kids weren't in school. They wouldn't mind, she was sure of that, Adam had filled the mum-shaped hole really well and he was better at her at fun and games. There. She'd said it. The strike had taught her she wasn't the be-all and end-all of their lives, they needed love and stimulation and it didn't matter if it was her or their dad giving it. This, she told herself, was all part of her survival pack for when they flew the nest. She had to do something for herself so she could reap the rewards later in life. Short-term pain, long-term gain. It'd hurt her for a bit but then, as it had turned out with this strike, she'd toughen up.

Tapping at the door, she pulled her cardie tighter as the remnants of yesterday's storm blew itself out.

And there was Mo, waving at her then scrabbling in her pocket for the keys.

'Morning!' she trilled, clicking her bright blue suede open-toed boots like a fashionista sergeant major. 'Bright and early, Lees, need a coffee?'

With a splash of Dutch courage, she thought, as she followed Mo to her office, with Mo chattering away about how grateful she was to Lisa for coming in on her day off, she had two meetings with suppliers and some new stock coming.

'No problem, honest. Erm, have you got a minute?' she asked, casually, with her back to her boss as she hung up her cardie.

Yes, as long as she wasn't resigning again, Mo told her. 'Quite the opposite, actually,' Lisa said, plunging into her speech about relishing the opportunity to step up to the mark.

Mo applauded: she was thrilled, how funny, she'd been planning on asking Lisa this week if she'd made her mind up. Was Adam OK with it, and the kids?

Lisa mumbled that he'd come round but it would be water off a duck's back for Rosie and George, that she now knew.

So, when could Lisa start? The sooner the better, Mo enthused, because she had some news of her own.

'I've decided,' she said, taking off her specs for emphasis, 'I'm going travelling. You, Miss, can stop gawping, it's not that shocking!'

Pushing her slack jaw closed with a finger, Lisa could see it now: Mo staggering in her heels under the weight of a backpack. Mo? The queen of interiors? Trekking through the jungle in a full face of make-up? Roughing it in a designer sleeping bag?

'Dear God, rather you than me, Mo,' Lisa said. 'You'd never catch me doing that. If I ever went travelling, which I wouldn't, I'd want a hairdryer, fluffed-up pillows and a butler, thank you very much.'

But Mo had always wanted to see the world; South America, India, China, she said, her hands spreading at the imaginary world map in her mind. And now was her perfect chance. Toby was at uni, he might even come out to meet her; the business was doing really well and she could seek out inspiration, look for new suppliers and sightsee at the same time. She hadn't done anything exciting for a while and she was coming up to a 'big birthday' so she wanted to do it while she could still work her bladder. Yes, it'd require a heartbreaking change of footwear, she didn't know how she'd cope in flats, but sacrifices had to be made.

There was just one problem: it left Lisa with the task of finding a deputy not only to train up but to share Saturdays with. Mo was sorry to drop the bombshell on her and she understood if she wanted to go back on accepting the job, but she trusted Lisa and didn't want to have to get in someone she didn't know to run the place.

'Besides, I'm only going for six months so I won't be abandoning you completely,' Mo said, putting her hands into a prayer position, her eyes imploring her employee to say yes.

That did throw a spanner in the works, Lisa agreed. It was a big ask, she thought – was she up to it? Was she prepared to put her family through more when things weren't exactly smooth at home? If only Adam would just give in, if only he would step down from his beloved high horse and concede to her terms. That would be a huge weight off her troubled mind.

'Oh, God, that is exciting stroke terrifying,' Lisa said, feeling flustered, wiping her sweaty palms on her thighs. Where was she going to get someone with experience so quickly?

Hang on. There was someone! Mo must've heard

the cogs turning in her head because she moved closer, as if hanging on her every word.

'Leave it with me, Mo,' Lisa said, getting her bag to find her phone, 'I think I know just the person we need.'

9.24a.m.
She'd done the drop-off so now the fun would start. To be honest, Cal thought, it's a relief to get out of the house for a bit.

Things with Rob were OK, they'd spent their evenings going through the finances, she'd drawn up spreadsheets and worked out what immediate cuts they could make. Her parents had offered a loan, which they'd accept so they could pay the mortgage for three months, so if they were lucky, they might be able to save their house.

But Rob wasn't taking it too well, he was quiet and she'd find him staring out into the garden when the kids were heckling him for attention, as though he was mentally not with them.

It must have been seismic, realising he couldn't dig them out of the hole alone. He said he felt a failure and he didn't know why she was staying with him. Bless him, she thought, pushing a wailing Dotty through Mandy's front gate and rapping the knocker. She'd had an insight into how he felt when she was so low and alone. That was why you had to accept

323

people's help when they offered, she'd told him, they were a team and that's all there was to it.

'Hiya!' Mandy said as she flung open the door.

'Sorry I'm a bit late, Dotty did a nasty one on the way here so I had to pop home and get her a change of clothes. Adam's going to drop off all of our stuff later on, he's the bag man, apparently, so that's why I'm here without anything other than nappies!'

That's fine, Mandy said, welcoming her in and immediately reassuring Cal she shouldn't feel bad about the baby crying – in fact if she could poke her to make her scream louder, it would wind up Sandro even more. And she shouldn't worry about the kids making a mess or breaking stuff; the more chaotic it was, the quicker he'd come to his senses and go.

She pointed upstairs to indicate he was in then rubbed her hands together with glee.

Cal laughed as she grabbed Dotty out of the push-chair and started an enthusiastic version of 'Row Your Boat' for Sandro's benefit. Mandy told her to mind the cordoned-off mouldy macaroni cheese area which Sandro had still refused to tidy up – then she stomped up the stairs for a wee, shouting down 'GO ON THROUGH, I'LL BE DOWN TO PUT THE KETTLE ON IN A MINUTE.'

A grunt filtered down from upstairs: Sandro was awake. Cal heard him tell Mandy to keep it down, it was his day off and he wanted a lie-in.

324

The TV was on in the lounge so Cal switched to CBeebies, plonked Dotty down on the floor and sighed. How was she going to leave her? The poor little mite. At least she was oblivious to it, she was too young to go through separation anxiety; it'd come, but the only one who'd feel it so brutally was Cal. And this was no time to feel sorry for herself, she had to go to work.

Her phone buzzed. A voicemail from Lisa. Did she want to work at Vintage? She could start straight away, she'd have to work Saturdays but they could alternate childcare and the money was good.

Cal felt elated then sick then anxious. It was all too real now. She'd secretly hoped it would take a while to find a job. But it was perfect timing, she had to admit that, and she couldn't think of anyone she'd rather work with than Lisa.

Lisa's voice gabbled on, she was clearly excited about it. Then Cal's heart jumped. Lisa said Mo had come up with an ingenious idea. Her boss had seen a programme about some companies letting mums bring their babies to work until they were walking and as Lisa was in charge Mo had said she was welcome to try it.

There was room for a cot in the office so Dotty could have her naps and, if it got too busy, they could stick Dotty in a playpen, the rushes didn't last long. She was sure customers wouldn't mind a baby in the shop, most of them were mums themselves and who didn't love holding a little one? Lisa would be there to help out and if it was too much they could have a rethink.

Cal had heard enough. She rang Lisa there and then and said yes and thank you and wow and Rob would be thrilled and she'd start next week if that was OK and she was so happy she could scream.

She picked up Dotty and blew raspberries on her neck, then chattered away about her news to Mandy when she came in with tea and biscuits.

'It's my turn for a wee now,' Cal said as she passed Dotty over to Mandy and stamped on every step with joy.

Upstairs, Mandy had switched a radio on in the bathroom, so Cal turned it up and sang along, mentally daring Sandro to complain.

It worked. As she came out of the loo, his bedroom door was thrown open. He was just about to begin a tirade of abuse when he realised it wasn't Mandy. His anger disappeared, his face went sheepish as he looked embarrassed to be caught in his pants.

'Didn't wake you, did I?' Cal asked innocently.

'No, no,' he answered, 'I was just getting up anyway.'

'Yeah, course you were,' she said, before clomping back down the stairs to his sniggering soon-to-be ex-wife.

3.45p.m.

Lisa had been looking forward to this all day.

She stood at Mandy's door with six ear-splittingly loud kids in tow: Rosie and George were proudly discussing what they'd had for their first ever school dinner, Franco and Lola were overjoyed by the mammoth sleepover and Ted and Molly were hoping all of them would get to sleep in the same bed, like the grandparents in *Charlie and the Chocolate Factory*.

'*Mamma mia*,' Sandro said as he opened the door, 'will someone tell me what's going on?'

He was pushed aside by the children's stampede as Lisa encouraged them at the top of her voice to go inside and have a play. She handed her coat to a speechless Sandro and sauntered past him as Mandy, Cal and Dotty appeared to greet her.

'Load them up with this lot,' Lisa said as she passed a bag of sugary drinks and sweets to Mandy, who peered inside then congratulated her with a 'good thinking'.

The noise was tremendous and so was the mess. Bags and shoes were abandoned, deliberately not picked up by the mums. Booming footsteps raced in and out of every room and up and down the stairs. Excited voices screamed and shouted as beds and chairs became a playground.

The mums took refuge in the kitchen as Sandro remained in the hallway, looking overwhelmed and terrified. On a high of their own, they gossiped and laughed over a cup of tea while discussing the sleeping arrangements.

Mandy called out to Sandro: 'You don't mind Franco and Lola going in our bed, do you? I'll go in with them. George and Rosie can go in Lola's bed, Ted and Molly in Franco's. Adam's bringing some blow-up beds over so Cal and Lisa can go on them. You'll be OK on the sofa, won't you?'

As Sandro walked towards them, Lisa could see an enlarged vein in his neck, a sure sign of his fury. The muscles in his cheeks were quivering as he clenched and unclenched his jaw.

Struggling to keep a straight face, Lisa couldn't resist asking if he was already in his pyjamas, pointing at his velour tracksuit.

Cal jumped in with an apology that he might not get much sleep in the lounge because she'd be down at any time from 5.30 tomorrow morning when Dotty woke up.

Sandro looked as if he was about to blow, Lisa thought. Good. Go for it, mate, then we'll eat you alive. Unintelligible Italian muttering poured from his mouth. Somehow he remained composed, spat out the word 'fine' and then stormed off.

'What was he saying?' Cal asked.

'He was swearing, mostly,' Mandy said, 'at me. That's about the only Italian I do understand.'

'The mark of a true gentleman,' Lisa said. 'At least we know we're getting to him. Phase One is complete, ladies, it's time to crank it up.'

She went to the bottom of the stairs and called up to the kids. 'Who wants to play "Just Dance" on the Wii?'

A deafening chorus of 'MEEEE', 'My favourite' and 'YESSSS' and then a race to get there first was the answer she'd been hoping for. The TV was switched on and turned up as hysteria gripped the children. Rosie was beyond happy – she and George were only allowed to play on it at the weekend so this was a complete bonus.

Mandy got on with the tea – Sandro's favourite spaghetti carbonara – as Lisa and Cal took it upon themselves to sit outside the master bedroom where Sandro was hiding to talk about periods, childbirth and breastfeeding in the most graphic of detail. Lisa could hear sighing and the muffled sound of something being pounded – probably the pillows, she thought – as she talked stitches and afterbirths.

A knock sounded – that'd be Adam or Rob – but instead of getting up herself, Lisa shouted 'Door!' in Sandro's direction and hugged herself as he went down to answer it.

'Mate!' Adam said to him as the rustle of sleeping bags announced he'd arrived to dump their stuff.

Then Rob's voice floated up too: he was clearly not taking any chances.

That makes six adults and seven children, Lisa calculated as she and Cal made their way to their husbands – this would make tea interesting.

With the men around, Sandro flipped his charming switch. He was the instant good host, welcoming them in, cracking jokes about 'the party atmosphere', telling them he'd made a mistake, he'd been stressed at work and Mandy was his dream woman, she'd always stood by him, he'd make it up to her, it was all a misunderstanding. His smile was unmistakably handsome. But, Lisa saw, his eyes were dead.

She watched Mandy as she dished up bowls of steaming pasta and garlic bread and told the kids to get theirs then go into the lounge. Not a hint of anger – she was performing too, unflustered by Sandro's act.

'Not eating, *amore*?' Sandro asked his wife, working out they were a plate short, holding a hand out for his.

'I am. You're not,' she said, looking him up and down while chewing on a huge spoonful.

Sandro grinned, adjusted his manhood, laughed and waited for her to produce a plate to show she was only mucking about.

Mandy shrugged then spoke through her mouthful. 'There might be some leftovers if the kids don't eat theirs.'

She'd played a blinder, Lisa thought. She'd not only humiliated him, but done so publicly. His face clouded over and his fists trembled with rage. But he couldn't lash out at her, not with all these people here.

He gave a roar of anger then punched the wall. With bleeding knuckles, his body contorted with pain.

'You bitch!' he shouted, spittle flying into the air, as Adam and Rob stood up and moved towards him.

Four adults wanted to deck him there and then. But there was an unspoken agreement that that privilege fell to the tiniest one of all, the one who'd lived through this for ten years.

Lisa held her breath as Mandy calmly put her bowl down, wiped her hands on a tea towel, swallowed what she was eating, and walked towards Sandro.

She stared him in the eyes then raised her hand as if she was about to slap him in the face. Then, calmly, she dropped her palm.

'I wouldn't stoop so low,' she said.

Day 20

5.45a.m., Tuesday, 3 June

Mandy hadn't slept well at all. A mixture of adrenalin and toasty-bodied kids had left her wide awake for hours, daring to dream of a new life.

A muted baby's cry was what she'd been waiting for all night. As soon as I hear someone moving about, I'll get up, there's no point lying here, she told herself. So she crept to the loo for a wee then hovered on the landing, wondering how Sandro would receive her.

She'd never seen him as angry as he was last night, she thought. He'd stormed out of the house after the near-slap but he'd come back in at ten, half an hour after the men had left, like a coward. He'd probably been watching the house. Without saying a word, he joined the women in the lounge, sat on one of the dining table chairs and stared at the wall, his arms crossed and his back straight. There was nowhere else he could go in the house. Once upon a time, I'd have been frightened of him in this mood, Mandy had thought, but now, nothing. He was clearly working out what he was going to do next. Knowing him, he'd be loath to leave for good, it was too much for his ego to bear. But as he jangled his keys the way he did when he was thinking, she hoped he was facing up to the fact that he had no other option.

She wasn't sad, she was just exhausted, mentally drained by a decade of drama; all she wanted now was a quiet life, a happy home for the kids and maybe one day, a normal bloke who cared about someone other than himself.

When the women had all gone up to bed Mandy listened out for his movements downstairs, but it was silent. The kids had been so worn out they'd only managed a half-hearted streak of excitement at bedtime so not even they were making a noise.

She must've drifted off at about 2a.m., she realised as she padded softly down the stairs. That's funny, she thought, the chain on the door is off, I swore I put it on last night.

Then she peeked round the sofa expecting to see Sandro drooling into one of her lovely cushions, his hair leaving a sheen on the cover. Never mind, I'll chuck them. But he wasn't there.

Into the kitchen, nope; back upstairs, checking all the rooms, nothing.

Back down and she found a key on the side in the hall. His key.

He'd left! They'd done it! Elation swept through her body as she fell to her knees and let out a sob.

It's over, Granny Glitter. Finally. Today was the start of the rest of her life.

She heard footsteps behind her, oh God, no, please tell me he hasn't been in the loo.

It was Cal, holding a beaming Dotty.

'He's gone, Cal,' Mandy croaked, getting up and embracing her new friend. 'We've done it, we did it. I never thought it would be that easy, I thought we'd have a stand-off for days.'

'Are you sure?' Cal whispered, her eyes still heavy with sleep, or lack of it.

Mandy was positive, she could just feel it. His coat had gone too, and his shoes, his orange motorbike helmet, his phone, wallet and – most tellingly of all – his beloved facial-hair sculpting razor! He'd left the blimming macaroni mess but you couldn't have it all.

A squinting Lisa emerged at the sound of their giggling, asking what's happened?

'Operation Davina has only bloody well worked!' Mandy said. 'You genius, you!'

Lisa gasped, put her hand over her mouth, dropped it then hissed 'noooooooo!' as the first ray of dusty sunlight streamed into the hall through the glass in the front door.

The three of them hugged, as Dotty, in the middle, took sweaty handfuls of their bed hair and poked their faces with pudgy fingers, believing this was a game for her pleasure.

Mandy was on cloud nine, she couldn't stop smiling. One night, that's all it had taken! Everyone could stand down now. She was chuffed to bits and grateful and they could go back to normal. What a relief for all of us, she thought.

'What are you going to tell the kids?' Lisa asked.

'Do you think you'll be all right tonight by your-self?' Cal wondered.

'These are very good questions,' Mandy said, 'but I haven't even had a cuppa yet! And I usually don't start thinking until at least my first coat of mascara is on.'

Soon the house was bouncing as the domino effect of a child waking set off another. All bleary-eyed and yawning, they looked adorable in their PJs. It was a shame they'd only come together under these circumstances, Mandy thought, she would definitely make sure they did this again when things had settled down. She'd told the kids Daddy had moved out for a bit because he wasn't very well; in time, she'd explain a child-friendly version of the truth.

It was lucky they were all up so early, she realised, because they had to do breakfast and teeth-cleaning in shifts, in between the mums getting ready themselves.

Amid the whirlwind of 'eat up', 'get dressed' and 'find your shoes', they found time for the second cuppa of the morning. After explaining she wasn't frightened of being home alone thanks to the girls, Mandy led a toast as they clanked their mugs together.

'To us!' she said.

'To friends!' Lisa added.

Cal could only offer a look of embarrassment as she chipped in with 'this is as good a time as any' and told Mandy she wouldn't be able to keep her on. She was really sorry but they were having money troubles. But Mandy wouldn't hear of it – she was going to offer a free clean every week because she'd helped her, a near enough stranger, and it was the least she could do.

Once Cal had been forced into accepting, Mandy noticed that Lisa was miles away; either that or she was suddenly very interested in that crack on the wall.

'What's up, hun?' she asked, softly.

Lisa's gaze returned to her friends. She'd been lost in thought, dwelling on something she'd kind of deliberately 'forgotten' this last day or so.

She was wondering how much longer she could go on.

'I've had enough. I'm going to end it today,' she said.

8.47a.m.
Lisa walked to work with a heavy heart.

Adam has won, she thought, her shoulders slack and her feet dragging on the pavement.

I miss the kids. I hate the bins stinking, the dirty worktop and table, the grotty floors and the heap of junk accumulating on every horizontal surface but I could live with that if I have to. What I can't bear is losing my place in the children's hearts. Adam was not her equal now, he was ahead in their affections. She'd seen that when he arrived yesterday and they flocked to him, telling him about their day, their dinners and the grazes on their knees.

Rosie had sealed her decision this morning when she chatted away to Lola about what she wanted for her birthday next month. 'I want a pony but if I can't have that then I want my mummy back,' she'd said, unaware that Lisa was listening in.

The truth is, she thought, I've taken this too far and for too long.

I thought I was teaching her and George about responsibility but in the end, they saw it as me ducking out of loving them and with this new job of mine it'll put even more distance between us. They've learned to go to Adam for reassurance in spite of me helping with homework and playing silly games with them. They'd even given up venting their post-school grumpiness on her, resorting to silence when she asked them what was wrong.

Going back to all the domestic work was worth it

for that alone: she couldn't care less about the loss of face at home or in public. People would understand. Even Mum had hinted that her support was wavering. She anticipated a backlash from all the women who'd joined her, she was supposed to be setting an example. If they managed to get on an equal footing at home good on them, she would say, it's just she needed her kids to need her. There'd be accusations that she was letting the side down and she was really only thinking of herself. She'd hold her hands up to both.

Maybe it's for another generation to try this; maybe Adam's changes of pocket money and school dinners were enough to take a little bit of pressure off her. And after all, it hadn't been a complete waste of time. She could reapply for her distance learning when the children were older. At least Mandy has got her house back, there's that. And Mum and me have a better relationship and Cal and I are besties again.

All that left was Adam; he was looking haggard these days, working hard at home and in all weathers. If she stuck to her guns she was frightened of where it would leave them. Already he was feeling emasculated. What if it drove them apart? No. Enough was enough. I've made my point, she thought.

What had happened to the weather? Lisa wondered recalling the blue skies of 6a.m. Now it was overcast and oppressive. Switching her brain back to domestic-in-chief, she began to work out her plan of attack on the house. Change every bed, bleach the toilets, mop the floors, hoover the carpets, shake the rugs. Maybe she should do it room by room, the kitchen would have to be first.

She sighed as she pushed the door to Vintage and said a weak hello to Mo, who for some reason was coming at her with her arms open wide. Crushed by her squeeze, Lisa managed to form a sentence out of her last breath: 'What's that for?'

'Haven't you seen the paper?' Mo said, rushing back to pick up her copy from the till.

'Adam's given in! Look at the headline: "I SURRENDER".'

Lisa took it in: a picture of her husband in his body-builder apron and the rubber gloves he'd given her on the front page in an 'exclusive interview', breaking the news in the paper first because he wanted everyone to know how proud he was of his wife. She scanned the words. He was agreeing to her terms of splitting the chores right down the middle, he'd asked a solicitor to draw up a housework contract which they'd both sign and he vowed never to take his wife for granted ever again.

He said he'd learned his lesson, he understood now how unappreciated she had felt, how unfair it was for her to do everything, and he didn't care if people thought he was a wimp – if they worked together they'd have more time for each other.

The worst bit had been staying on top of the washing, it was endless; the best bit was getting to know his children, learning their funny little ways.

He'd been determined to stick it out as recently as the weekend because he wanted to make her suffer – he could see how the mess was driving her mad and it 'just wasn't on' to expect him, the breadwinner, to pull his weight. Why should he? She wasn't earning much and the kids were getting more capable of helping out.

He even admitted he'd enjoyed it at times. The feeling of achievement when everyone had clean clothes and full tummies. And yes, he'd loved being the martyr.

But then when he spoke to his mother yesterday he found out that Lisa had been doing her housework for her without telling him because Mum was too unwell to do it. Then she helped a friend out of a sticky situation on top of all that.

It was then he realised she deserved equality, and he finished with a call to dads to seriously consider signing a housework contract like him.

Lisa felt faint.

'It's worked, the strike's worked, he's going to help me, we'll help each other, the kids,' she said aloud as Mo nodded with excitement.

'Pinch me, Mo, go on.'

No need, it's right there in black and white, her boss said pointing at the paper with scarlet nails.

'You've won, girl, you've done it, now go and find him and celebrate.'

Everything was blurred, she had to be convinced several times that Mo meant she could nip out. The door, her bag, her phone, her hand was shaking, contacts, Adam, call, it's me, where are you? At the café, I'm coming.

Racing up the street, heads turning, a smatter of applause as people recognised her, her heart pounding, breathing fast, dodging a dog, sidestepping a pensioner, there was the café, almost there, the door, Adam.

She fell into his chest, gulping for air, tears coming, her nose running, unable to believe it.

'Adam,' she said into his overalls.

'Lisa,' he said back, pulling her face up to cover it in kisses.

She sobbed.

'Jesus Christ, Lees, I thought you'd be happy,' he joked, knowing full well she was beyond that.

As her senses steadied, she smiled, then started laughing, then guffawing, her sides splitting, her cheeks aching.

'I'm so happy! And I'm so sorry for making you feel like a child and for being so obsessed with things being "just-so". I love you, Mr Stratton.'

'Yeah, I am pretty amazing,' he said. 'Hats off to you, Lees, you did it, you actually turned this lump of laziness into a lean mean cleaning machine.'

341

Thank God it's over, she thought. Well, almost over.

She asked Adam if he minded being 'her' for the rest of the day because she had one more thing she needed to do.

'Unbelievable,' he said, 'I give in and you want one more day. Go on then, do whatever it is you have to do and we'll start our Brave New World tomorrow.'

3.21p.m.

Lisa felt like a hero when she arrived at pick-up.

A throng of mums hugged and high-fived her when she walked into the playground – it was incredible the reception she received. Everyone was talking at once, congratulating her on her achievement; those who were on strike were thrilled and told her that was it, there was no way they'd stop until their husbands gave in too, while others told her they were going to give it a go now.

Cal pushed her way through and gave her the biggest hug of all. 'I'm so proud of you, Lees. I'll be honest, I didn't know if you were doing the right thing at first but I can see now things are going to have to change at home when I start work. You're a bloody star!'

Her words meant the most of all. Not far behind were the thumbs up and nods of the head she received from some of the dads who'd given her a tongue-in-cheek hard time over the last weeks,

342

accusing her of giving their wives silly ideas. They'd always maintained they were doing their bit by being there at drop-off or pick-up, their dads wouldn't have been seen dead in the playground so what was the problem? Their begrudging respect of sorts gave her a thrill – she wanted to tell them their time was up, their wives were coming to get them!

The kids piled out and George and Rosie wanted to know why the other mummies were kissing her. She told them it was a surprise – she didn't want to say any more because she and Adam had to do the explaining side by side. That's what this had been all about, joint responsibility, and she didn't want to steal Adam's thunder or put a negative spin on it.

'Come on, we're off to Nanny Stratton's for a bit,' she said instead, 'I need a quick chat with her. You can play in the garden when we're there.'

Lesley was bowled over by the surprise visit from her grandchildren.

'Hello, dears, how lovely to see you,' she said, kissing their heads and watching them scamper around the hallway in a game of tag. 'Shall we see if Nanny's got some treats for you? I might just have some choc ices in the freezer.'

Lisa trailed after her mother-in-law. Once the kids had been praised and spoiled and sent off into the garden to play, Lesley's glow left her. Anxiety clouded her face as she began to apologise.

'Now I know you told me not to say anything to Adam,' she said, adjusting her sling, 'but it slipped out.'

Apparently he'd been having a whinge to her the other day on the phone because he felt so put upon and he was really missing his mother's input since she'd broken her arm. Lesley had leapt to Lisa's defence, which Adam didn't take kindly to. That was when she'd said he should count himself lucky because Lisa was a wonderful woman and she'd been a life-saver, what with doing her housework and cooking for her.

Smoothing down her M&S twinset, she said she hadn't meant to break her confidence and she was ever so sorry.

Lisa picked a bit of fluff off Lesley's jacket and told her it was thanks to her that Adam had agreed to share the domestic duties – in effect, her victory was down to Lesley.

Confusion then; Lesley didn't know what to make of that. 'Oh dear, it seems I inadvertently undermined my son.'

Never mind, at least this business was over, because it had worried her, she'd feared it would cause problems, you know, between them.

'We can all go back to normal now although I expect it means I'll see less of you,' she said, her voice trailing off and her eyes filling with sadness.

Well, not exactly, that was why Lisa had come

round. As well as to do a quick hoover and make a stew.

She had a proposition for Lesley and she didn't want her to think she was taking advantage: she was only suggesting it because she remembered Lesley offering.

'How would you feel about helping out?' Lisa said, busying herself at the worktop as she chopped away. This had to seem casual or Lesley might feel they pitied her. In truth, her mother-in-law's words when Lisa had caught her ironing at her house hadn't left her: she obviously wanted to be more involved in their life and it was a simple gesture that would help Lisa and Adam and Lesley. A win-win, if you like.

She turned around and caught Lesley with her eyebrows almost at the Artex ceiling, her good hand patting her hair. Great, she liked the idea.

'Once a week you could come over and do a few jobs, stay for tea and Adam would take you home, we'd pay you of course, but if you didn't want any money then we could buy you vouchers or pay for something, like a weekly set and blow-dry?'

Lesley's face lit up – it was as if they'd offered her a key to Buckingham Palace!

'That would mean so much to me,' she said. 'It'd be lovely to help and it'd do Roy good to fend for himself once a week.'

Ha! Lisa hadn't meant to exclude Roy; her

invitation was for both of them should he fancy coming for a meal. But obviously Lesley loved the prospect of doing this alone, of having a valid excuse to be amongst her family and away from him for a break.

Lesley accepted on the spot with the caveat that (a) they weren't doing this because they felt sorry for her, and (b) she didn't want any payment, but being cooked for would be wonderful.

Lisa looked at her sternly. 'Don't you go thinking we're doing you a favour – you're one of the most fastidious workers going, I'll be checking the top of the picture frames for dust! And frankly I think me and Adam will benefit the most from this. So before you change your mind, I think we've got ourselves a deal. When can you start?'

Lesley made a fuss of checking her National Trust calendar; she had appointments here and there, coffee with 'the girls' that day, lunch with some of 'the ladies' then and oh, what about this? she said, holding her plaster cast aloft. A one-armed housekeeper wasn't much help.

'Pah!' Lisa said, waving her gesture away. 'Just do what you can manage for now. It'll be healed in no time and I tell you something – with one arm you'll be a darn sight more able than your son with two.'

A bashful look came over Lesley, she looked

flattered to be considered useful – probably no one had ever told her how valuable she was. Certainly not Roy, and her daughter didn't depend on her because she lived miles away. Before this strike, that was exactly how Lisa had felt.

'Just let me know what day you want to do,' she said. 'It has to be the same day every week, no excuses, this must be a regular thing. I'm really going to rely on you now I've got this manager's job.'

Lesley nodded vigorously and started to talk of buying a new overall and some dusters – she'd go to the pound shop because they always had a few bargains. She opened cupboards and drawers in a stocktake of cleaning tools and started a list in her lovely, curling, old-fashioned handwriting.

When it was time to go and she'd rounded up the kids, Lisa caught Lesley on the phone to a friend.

'Yes, they want me to help out, I'm thrilled. Lisa said I was very much needed,' she said, in an important voice.

Lisa tapped her on the shoulder, to let her know they were leaving. She gesticulated 'no need to end your call' and waved goodbye.

Lesley followed them to the hall, blowing kisses before she returned to her conversation, which Lisa caught just before the door shut: 'Modern women, they do have it hard.'

5.30p.m.

Adam walked into the lounge where Lisa and the kids were in the process of building a den, coughed and then announced: 'Ladies and gentleman, dinner is served.'

He had a folded tea towel hanging from his left forearm, and sandwiched between his raised chin and grubby work T-shirt was a dicky bow.

'Hey that's my *Doctor Who* bow tie!' George said, unamused by his dad's fancy-dress hijack, as he got up to aim a swipe at him.

'Order. ORDER!' Adam replied, which did the trick as Rosie and her brother collapsed into giggles. Lisa wondered what he was playing at as she swept the kids into the kitchen.

She clapped her hands in delight when she saw the table had been dolled up to the nines with whatever he could lay his hands on from the cupboards, starting with a riotously colourful Moshi Monsters plastic cloth from Rosie's last birthday. Their green shatterproof picnic wine glasses contained leftover party poppers from Christmas and their knives rested on Lightning McQueen serviettes dating from either George's third or fourth birthday, Lisa couldn't remember. A string of pink £2 Ikea fairy lights from Rosie's bedroom snaked its way up and down the middle of the table.

The kids squealed as Adam welcomed them to The Last Supper at Daddy's Bistro before reading out tonight's menu, which was spag bol, spog bal or bog spal. 'BOG spal,' Rosie shouted, delighted to be able to get away with using a 'rude' word, which predictably made George follow suit even though he hadn't a clue what it meant. Lisa thought, what the hell, adding 'make that three' as Adam tucked their napkins into the necks of their shirts then dished up.

'Right,' he said, sprinkling Parmesan on Rosie's, Lisa's and his and Cheddar on George's, 'this is a celebratory last supper because Mummy and Daddy have got something to tell you.'

Cue a series of questions from the kids: what's a last supper, what's celery bravery, are we going to have a little brother or sister or a puppy?

'Shhh,' he said as he prompted his wife with an arch of his eyebrows. He obviously thinks I want a taste of glory and to rub his nose in it! Not a chance, she thought, taking a breath.

'You know I've been playing that game with Daddy?' Lisa said. 'Well, we've finished it and, no, Rosie, no one lost, we both won, in fact. We've decided that from now on we're going to share all the housework. It means Daddy won't be doing everything like he has done over the last few weeks and I won't be doing everything like I did before that. We wanted you to know things are going to change again, but this time we're going to be doing it equally so it'll be better for all of us.'

George burst into tears at the prospect of no more school dinners and pocket money. Then stopped when Lisa told him it meant nothing of the sort – she had the grace to admit Daddy had been right to start both, at which Adam huffed on his fingernails and rubbed them on his top.

Rosie said: 'I hope you two won't be arguing any more. George and me didn't like it. Daddy, can you promise you'll try to be a bit more organised checking the school bags and Mummy can you try not to be so fussy like you were before about mess and stuff?'

Out of the mouths of babes or what, Lisa thought: trust a child to offer such an insight into the nub of the issue. Adam has to anticipate more while I have to chill out a bit – that just about sums it up.

After they'd eaten, Adam asked Rosie for her very best pen for Mummy and Daddy to use so she scurried off for her pencil case and picked a pink highlighter.

'This, kids, is a Housework Contract,' he said, as he produced a folded-up piece of paper from his pocket. 'Both Mummy and I need to sign it and you two have to give it your autograph too because you're going to be our witnesses.'

Adam smoothed out the document and, with a prime ministerial flourish, scrawled his name. Then with a solemn look on his face, he passed the pen to Lisa, who took a moment to study the wording.

Signatories will agree to draw up a housework rota,

agreed by all parties, blah blah, ensuring equal division of labour and responsibility for domestic duties, blah blah blah, either party can terminate but face a penalty to be decided by the opposite party, this agreement is binding, comes into effect at time to be specified by both parties – 'midnight, Ad?' – yes, it all seemed reasonable.

'Just checking there's nothing untoward in the small print, like making me the sole toilet cleaner,' Lisa said as she scribbled her name.

Rosie chose a gold metallic pen to do her bit while George picked a green felt tip but as they got down, their daughter froze and swivelled round with a pressing question. 'So who do we call for first from tomorrow? Because if you're both in charge now . . .' she said, her little forehead ruched with worry.

That's a good question, Lisa thought as she looked to Adam to see if he had any ideas.

'Tell you what,' he said, mischievously, 'if you combine the words "mum" and "dad", you get the word "mad". You could try that, maybe? Whoever's the nearest will sort you out then.'

Predictably, she loved that and shouted 'mum and dad equals MAD' several times before George asked her to help him build some Lego.

Making the most of her last night, Lisa watched Adam tidy up and reflected on the strike.

'You know, Rosie was right earlier. About you

needing to think a bit more and me needing to be less obsessive.'

'Yep,' Adam replied, fiddling about with the buttons on the dishwasher which, Lisa noted, had been beautifully stacked. 'We need to meet in the middle. How are we going to do the rota then? Write down all the jobs or classify them into rooms and swap each week or what?'

Lisa said she'd have a think and work on it once the kids were in bed.

'Oh, it nearly slipped my mind,' she said, 'but had you held it together for one more day, you'd have won.'

Adam whirled round and clutched his heart. 'What? You've only just remembered to tell me? Funny that, after we've just signed the deal. You mean I was this close?' he said, making the smallest gap between his thumb and forefinger.

Lisa feigned innocence as she ripped her tattered 'How To Be Me' list off the fridge. Screwing it up into a ball, she explained how illuminating the strike had been.

Adam, serious for once, agreed and revealed he'd found it harder than he'd ever imagined. Then those words she'd been waiting to hear for what seemed like years.

'I just didn't realise how much you did, it was a nightmare if I'm going to be completely honest. There were points when I enjoyed it, becoming more in tune with the kids, and the longer it went on the more I felt I had to prove to you I could do it, and there's something gratifying about being the martyr. But in the end, I gave in not just because of what you did for Mum and Mandy and Cal but because I didn't think it fair for one person to do everything.'

Finally, she thought, finally he's seen the light. 'So now you understand I wasn't nagging you all those years,' she said.

'Yes. But this is the only time you'll ever hear me admitting it,' he said, returning to the dishwasher to puzzle over the controls. 'And, by the way, I am proud of you for wanting to study,' he said to the buttons. 'I was just scared of you turning into a butterfly, leaving me a boring old moth. You can't have history repeating itself, not after what your mum went through.'

Lisa got up, cuddled him from behind and told him she loved him more than ever.

Then as she went to walk off, she thought she'd go for one last dig. In a can't-you-do-anything voice, she said: 'You might want to put some salt and rinse-aid in there, that's why the buttons are flashing.'

Adam just managed to flick her bum with a tea towel on her way out of the room.

10.41p.m.
It'd been a job for Lisa to get the housework rota down in full what with the constant distraction of

her beeping phone and flashing inbox. Facebook was in meltdown with all the 'likes' and good wishes, The *Herald*'s online story on Adam was the website's 'most read', and individual texts from friends and family were proving too numerous to respond to.

Most impressive of all was an official email from someone to do with the Government, an adviser on motherhood called Stella Smith, who'd heard about her plight and wanted to have a meeting because she was very interested in what had gone on under Lisa's roof.

Obviously there were a few snarky comments here and there from husbands who did the lion's share of the chores as well as from idle men and a few women who took pride in their homes.

But you couldn't please them all. And Lisa's only concern was to please her family.

Her left forefinger tucked between her nose and her top lip, she pondered on the rota lit up on her laptop screen as she sat in bed in her pyjamas.

I think that's everything, she thought, scrolling down the list of jobs, which she'd divided into 'daily', 'weekly' and 'extras'. Every morning, they'd take it in turns to do breakfast, load a wash, sort the dishwasher and get the kids ready for school. The other one would then be responsible for checking school bags, tea, bathtime and bed. The person who did brekkie would be responsible for hanging out or putting away the washing and tidying while the other one cleared away upstairs.

By Lisa's calculations, it would mean both of them would be able to sit down together by 8p.m. at the latest and relax.

Weekly chores were changing the beds, meal planning, hoovering, shopping, toilet cleaning, ironing, mowing the lawn, putting the bins out, etc, while 'extras' took in cleaning the car, school events, special planning for birthdays, Christmas and holidays, which they'd work out when they crossed those bridges. As long as Adam agreed with it, tasks would be allocated according to expertise – it made no sense to get Lisa to finish that cupboard door – she was woman enough to admit she'd cocked it up. Any slack would be picked up by Lesley, such as cleaning the windows and dusting.

'Here,' Lisa said, handing the computer to Adam when he walked in with his dressing gown, 'see what you think, it's not that detailed yet and we won't know if it's going to work until we do it but at least it's a start.'

'Sounds good. Oh, I meant to give you this earlier, came in the post,' Adam said, pulling something out of his gown pocket as he settled down next to his wife under the duvet.

He handed her an official-looking envelope which made her heart thud. It was stamped with the logo of the long-distance-learning company she'd applied to. 'Adam!' she hissed. 'How could you forget this?' Tearing it open, she unfolded the letter and speed-read the lines of text to get to the point as quickly as possible.

'I've been accepted!' she whispered. 'I can't believe it, Adam, I've got a place on the September business course and they've invited me to an open day.'

Adam looked as chuffed as Lisa as he pulled her in for a kiss and a hug. 'Never doubted it,' he said, which earned him a shove in the ribs.

'New job, new course and a new husband, I'm one lucky woman!' she laughed.

It was the icing on the cake; what a few weeks they'd been through. Life had completely changed. Her head whirled with textbooks and mortar boards as Adam brought her back to the rota.

She'd left out a few key rules, he said, namely that the kids should be roped in wherever possible and anyone who noticed they were about to run out of something had to write it on the whiteboard in the kitchen, the whiteboard, he reminded her, that he'd introduced in what he called 'my era'.

'Good call,' she said, switching off the light, snuggling down, relieved they'd reached a consensus, seeing as it was almost 11p.m. and she was suddenly exhausted.

Talking of which, Adam said, he'd had a text from

Ginger Steve tonight. He'd bumped into Mandy in the supermarket after work and he'd offered his services as a handyman now she was on her own. She'd accepted and he was going over tomorrow night and she said she'd cook something as a thank you.

'Dirty buggers,' he muttered as his breath became heavier and he drifted off just like that.

Lisa smiled into the darkness. Who'd have thought so much goodness would come out of a squashed grape?

The Day After

5.15p.m., Wednesday, 4 June

Lisa shouted 'Tea's ready!' as she dished up home-made burgers, salad and wedges onto four plates.

Silence. Apart from the telly blaring in the lounge.

'Tea's ready!' she called again, slightly louder, putting ketchup, mayo and mustard on the table, checking the baps weren't burning under the grill. Nothing like toasting them to top it off, she thought, taking pleasure not pride in her job.

Adam had done the breakfast run this morning, loaded a wash, emptied the dishwasher and got the kids ready for school. She'd checked the school bags and found two slips relating to the school cake sale on Friday. She'd made a note of it on the whiteboard and wrote Adam's initials alongside – there was to be no honeymoon for him, she'd decided, she needed to keep him on his toes.

Not that Adam had let her off lightly, telling her with glee he expected a slap-up meal at teatime, it was the least she could do, considering. He'd fulfilled his part of the bargain so far, hanging the washing on the line when he got in from work, aided by the kids, who each passed him the next piece of clothing or pegs when he was ready.

Switching the heat off, Lisa pulled the grill out and dropped the hot rolls on each plate. Going to the fridge for the kids' juice, she managed to stop herself in time – it was water now, of course it was.

Drawing breath to shout once more, she instead said, 'Oh, good, there you are' as they entered the kitchen and sat down.

'Mu-uum, you've got my knife and fork wrong,' George said. 'Not the *Star Wars* ones any more, I'm a big boy.'

'He has the same as us,' Rosie added for clarity, inspecting the table to see if there was anything else which would count as a fail.

Adam rubbed his palms together, admiring his triple-decked burger, before insisting the kids had salad – not just one piece of lettuce, George, and more than two slices of cucumber, Rosie.

Once they'd devoured their afters of ice cream – still chocolate sauce for George and raspberry for Rosie – the kids helped carry the dirties to the dishwasher while Lisa wiped the surfaces enough to pick up the crumbs but not as before, when she'd threatened to scorch holes in them.

God, it felt good to be back at the helm, well that wasn't strictly true now, was it? She was a co-pilot this time and she couldn't be happier. She mopped the floor, getting down to pick at bits with her fingers but surprising herself when she gave up on the more stubborn stains. Then she announced she was going up to run the bath and she'd shout down in five minutes.

As the taps ran, she did a tour of upstairs and made a note of some jobs Lesley could do, such as giving the kids' rooms a thorough cleaning. There were new blobs of probably toothpaste or milk on George's carpet, and Rosie's drawers were a jumbled mess of vests strangling T-shirts and inside-out jeans. Adam's side of the bed was a smelly pile of discarded work stuff while the loft needed a good dust.

Back in the bathroom, she laid out clean pyjamas then shouted down for the kids.

For once, they both came straight away, happy to have their mum all to themselves at bathtime. The old her would've reprimanded them for the surging waves of water spilling onto the floor. The new her threw a towel down to soak it up and let them make daddy beards with Adam's shaving foam.

'LEEEEEEES,' came a shout. Instinctively, she rolled her eyes. What on earth did he want? Couldn't he see she was busy with the kids? Stop right there, Lisa! This is a new dawn, OK? She got up from the loo seat and walked to the top of the stairs.

'What is it, love?' she said, all nice and warm.

'Quick, come here, you need to see this!' he shouted before adding, 'Pull the plug out of the bath, don't let them drown.'

Honestly! Talk about paranoid. And as if she wouldn't think of that. My God, he's thinking ahead – he really is a changed man!

Shouting at the kids to pull out the plug, Lisa galloped down the stairs and burst into the lounge where Adam was frozen to the spot, his hands suspended mid-tidy, watching Sky News. 'I just switched over to get the headlines.'

She went to speak and he violently shushed her. What on earth was he on about?

Then she caught sight of the breaking-news ticker scrolling along the bottom of the screen.

COPYCAT STRIKES BREAK OUT ACROSS COUNTRY . . . MUMS DOWN TOOLS AFTER LISA STRATTON'S HOUSEWORK VICTORY . . .

Adam turned his head to hers. Excitement, shock and awe were written all over his face.

Lisa blinked hard to double-check. 'Bloody hell,' she said slowly as the landline started ringing and her phone began to vibrate on the sideboard in the hall.

Adam stood up. And gulped. Then blew air out of his cheeks before he said: 'I reckon I better do bedtime, don't you, love?'

THREE WEEKS LATER

Wednesday, 25 June

8a.m.

As Cal unlocked the door to Vintage, it dawned on her that something was missing.

The knot she'd had in her stomach in the first fortnight here had disappeared and she was actually enjoying herself.

Especially the early shifts, she thought, raising her shoulders with glee. Knowing she could have a coffee in a moment of quiet got her through the hectic morning rush.

It was a surprise, she realised, putting her handbag in the office. She'd never expected to be happy at work. The most she'd hoped for was to not mind it too much. Even dressing up for it, nothing fancy, just a nice skirt and a clean top, had made her feel she was doing more by working than just bringing in money.

And even though she was late to it, she felt part of the post-strike buzz, which was still going strong three weeks after Lisa's victory. Takings were up because of the sheer number of people coming through the door curious to see the woman who'd won equality by hanging up her dusters.

Cal threw her cardie onto the desk and peered up at a map of Great Britain which Lisa had Blu-Tacked to the wall. It was covered in drawing pins, each denoting the location of an outbreak of industrial mum action. Mushrooms of silver and gold covered cities, with more added every day. You couldn't turn the radio on or read a paper without some mention of the effects of the strike. Where mums were taking industrial action, pubs were reporting a drop in business, whereas wine bars were booming. There were signs that productivity had taken a dip in male industries but was spiking in female ones. Experts were predicting a boom in the birth rate should men share the housework. Some women MPs were tweeting pictures of their husbands doing the ironing. And a group of men somewhere up north had had enough and formed a group called Dads Strike Back.

Back into the shop and little more than a fortnight in, Cal already had a routine. Press 'play' and 'loud-speaker' on the answerphone to check for messages while walking around switching on lights and straightening stock.

As she went about it, she considered the story so

far. It was still at the 'suck it and see' stage, of course, but at least she had a sympathetic boss; they were both in the same boat should one of their kids fall ill. Their mantra was 'Make the best of it' and if there were queues, well, so be it. And to top it off, she still got to see Dotty in the day.

Replacing the till roll, Cal recalled with satisfaction the way she and Lisa had put their heads together the weekend after the strike ended and drawn up a plan in the café upstairs.

Taking it in turns, one would come in at 8a.m. and leave at 3p.m., the other started at 10a.m. and shut up shop at 5p.m. It was so simple; they were each other's childcare safety net should their regular arrangements falter.

In the first few days, Cal discovered she couldn't simultaneously give Dotty her all and fulfil her role, particularly if she had to help a customer and the baby was grouchy.

So she visited a few nurseries and knew she'd found the right one when a softly spoken woman in her fifties scooped up her bawling baby and instantly stopped her crying. Dotty now gave Grace a gummy grin every time she saw her. And she was handed back, calm and contented, at lunchtimes so Cal could put her down for a nap in the office, where she would do paperwork. Not that four-month-olds could be expected not to cry when she was making a call! But this was the best compromise going. Cal's days off from the shop would be covered by Babs, who had been itching to step out of the kitchen for years, and her daughter, who was their 'worth her weight in gold' Saturday girl.

The emotional turmoil Cal had felt putting the kids in breakfast club when she was on earlies was replaced by a bit of a huff when it turned out they loved it. When Cal worked lates, Rob would work flexi and first pick up Dotty from her then get the kids from school. Looking back, he'd been on a precipice, retreating from them, so this had forced him to get back on his bike and his confidence had grown. My God, Cal thought, two weeks ago he wouldn't have been able to make beans on toast and now he can whip up a lasagne.

As for Lisa, she was only just saying yesterday how much she'd dreaded putting the kids in after-school club when she was on lates but they were always annoyed to find it was home time when she or Adam went to collect them.

The sound of jangling keys behind her told Cal that Mandy had arrived to do her daily clean.

'Hi, Mand! Coffee?' Cal said, going upstairs to see Babs, without waiting to hear her answer, knowing full well she'd be 'gagging', as she put it.

'Ooh, yes please. Tell you what, how anyone can call this "work", I don't know!' Mandy laughed, setting down her Housework Fairy bag of tricks and pulling her vac in behind.

This was another benefit of an 8a.m. start, Cal thought as she put in their order with Babs and came back down for a chat. Mandy was now 'one of us'; it was as if she'd always been there. Bringing her on-board as official cleaner meant the best friends could spend more time with customers, something Mo had agreed with, judging by a text she'd sent from Rio in response: 'Do what you want, I'm being shown the sights by Rafael, my 30-something personal tour guide!!!'

Mandy's optimism and warmth were infectious.

'So. How's it going then?' Cal said, arching her eyebrows, fishing for info.

Mandy blushed as she fought a huge smile. A little cough, a big swallow and a dry mouth.

'Oh my God! You've got it baaaad, girlfriend!' Cal teased, her left hand on her hip, her right forefinger pointing at the accused.

'Yeah, guilty as charged,' Mandy admitted, finally giving in to her elation. 'It's early days, very early days but, yeah, Ginger Steve is lovely.'

'Good,' Cal said, nodding with emphasis, 'you deserve it.'

But it wasn't just him, Mandy added, it was her independence and the kids not being frightened. Sandro had sent a few abusive texts after he'd moved out but they'd stopped when the police had 'a word' so for once, at last, things were good. Even better, she'd heard he'd had his motorbike nicked.

The phone rang as Babs delivered their coffee.

'Hello, Vintage!' Cal sang, wondering what was in store for them today.

'Hi, yep, yep, OK, I've got you, no problem,' she answered, mouthing 'Lisa' to Babs and Mandy who'd gone quiet for the call. 'OK, see you in a bit.'

'Well, that's the lamest excuse I've ever heard for being late to work,' Cal said, over-rolling her eyes, pretending to be in a strop. 'She's going to be in at half ten.'

Then, her face exploding with joy, she added: 'There's been a development. Lisa's been asked to do an interview for the BBC. The Football Association has apparently been in touch with the Government – they're worried that if the strikes gather pace attendance will be down when the season starts.

'Do you know something, girls, I don't think we've heard the last of this.'